Quantum Tangle

Chris Reher

Chris Reher

Quantum Tangle

Terminus Shift

Entropy's End

Also by Chris Reher

Sky Hunter

The Catalyst

Only Human

Rebel Alliances

Delphi Promised

ACKNOWLEDGMENTS

Thank you to Dee Solberg, Tracy Leach,
Hugh and Cypher

Chris Reher

ONE

Was it morning yet? It felt like morning. There was something weirdly natural about the beam of light that played over his chest. He blinked slowly and gazed at the small shadows shifting around like they had some purpose.

Frowning, Sethran Kada shifted his violet eyes to the cockpit console before him. Inactive. Then to the com panel to his right. Silent and dark. It all looked an awful lot like an emergency shutdown. Finally, he peered up at the small window set into the ceiling to find the perpetrator of the sunbeam on his chest.

Why was a white star wandering around out there? He was supposed to be in the vicinity of a red dwarf. A couple of days from now he'd enter the jumpsite to Aram where Timo was currently freezing his scales off, waiting for the drop. Somehow he thought he might have missed the turn to Aram. The shadows in the cockpit weren't thrown by any red dwarf star.

"Isn't this embarrassing," he muttered, mostly to assure himself that everything was in working order. "Good thing nobody saw that."

He released the restraints of the pilot bench and sat up, suspecting that the subspace leap through that gate had taken him far deeper than he meant to go. Although just minutes had passed since he let the *Dutchman* fall into the jumpsite, he had that disoriented, hung-over feeling one got after a long jump.

No one doubted that it was possible to take a wrong turn inside subspace. Perhaps some split-second glitch could shift the exit point by a fraction. Of course, no one ever returned to tell about such miscalculation. Any sensible navigator plotted an exit before entering a jumpsite to make sure that didn't happen. But clearly this wasn't anywhere near Aram Gate and he just hadn't taken a simple chart jump. He felt it in every bit of his long-limbed body.

Seth rubbed his eyes and sent a mental directive to the *Dutchman* to begin a reset and diagnostic. He listened to the blips and buzzes as it groomed itself to check for damage. Something worried the ship enough to rerun some routine repeatedly. He resolved to spring for a more thorough overhaul of all systems when he returned to Magra.

What happened back there? As subspace leaps went, this span should have been an easy hop, fully mapped and one he'd taken before. He prided himself on his skills as pilot and on the quality of his ship. It made it possible for him to travel without crew, a definite advantage in his line of work. This jump, however, felt like someone tried to crack his ship like a seed pod to get at the chewy morsel inside.

"Where are we?" he said although the controls were not set to voice command, a system too easily compromised. It was the neural interface embedded at his temple, connected to the main processor, that relayed his inquiry. The ship's scanners took a look around the sector and scrolled information onto the display screen in front of him. Two stars nearby. Some planets. Definite signs of traffic and habitation. Atmospheric conditions, life forms, environmental threats, evidence of technology and sentient populations were analyzed, recorded and then the *Dutchman* decided on the most likely location.

"Rishabel," Seth said, unconvinced and not at all happy. Another thing the *Dutchman* displayed as routinely as the cabin temperature was that his coolant supply was utterly drained. And so unless he found a way to keep the ship's processors from disintegrating during a subspace jump he had one hell of a long walk home.

He called up information about Rishabel. Part of the Benstar system, the planet lay so far outside any point of interest that it had been mapped and then immediately forgotten by everyone back in the Trans-Targon sector. At some point it had supported a few colonies that eventually failed and were abandoned. Still, habitable planets were hard to find and so this one still played host to a fair bit of traffic moving through this sub-sector. Like a crowded harbor in the middle of an empty sea, people came and went on their way elsewhere. Rebels, mostly, and folks whose welcome in more civilized places had worn out. Trading fleets, heavily armed to ward off pirates, also shifted goods and personnel here before heading into other parts of the sector.

Sighing, he set course for Rishabel, choosing an orbiting spaceport unlikely to ask why he wanted to enter their airspace. Perhaps it was wise to find out how he got here, or why, before announcing his presence. He suspected that paying for a supply of coolant tubes in this place was going to sting.

He looked up when the com console alerted him to an incoming message. Who was calling at this hour? This wasn't the type of neighborhood where travelers were stopped and frisked.

He tapped the receiver. "Kinda busy here," he said, offering no identification.

Instead of a reply, every alarm on the controls surrounding his pilot bench went into alert mode. Programs ran for no particular reason and things flashed that he'd never seen flashing before. Audible warnings added another layer of mayhem as the *Dutchman* tried to determine the nature of the threat.

Seth winced when a spike of pain drove through his skull. His headset was little more than a thin wire comfortably slung from one temple to the other but now he could not even tip his head to push it away. His body arched as if through some electrical charge but the only pain he felt was in his head. The field of his vision closed in and he thought that passing out was likely the next experience he was to have today.

He watched helplessly, both on the screens and via his mental link, as one system after another was accessed and scanned. His ship possessed the anti-intruder programs used by Air Command's most complex systems and had never been breached. Right now, however, it seemed like someone was looting everything he possessed. The fact that his own brain was plugged directly into the compromised technology filled him with gut-wrenching dread.

Don't fear.

The words appeared in his mind and he was unsure if he heard or dreamed them. They were certainly not his own. Giving up his fear at this moment was not an option.

The cockpit calmed. One by one, the alarm systems ceased their protest, lights dimmed again, and the *Dutchman* returned to its diagnostic mode as if it had never been interrupted. Seth exhaled shakily and immediately breathed in again, suddenly aware that he had not been doing that for several minutes. He pried his hands from the armrests of his bench and tested his limbs.

Sleep.

"I don't think so!" he said. But then he did.

* * *

More time had passed, of that he was sure. Seth drifted out of whatever deep sleep had claimed him to glance warily around the cockpit. Standby mode now. Mostly. No indicators nagging him that something wasn't right with the *Dutchman*. That was reassuring, at least. He checked the ship's timers. He had been asleep, passed out, whatever, for nearly five hours.

"What the hell was that?" he said.

The *Dutchman*, long used to his mental vernacular, responded by listing the results of the systems-check on a screen.

"Did I hurt you?"

Seth twisted in his seat so abruptly that something in the back of his neck cracked alarmingly. "What? Who's there?" He peered into the cabin that made up the central space of the *Dutchman*'s interior and served as main living quarters for the tiny crew meant to live aboard. Whoever had spoken was not back there. Nor did it seem likely that anyone would be, given that he was the only person within twenty thousand marks of this place.

"Wait."

He removed his headset and used an overhead grip to pull himself out of his couch to stumble into the cabin, still groggy and disoriented. Despite the recent tumble through subspace, nothing seemed out of place in what was essentially his home. Actually, he thought, much of it *was* out of place, but that was the usual state of things here. "Wait for what?" He glanced into the tiny galley. No one there.

"Learning language. You are Centauri."

"So I've been told." Seth returned to the cockpit. "Where are you?" He reran the scanners to look for ships in the vicinity. His curiosity, easily the greatest source of his troubles, had taken over. He liked it better than fear, anyway. Whoever was accessing his system was doing it in a way that the *Dutchman* didn't even notice now. The intruder remained undetectable. Impressive, whatever it was. Then again, he was a long way from home. "Closest ship is a Feydan trader. Not exactly something that can break into this place."

"I did not break anything."

"Not literally."

There was a brief pause. "Wait. Learning language."

Seth raised both eyebrows and made a placating gesture. If the *Dutchman* hadn't found a way to keep these people out of here, there certainly wasn't anything he could do about it. He looked up at the monitors, uneager to re-establish his mental connection with his ship. Nothing was going on there other than heightened activity in his data bank. "You can look at Union mainvoice," he suggested. "Easier than Centauri language."

"I only need one?"

"At a time, yes. What language do *you* speak?"

"We do not have language. Now I have many."

"So fast? How many?"

"Centauri, Feyd, Delphian, Magra Torley, Magra Alaric, Phi Nine, mainvoice."

Seth considered a quick emergency signal. The chance of that lone freighter rushing to his rescue, here in this pirate-infested sub-sector, didn't seem very good. "You're an artificial system? A program? Where did I pick you up? When?"

"Is that a question?" the intruder replied. Seth noticed the beginnings of an undefinable dialect, likely a blend of those on file on his ship. "Still learning... stuff."

"Stuff?" Seth grinned. "It's not really polite, whoever you are. You should ask before breaking... before looking at other people's stuff."

"Can I look at your stuff?" The database scan continued without pause.

Seth sighed. "Help yourself. Don't break things." He sat down and engaged another diagnostic to see if whatever AI had invaded his system left any traces. There was no new code, no changes, nothing deleted. It really did seem as if someone was merely browsing through his library. That was not especially worrisome. Having seen the inside of a few prison cells, he stored nothing there that was better left unshared. "Mind if I head for Rishabel now?"

"Rephrase."

"Can I go... Why am I asking you, anyway?" He directed the *Dutchman* to resume his journey to the nearby planet. "So where are you, really?"

"Here."

"In my processors? You're a program, then?"

"No."

He pursed his lips. "Let's pretend I don't know who or what you are, shall we?"

"That is sarcasm?"

"Yes."

"All right."

"Who are you?"

"I just am. We don't have words like this. I like them. But I understand your confusion. I found you in-between, when you went by."

"In-between? You mean subspace?"

Pause. "Yes."

"That's not possible."

"If it were not possible I would not be here." Another lengthy pause ensued. "Oh," the intruder said. Then said it again, with a different inflection as if tasting the word. "Oh, you think I am lying. Exaggerating. Subterfuging."

"Yes, subterfuging," Seth replied, amused. "We do that."

"We do not."

"The ship doesn't recognize you in there."

"I am in your head."

Seth blinked, then frowned. "You're in my head?"

"Yes. You have a door there."

He felt for the small, triangular interface node at his temple. "My neural tap?"

"Yes. Your interface and the devices on your wrist and this vehicle all connect. And something inside."

He touched the spot above his elbow where a thin circuit sheet served as backup for his neural implant. Although the data array on his forearm sleeve contained scanning devices, receivers and transmitters, the more limited relay embedded under his skin had gotten him out of more than one scrape in the past. "You are scanning me, too?"

"Yes. Interesting. You are experiencing stress indicators."

"You don't say. So are you a life form? Living in subspace? There is nothing in subspace."

"You don't know that. You only pass by. You never look

11

inside."

"We can't."

"True. Organics. You need too much to live. Gas, food, space." Another pause for a data scan. "I don't understand sleep."

"You're not organic?"

"Nope."

"Nope?" he repeated with a smile.

"Does that bother you?"

"Not really. Not as much as the thought that you're in my head. We call that mental illness." As he said that, Seth wondered if his glib comment might, indeed, be true. Was he even having this conversation? It still didn't seem as though he was actually hearing that voice and, if he was, where it came from. Had he suffered some sort of brain injury during the jump? Perhaps he was the one in need of a diagnostic.

Seth, like most people living in the Trans-Targon sector, assumed there to be two types of sentient life forms. What were commonly and arrogantly called a Prime species appeared to be actually a single species, scattered over several planets. Their evolution diverged a little over time to suit their environment but their DNA did not vary by much, hinting at some common origin. And then there were the true, indigenous species whose anatomy and mental processes barely resembled the Primes. Seth had met a few of those. Possibly, and unless he had indeed gone crazy, this strange interaction he was having could well be a first contact event. He decided to assume that he had not utterly lost his mind.

"I don't want to bother you," it said. "Do you fear harm from me?"

"That would be my first instinct, yes," he admitted. "Is this how your people travel around out here? In people's heads?"

"No. We don't travel around out here. It's dangerous. This is new. Your ship tells me your name is Sethran Kada. Right?"

He nodded although there was no one to nod to. "Seth. Do you have a name?"

"We don't have words, remember?"

"So make one up."

"I can have any name?"

"Well, something you like. There are stories, made-up ones, in the database. See if there is something in there."

"Stories. They are not factual? Not true?"

"Yes. But they are amusing." He looked up to see the rapid flicker of something scrolling through the sector's astronomical database. "And they'll tell you more about us than nav charts."

"All right."

Seth got up and went back into the galley to brew a cup of tea, warming to the idea that he had a visitor on board who apparently meant no harm. First contact, as approved by the Commonwealth of United Planets, was a complex and formal process, rife with protocol and well-meant advice. But in fact it was mostly the traders, rebels and privateers that stumbled upon new species, not always to the benefit of both sides. He reminded himself to step carefully around this one, especially since he seemed to have no effective means to keep it out of his systems.

"Why do you have stories about copulation?"

Seth winced. He might have been blushing. "Try another story," he said quickly. "Please."

"All right. Oh. Khoe. I like Khoe."

"That's a nice name. Delphian, I think. It's a girl's name."

"Girls seem more interesting in your stories."

"I think so, too," he said.

"Then why are you a boy?"

Seth wondered if perhaps he was not the most suitable Trans-Targon representative for a first contact situation. A Union xenologist would know what to make of this individual. And perhaps know how to get it off his ship. "You're going to have to read some more," he said finally. "It's difficult to explain."

The hours, days and weeks he spent traveling through real-space between jumpsites left him with little to do but study and learn. Over these past dozen years or so, the database he had amassed had made him as much of an ethnologist as any of the Union's experts. But, considering the rate at which this creature absorbed information, there was probably little he could explain better than his library could.

"All right," the newly female visitor said in a voice to match.

"So what do you look like?"

"Nothing. Not to your eyes."

"Nothing? Just energy? A neural net of some sort?"

She seemed to think about that. Or perhaps consult his archive. "Particles. Composite particles. As you think of them. Not physical. But it works like that. Your particles need to be together in one place to function. Ours don't."

"Something must be holding your cognitive process together."

"Energy does. Out here you do. Does that bother you?"

Oh, yes, he thought. "Just curious."

"I can look like something, if you need that."

Seth frowned when a vague distortion of light and air coalesced before him. He stepped around the counter separating the galley from the cabin and circled the thing taking shape there. He gasped when a small Prime formed, growing arms, legs, torso, head. It moved slowly as if discovering its limbs as they appeared. Details emerged as it sprouted hair and sharpened its features. "Cazun..." he evoked for the second time that day.

The small being taking form looked toward him, its eyes not quite focused on his face. "You have so many shapes. Is this correct?"

"Hmm, looks like a Feydan juvenile. Female child. But the hair is Human, maybe Centauri."

The stranger grew in size, changing her form several times along with hair and skin color. Seth's eyes widened in surprise and a slow grin tugged on his lips. He turned away with some reluctance.

"Don't do that," Khoe said. "I'm using your eyes. I cannot see me if you're not looking at me."

"Put some clothes on," he said, feeling the absurdity of the moment.

"I'm in your head. I can't feel cold if you don't." She fell silent for a moment. "Oh. Cultural idiosyncrasy. You can look now."

He turned back, a little sorry that the pleasantly curved shape she had flashed at him was now covered by what looked like a mix of Magran and Feydan clothes, fetchingly arranged.

She inspected herself through his eyes while she changed a few things to her liking. "Is this funny?" she said when he smiled.

"Green hair? That is… rare among our species."

"You don't like it?"

"Doesn't matter what I like," he said diplomatically.

She went through another series of changes, picking individuals seemingly at random from his database.

"Not that," he said when a tall redhead, Human and in uniform, appeared before him.

"You said it doesn't matter."

"That one does."

She changed her hair to blue and her features to the sharp contours of a Delphian. Finally she decided, perhaps in deference to his own origin, to present herself as mostly Centauri, with the characteristic violet eyes that reflected the dim light of the cabin. She settled on Bellac Tau for a source of her hair, which now hung in long white ropes from her head.

He watched her play with some gestures and facial expressions she found among his data files. Why was it that even a gender-neutral wisp of energy escaping subspace managed to figure out what female traits unerringly hit their target?

"So if you're only in my head and in my processors, you're not actually there?" He pointed at the spot where she stood, her feet not quite touching the floor.

"That's right. You only think you see me."

His brows drew together as he contemplated this. "You seem awfully real. I can hear you, see you, like I would anyone." He stepped closer and cautiously touched her arm.

Both of them recoiled when he encountered solid substance under his fingers. Clearly, he had felt the soft fabric of the shirt she created out of nothing. She seemed as surprised as he.

"You felt that?" he asked.

"Yes. No. I felt what you felt. What your fingers felt. It's a strange thing."

"Guess that isn't something you can read up on."

"I can't see your face, though." She reached out to find his chin, rubbed awkwardly over his nose, and then lingered over a scar above his eye. Seth had to smile when she touched her own face and then leaned closer to turn left and right as if examining herself in a mirror.

He winced when she jabbed a finger into his midriff. She did, too, but whether in response to the touch or to copy his reflex was unclear. Seth considered once again the possibility that he was suffering a mental collapse. How could any of this be real? It wasn't real, of course. She created every sound and sight and now this touch in his mind. What difference did it make if a sensation was real or if his brain simply told him it was? It was the same, in the end, wasn't it? Neurons reacting to stimuli, real or imagined.

Something even more disturbing came to mind. "You... I mean, can you tell what I'm thinking? My thoughts?"

"No, I cannot. You're worried that I'm spying into your mind? Do you have secrets?"

"Everyone does." He watched her experiment with hand motions that looked like various forms of greeting. "How do your people sustain yourselves?"

"Out here? Your thorium. And you, a little." She clapped

her hands, apparently pleased by the sound it created.

Seth hurried into the cockpit. Indeed, the monitors there showed a slight drain of the ship's thorium levels. Not yet alarming, but noticeable. "Me?" he said, a little worried.

"Yes. I don't need much. Most of the time."

"Most of the time?" He looked up and then did a quick double-take when she appeared to be floating in the air. He supposed there was no real need for her to be standing on the *Dutchman*'s deck plates.

"I expect that if you do more, you have to eat more," Khoe said philosophically. "Holding this shape for you is taking up energy. Is this making you tired? Hungry?"

"A little."

"Then you must eat. I need more words. I will look at more stuff now." As soon as she said this, she simply winked out of sight.

"Didn't mean to bore you," he grumbled.

TWO

When Seth awoke hours later he smiled with the realization that all of this had been a very strange dream. The breach into the *Dutchman*'s tightly-guarded systems, the girl, everything. He blinked up the ceiling, having as usual simply fallen asleep on the main cabin's lounger rather than one of the bunks in the cramped and untidy crew quarters. He stretched and turned to find himself nose to nose with Khoe.

"Damn!" he exclaimed and jerked back. "What are you doing?"

"Practicing sleep."

"You have to sleep?"

"No. But your brain does interesting things when you do."

He sat on the edge of the lounger and ran his hands through his tousled hair. "You don't just crawl into someone's bed uninvited."

"Oh," she said as if making note of that. "I was bored."

He turned to look at her, unsure if he should be amused or annoyed. "You live in subspace. We call that the Big Empty. What's more boring than that?"

"It's not empty. And turning yourself off for hours at a time seems pretty boring to me." She drifted past him to hover near the cockpit entrance. Her language skills had improved over these past few hours and had taken on a pleasant twang. "Besides, we don't count time. We're almost at Rishabel."

"We're not landing *on* Rishabel. There is a station in orbit I need to visit to top up the coolant. And maybe thorium, if I can get some there."

"I know your flight plan. You are going to the correct place."

"I am definitely *not* in the correct place."

"You are. I brought you here."

"You what? How? And, just to round things out, why?"

"There's no need to shout. I will put you back. I need to find... something. I can't get there on my own. Obviously."

"Nothing is obvious right now. Who are you looking for? How would you know who is on that orbiter?"

"Some people there took something from us. I can feel its presence from here." She shrugged as if there was no more to the story.

Seth stared at her for a while, digesting this bit of news. "Who took what?"

"I don't know who. One of your ships passed and some of my people got stuck. One of them is very important. They took them all to Rishabel."

"Important?" Seth said, still not even close to understanding how subspace could possibly give rise to sentient beings.

"Very. Without it we can't be."

"Can't be what?"

"Just *be*. We need it to exist. It makes us live, I suppose."

"So what happens if you don't get it back?"

"We stop being," she said as if surprised by the simple-mindedness of his question. "Eventually. And there won't be new ones. Without it, we're just particles scattered around subspace."

"You don't seem worried."

She fell silent while, he assumed, she checked his archives for some reference. "I am, I think." She pondered this a little more. "I will combine emotions with physical symptoms. Is that correct?"

Seth winced. "Within reason."

"I will study that. But, yes, I am afraid for my kind. We are fragile."

"And so you are going to... do what? Ask the people on Rishabel nicely to give your friend back?"

"Or maybe you could. I'm sure they didn't mean to. We would like to learn how they did that. And maybe not have that happen again."

He scratched his head. "If they're out here they're likely rebels or pirates. Not the sort of people you ask nicely."

"You're out here."

He sighed. "For someone who's learned six languages in a matter of hours you're being awfully obtuse."

"Are you going to help me?"

"We'll have a look around, since I have no choice but to go there, anyway. I don't promise anything. And then you're going back to wherever you came from." Technically, he supposed, the thing to do was to contact one of the Union's research stations to report a sighting of what may well be a heretofore unknown species. Of course, since he was the only one who could actually communicate with this one, reporting it might just waste a perfectly good opportunity to stay far, far away from Union concerns. "Do you have to do that? Float around like that? It's a bit creepy."

"I don't know where the floor is unless you're looking at it."

He dropped his eyes and, indeed, she lowered herself to let her feet touch the floor. They were bare, he noted, but then there was no real need for her to wear shoes, anyway.

He stood up. "You really only see what I see?"

She moved farther away from him and carefully put one foot in front of the other to walk around the small space between the cockpit and the lounge. "And your ship's cameras, but they're not on. Don't worry, I won't look at your stuff if you have to go bathe yourself or whatever you do."

"Thank you," he said, a little primly and with a growing suspicion that she was enjoying herself tremendously, as he left for the crew cabin.

He made use of the ship's hygiene chamber and then dug through his inventory for something suitable for Rishabel. He normally slouched around the *Dutchman* in well-worn coveralls but now slipped into a clean shirt and lightly armored jacket, sturdy leather trousers and boots. Doing that, he wondered if his passenger was actually and tactfully averting her eyes. He doubted that he would.

Before nodding off on the lounger, he had spent a few hours poring through his database as well, looking for any instance of an unknown entity emerging from subspace or of any sentient species known to live in there. He had found nothing. Was she telling the truth? Or was he victim to the intrusion of some sophisticated artificial intelligence? If so, where was the program? Who would send a shape-shifting apparition to watch him sleep? That someone had become interested in his movements presented more of a problem than having an alien aboard.

An hour later he received permission to dock onto one of the piers stretching out from the orbiter's central, domed hub like the legs of a dark arachnid. He swung the *Dutchman* around a bit to see what else was parked there and saw mostly private cruisers and small transports lining the covered concourse. In the distance, a curved platform accommodated freighters and black sky travelers. The interior of the massive dome enclosing a town of sorts was coated with something no one ought to be breathing in. It was night on this side of the planet and most of what he saw was outlined in multi-colored lights, dimmer inside the dome.

He approached the upper level of the two-tiered dock when a plane below caught the attention of the *Dutchman*'s scanners. It was always prudent to be alert to the presence of Air Command patrols in case one wanted to avoid them. Seth usually did. And now his sensors picked up a definite scent of military among the hardware on the pier.

"Now what brought that bird down here," he muttered to himself as he eased the *Dutchman* into its assigned berth.

"Birds?" Khoe said, making him flinch in surprise at her sudden appearance beside him. "Where?"

"Not a real bird. There is a military ship down there."

She followed him to the airlock where he picked up his weapons. "Are you going to shoot them?"

"What? No."

"Are you going to shoot rebels?"

He sighed. "When are you going home again?"

She shrugged.

"I'm going to have a look around. Go scan some more stuff. I won't be long."

She laughed. It was an agreeable sound, taken from a Feydan recording, he suspected. "You still think I'm some program living in this flying machine? I'm in your head, Sethran. Where you go, I go. Besides, you don't really think I'd wait around here while you're exploring out there, do you?"

"You don't need the plane to... for energy?"

"No. You're enough. And I can tap into other things here, I'm sure."

"All right. As long as nobody notices you doing that."

Outside, Seth tested his legs for a moment, finding the gravity reasonable. The air in this tunnel leading to the hub tasted humid and stale. Whatever kept it moving up here created unpleasant turbulence that chased garbage along the concourse and people hurried by with their heads tucked between their shoulders. The Genen native stalking past him had no shoulders and Seth felt mildly sympathetic.

After haggling over the coolant he needed to get back to civilization, he crossed over to the vehicle rental at the perimeter of the concourse and signed out a skimmer, a small two-seat sled. He paid real currency, as always. His favorite kind of money included bits that were not easily traced.

The sled took him to the lower dock to where his sensors had detected that suspicious cruiser. He trundled past the ship, looking for signs that this was not just the sort of nondescript private traveler favored by those who could afford them. The crossdrive port markings looked familiar, as did the rear shield assembly. Someone had taken pains to disguise it but he knew enough about Targon-built technology to recognize this as Air Command issue.

He put his foot on the ground to steady the skimmer just outside the perimeter scan range. This boat had seen action, that much was clear. Eagle class, he suspected, which meant Vanguard agents. What were they doing all the way out here on Rishabel? So far, Air Command, the Union's military arm, had shown little interest in this planet. Their jurisdiction did not extend out here and, while Rishabel's leaders tolerated rebels and smugglers, none of the Union's firepower was welcome here. Smugglers brought revenue; military brought trouble.

"What are you doing?" Khoe said, peering over his shoulder where only a moment ago she had hovered in front of him.

He ducked out of the way. "Must you do that? You don't need to move around at all, do you?"

"No. Just having fun. This all so new. You have no idea how exciting this is." She spun in front of his sled, long braids flying somewhat contrary to the laws of local gravity, her arms stretched out to encompass all he saw.

He looked around the dreary concourse as he started the vehicle up again. "I admire your attitude. So where is this ship you're looking for?"

She pointed at his data sleeve and waited while he ran the mapper. Guided by her, it scrolled through the hub of the orbital station, laid out like the spokes of a wheel. Their destination appeared to be the edge of the shipping platform near the shield generators. Probably not the finest part of town. Likely popular as a place where the generators would nicely confound most scanners.

"Do you know what sort of ship it is?"

She pondered a moment, recalling his archives. "Transport class. Fleetfoot, I think."

"That's a small cargo vessel. Black?"

"I don't know. We don't have color. I just recently got eyes." She pointed at his face. He waved her hand away before realizing that, to someone watching them, that probably looked odd.

"Likely smugglers in that class of ship," he said. "Let's go take a look."

Considering the distance from the ground to this city in orbit, the temperature of the stale air up here felt oppressive. By the time Seth threaded his way through the increasing commercial traffic on the loading dock, his hair clung to the skin of his neck and visions of a long bath shifted around his thoughts. Or maybe just a nice hot shower instead of the stinging decon cycle aboard his *Dutchman*. He looked up along the vast, curving wall of the dome to see its apex lost in a haze of pollutants and moisture. It occurred to him that any water available for bathing up here was probably poorly recycled or condensate. He decided to wait for friendlier shores before looking for a swim.

The dock turned out to be an expanse of multi-level rail systems along dismal racks of storage units used for warehousing as well as shipping. A few of those moved around overhead, hinting by the creaks issuing from their derricks that walking beneath them was ill advised.

"How do you know which ship you're looking for?" Seth said, slowing to cruise past the air locks leading into the parked transports. Some of the massive hulks looked like they had felt one too many debris fields. Outside the transparent dome larger vessels hovered at a distance, using cargo tugs to exchange crews and merchandise.

"I can feel… my friend. It's near here." She had decided to sit on the console of the skimmer and he noticed a few loose wisps of her hair moving with the air flow around the sled. He wondered if she made him see it like that or if his

24

brain just imagined it that way. Like in a dream, there was nothing about her that did not seem absolutely real. "Over there!"

"Huh? Where?"

"They've taken it this way." She changed the display on his mapper.

Seth turned into a narrow alley lined with dilapidated businesses and residences for hire. Most were housed in identical, box-shaped pre-fabs, stacked three or four high, festooned with elaborate artwork, signage, lights and flags to catch the attention of passersby. The garish lights and colors only seemed to emphasize the orbiting harbor's pervasive shades of gray.

They cruised by a shop offering engine and generator repairs. Not very profitably, judging by the state of the shop front. He pulled around the back of the building next to this one, out of sight of the people crowding the narrow street, and walked back.

Mildly bothered by the smell of sewage, he paused and listened. Through the surging, ceaseless sound of the city, he heard voices, shouts, laughter; none of it worrisome. Something thumped a slow rhythm somewhere and he guessed it to be a part of the ventilation system, obviously not doing a very good job. He fancied it as some massive, lumbering creature looming over them all and wondered why this place was putting such morbid thoughts in his head.

He entered the shop. Khoe moved ahead of him to look around the cluttered interior.

"What are you doing?" he whispered.

"Being a person. Doing person-things. There are people upstairs, according to your scanner. They have what I'm looking for." She froze, then cocked her head to the side. "Turn around."

"What? Why?" He turned to the window. There was nothing to see outside as most of the shop's interior was reflected by the glass.

She studied his reflection through his eyes. "You're

handsome."

A smile tugged on his lips. "How would you know?"

"From your literature. Stories. Some of your traits are admired."

"Just some?" he said in mock dejection.

"Hello?" An elder Human shuffled into the shop from a hallway, regarding Seth with curiosity and a considerable amount of suspicion.

"You don't have to talk out loud to me," Khoe said.

Now you tell me. Seth walked over to the rack of engines where the man took shelter as if about to be physically attacked. "Looking for some friends that might have come by here," he said meaningfully and handed over a vial containing a few grains of ordium.

"What's that?" Khoe asked.

Around here that's money.

The shopkeeper's expression changed immediately. "You need to get out. Three Vanguard agents showed up just a bit ago. Went upstairs. No idea why."

Seth's eyes went to the ceiling. "Just the one staircase?"

"Yes. You people are nothing but trouble. Nobody said anything about Air Command sticking their noses in. I'm closing up."

Seth allowed himself to be hustled out onto the street. Instead of returning to his sled, he sauntered along the shop front, nodded pleasantly at a trio of hookers, and then slipped into the service gap between the buildings. Keeping his head down to obscure the telltale glow of his Centauri eyes, he scaled a metal fence to reach the second floor. It only took a few moments to pry a window and slip into the building, using years of experience and a handy tool acquired on Feron.

Gun in hand, he crept through gray and empty rooms, his steps muffled by the compounds used to encase the sheets of metal and plastics of which the city was built. He circled around a hoist used to move machinery for repair or cleaning or whatever it was that happened up here. There were voices ahead, not sounding very friendly.

Once as close as he was likely to get, fished a crawler from his pocket and set it on the ground. The insect-size device, another of his favorite tools, scurried along the wall, guided by Seth's neural implant, into a partitioned area at the rear of the building. He inserted a small speaker into his ear and then tilted the crawler's minute sensor upward to study the people that now appeared on the monitor of his data sleeve.

"I could have done that."

Seth flattened himself against the wall, catching his breath after these words nearly startled him into pulling the trigger of his pistol. "Don't do that!" he gasped.

She put a finger to her lips. "Shh. They'll hear you."

Look, just because you can't get your head shot off doesn't mean I can't. So please be quiet and quit jumping out at me when I'm trying to concentrate.

"Actually, if you get your head shot off I'm in a whole lot of trouble," she said. "You're not used to having people around, are you? I just wanted to point out that I can ride that thingie you're using and show you what I see in there."

Don't get involved. That crawler is working just fine.

She sighed dramatically as she stalked away and he wondered where she had learned that trick. *Thingie?* What else was she digging up in his database?

He returned his attention to his crawler. It actually wasn't working just fine as the electromagnetic interference in this part of town turned things into a bleary haze over there. He wondered if more significant radiation was currently working on reducing his lifespan. Getting off this orbiter as soon as he had something that satisfied the alien seemed like a sensible strategy.

Things weren't going so well in that room. Two Centauri civilians sat on the floor in what seemed to be a squatter's hideaway. The three Vanguard officers loomed over them, weapons drawn. Unlike the plane they had left on the air field, none of the agents hid the fact that Air Command had arrived. Although dressed in a mix of civilian clothing from a number of distant worlds, their weapons were high-grade military issue and the small badge at their shoulder was something that lesser beings were supposed to heed. The calculated arrogance borne by Vanguard usually served well to intimidate and prompt compliance. Their authority was absolute on Union planets and not trifled with in more neutral areas.

Seth raised the sound level for his earpiece. *How did Air Command get mixed up in this?*

"You sort of have a choice, Pirate," one of the Vanguard officers, a powerfully-built Centauri woman, said to one of the men. "We can arrest you and lose you somewhere along the way, or you can just tell us where you were taking this thing."

"That's it," Khoe said. "That wheel in that man's hand."

What about it?

"That's what I need to get back."

Your person is inside that? Seth shifted the crawler's focus to the Human officer standing nearby. The man was studying the thick, disk-shaped object curiously as he hefted it from one hand to the other. It was thinner along the edge and the prongs extending from it seemed to connect to something else.

"Go get it, please."

Did you notice those guns? What makes you think they'll hand it over?

"It doesn't belong to them."

You're sweet. In a naïve sort of way. He turned his attention back to the Centauri soldier and her captives.

"We're traders," the man accused of being a pirate told her sullenly.

"Smugglers."

"Telling you nothing. You're going to off us anyway."

She raised a foot and tipped him over. His hands were bound behind him and his head met the floor with a bang. She put her boot on his shoulder and, judging by his expression, a lot of her weight, too. "What gave you such a low opinion of us?" she said amicably. "How about we just lock you up until we can get there? Deal?"

"We don't know where it's going! We deployed it during the jump and get paid for doing that. Some kind of experiment. No law against that, is there? Just trying to make a living and you come down heavy. Get your foot off me."

"Seth?" Khoe said. "Not trying to get involved here, but there's someone downstairs."

Seth crouched deeper into the shadows. The shopkeeper had left his cluttered lair when Seth had, so who was down there now? When Khoe boosted his scanner's signal he saw someone, several someones, approaching with stealth. Belatedly, he felt the gentle buzz of the alarm on his skin beneath the data sleeve.

"Who's that?" Khoe said when he peered down into the stairwell.

A beam of light stabbed through the dusty gloom as a tracer came looking for him. The silent shot that followed burned a ragged scratch into the plastic wall behind him. Seth spun around, debating only for a second between racing for the window where he had entered and the room at the end of the hall.

He burst through the door. "Incoming!" he shouted and shoved the Centauri out of the way. Only moments behind him, four armed men and women stormed the hallway, firing without prejudice. Seth lurched aside and saw the bound smugglers and one of the officers turn into a bullet-riddled mass of gore. He returned the fire, the Centauri at his side, but then the second soldier fell, his body crisscrossed by laser fire. They were driven back behind a tiled partition at the rear of the loft. Khoe hovered wide-eyed in the room and he had to restrain himself from pulling her to safety.

The Centauri officer, still standing but with a bullet wound to the thigh, shoved him against the wall. "Who the hell are you," she snapped, violet eyes blazing with fury, and punched her gun under his chin.

"No!" Seth felt Khoe's scream stab into his brain more than he heard it. It seemed to reverberate through his mind and body, filling him with a strange, electric sensation racing like a swarm of insects through his veins. He gripped the woman's arm, ready to defend himself, but she suddenly went rigid under his hands and her eyes widened in pain and fear. A mighty thunderclap ripped through his chest and the officer crumpled to the ground.

He, too, slumped to the floor, gasping, trying to comprehend what had just happened. The massive burst of energy surging through his body ebbed as quickly as it had begun and he felt himself fading along with it.

* * *

"Seth? Are you awake?"

Seth groaned as he sat up, taking a quick inventory of his body parts. There was a pain in his head that wasn't there before, but he seemed undamaged. "What the..?" Bodies on the floor. Blood. Nobody moving. Especially not the Centauri officer lying beneath him. He took a closer look, squinting through the gloom and his headache. "Dead. Gods, Khoe, what happened here?"

"Dead?"

"What did you do? To me? To her!"

"I don't know! I was scared. I thought she was hurting you."

He heaved himself upright. A laser had scorched the side of his jacket but not his skin. Among the dead were the two smugglers, their hands still tied behind their backs. "We better get out of here." The officers' Eagle would have sent an emergency message as soon as their neural implant failed to transmit their unique cerebral signature. Air Command would soon descend upon Rishabel in full force and he wanted to be long gone before that happened.

"They took it. The disk. Seth, they're gone!"

"I can see that." Besides missing the disk, none of the bodies seemed looted of valuables. Seth removed the

Centauri's data sleeve and used his gun to destroy those of the other officers. He made his way back to the window and out onto the fence which creaked alarmingly under his weight. It seemed forever before he was on his sled and racing back to his ship.

"You're angry," Khoe said after a while.

"That about describes it." He kept his eyes on the mapper while he took a small detour and varied his speed. None of the vehicles moving between this quarter and the docks seemed to be in pursuit of him.

"Why?"

"Don't pretend you don't know. I don't know how, but you killed someone today. You damn well understand what that means. And not just anyone. A Vanguard officer."

"But they're Union people. Air Command. You don't like them."

"What makes you think that?"

"You're a rebel, aren't you?"

"What? No, I'm not a rebel." He lowered the skimmer when they entered the airfield tunnels. There were fewer people around here now. The turbulence whipped refuse across the tarmac, making sounds like whispers in the dark. He shivered despite the cloying humidity, wanting only to be back inside his ship and a long way from here.

"Maybe you could have told me that before you sneak up on Air Command officers," she said and the voice in his head sounded clearly on the brink of tears. "There is nothing about you in your own database. How am I supposed to know? I thought she was going to kill you."

He closed his eyes for a moment and took a deep breath. She was right. The Vanguard officer hadn't known, the attacking rebels hadn't known. Because they weren't supposed to. How would Khoe have known?

He moved across the lower concourse of the small-craft docks and came to a halt by the Vanguard's Eagle parked there.

"That's not your ship."

"No. It belongs to that Vanguard team back there." He pulled the officer's data sleeve from a pocket. "You're going to get some info for me. This should get you into there."

"Me? You told me not to get involved. I don't want to be involved." She paused. "You saw what happened when I do."

"Are you going to snivel or are you going to help me?"

Another pause. "How?"

"Get into that ship and download anything that mentions Rishabel to my data sleeve. And anything else from the last few days. Conversations, records, messages sent and received." He turned when a buzzing sound alerted him to the arrival of a small sentinel, sent by whoever found his presence on the docks interesting.

"Evening," Seth said politely. He pulled a square of flavored gum from a pocket and chewed it slowly. The air here tasted as dirty as it looked.

The floating camera circled him once before halting in front of his face. He swatted it and it backed off.

"Is there something you need?" a tinny voice reached him from the speaker of his data sleeve.

"No."

There was a brief pause. "Then why are you out there?" the air field guard finally said.

"Waiting for a date."

"You have no business near that ship. Move along."

"Thinking of making an offer for this one," Seth nodded toward the Eagle. "Any idea who it belongs to?"

"It's not for sale," he was told after a moment.

"Everything is for sale." Seth swung a long leg over the back of the sled and then ambled to the plane. The sentinel followed close enough to whip his hair into his face.

"Tough protocols in place," Khoe said. "Too tough for your transmitter, with this interference. Try touching the ship. The keyplate by the door."

Seth leaned toward the guard bot as if taking a closer look at it. "You've got something on your lens. Let me get that for you." He snatched the sentinel out of the air before its sensors could react. Carefully, he pasted his gum over its single eye. "There you go." He released it and watched it spin away.

"Clear that visor immediately!" the guard's voice rose several notches.

"All right, all right. You need to grow a sense of humor." Seth pretended to chase the disoriented drone, moving close enough to touch the stolen sleeve to the Eagle's key plate. Khoe's image wavered momentarily as she shifted her attention to the plane's system. A series of lights flashed on the key panel but the ship remained quiet.

With hopefully enough information gathered about the ship, Seth strode back to his sled and climbed aboard. A door on the guardhouse at the edge of the concourse opened to release a rather capable-looking Centauri, apparently less than pleased with the situation. "Sorry, it's too quick for me," Seth said to the sentinel. "I'm late for my date. Have a nice evening."

* * *

Soon back aboard the *Dutchman*, now fully supplied with fresh coolant, Seth wasted no time in requesting clearance for departure. He set course for the nearest jumpsite, back the way he had come. He flew manually for a while, brooding in silence. Khoe also seemed uneager to communicate.

Finally, he engaged the autopilot and moved into the main cabin. Khoe appeared as if he had called to her, but she curled up in one of the bucket chairs and did not look at him. He regarded her silently for a moment, wondering if she struck that pose because of what she had learned from his files or if the image she presented to him was beginning to correspond to her mood on its own.

He sat down on the lounger, again aware that he was unqualified to deal with this first contact situation. This stranger had reacted to a threat in ways no one, including she, could have foreseen. Obviously, Khoe was not as harmless as she appeared and that discovery had cost someone's life. The xenobiologists on Targon would probably trade their first-born for a chance to study this individual.

"Can you tell me what happened back there?" he said without making the question sound like an accusation.

She lifted her shoulders. "I told you. I was scared. Maybe angry. I just meant to... to weaken her I guess. Push her away from you."

"I believe you." He recalled the pain of a whole lot of power surging through him. "You took her... her energy somehow? Neural energy? Through me? You said before that you can take that from me."

She didn't reply for a while. "I think so. I didn't know that would happen. I was just so scared. I didn't mean to hurt you. Or her."

"Your next dip into my archives is going to be physiology. Try to figure out how you affect us out here."

She finally lifted her head. Her haunted expression seemed far too pained to be anything but genuine and Seth felt a stab of compassion for his visitor. "You want me to go away," she said.

He looked into that sad face, that pleasing assembly of whatever traits she had come to like among his species, and found himself entirely unsure of what he wanted. There was something undeniably fascinating about this creature and he, a lifelong scholar of the races inhabiting Trans-Targon's many worlds, yearned to learn more about it.

What he was not prepared to admit to himself was that this unique person, evolving by the hour, also held considerable appeal. He spent much of his time alone here on the *Dutchman*. And when among people he was often in the rough company of felons and rebels or the fleeting comfort of women he never knew long enough to care for. Khoe's unpredictable and vexing presence here felt like a little sunlight in the night.

"I don't know if this is a good place for you," he said carefully. "You will need to go home sometime."

"I need to find that disk! You don't understand. I have no home without it. None of us do."

"Do you know what those smugglers want with your... person?"

"No."

Seth thought back to the horrific blast of energy surging through him to kill the officer. And the intense pain he suffered when Khoe first entered his brain and the way she had put him instantly to sleep. Of course, the ease with which she had cut through the *Dutchman*'s encryptions was the most remarkable thing of all. He had no trouble imagining how these entities might be very useful. And valuable. "I think you do," he said. "You're dangerous out here. To us. You saw that." He raised his hands when she started to protest. "I believe that you didn't mean to do that. But there is some powerful energy transfer going on. People will be interested. And frightened by it."

"Are you?"

He tipped his head back and looked for answers on the ceiling. "You took a chance when you came aboard this ship. Hoping I'd be useful. That I'd help you. What would you have done if I hadn't agreed? If I wasn't able?"

"Another of my people would try again with another pilot, I guess," she said. "Before those smugglers leave this sub-sector. We won't be able to find them if they get too far. Your... space is so, uh, unconnected."

"So should I be frightened? I am, I guess, your prisoner now. Stuck with you in my head."

She sat up. "I don't want you to be stuck. That wasn't our intent. We need you. And I trust you. You tried to help those soldiers when you could have just escaped. You were upset when they died. I think you could help me because you want to." She allowed herself a small smile. "And you have more curiosity than good sense, I think."

He grinned. "That has been problematic in the past."

"If you want me to go away, I will. You don't have to do this. You're not a prisoner."

"What'll happen to you if I ask you to leave?"

She shrugged. "I don't know. I could try to join with another of your people. Although now I know to ask, first. Or maybe I'll just stop being."

He winced.

"I don't think I'm wrong about—" She suddenly leaped out of her chair, eyes wide.

"What? Khoe?"

"They're opening a keyhole. They're going to jump!"

"A keyhole? Not the jumpsite?"

"No. They're going into the breach. Now. We won't get there on time."

He hurried into the cockpit and sat down to engage the *Dutchman*'s neural interface. "Where?"

She accessed his navigator to show him coordinates much closer than the charted and stable gateway into other parts of Trans-Targon, the one that most pilots used to travel the immense distances separating the explored areas of their sector. But these new coordinates lay nowhere near those. The *Dutchman* reported a keyhole, difficult to detect and even more difficult to navigate. There were several such breaches in this area but using those required a tremendous amount of coolant, a very capable ship and, most importantly, a navigator with the necessary mental ability to find his way out again.

Seth changed their course. "It's not that far. But I'm just a chartjumper. I can open that keyhole but I won't be able to span it. It takes a special talent to do that. Most of us don't have that."

"I do," she said, her attention on the ship's sensors. "There they are. Too far."

"We'll get there soon," he said, looking up into her tense face. "Don't worry."

"Yes, but that span has three possible exits. They could emerge anywhere. Too far for me to follow." She closed her eyes and her shoulders slumped. "Gone. They jumped. Too late."

He surprised himself by reaching out to take her hand. She flinched when she felt her skin under his touch. "We'll get some advice," he said, half expecting her hand to melt through his fingers. But it was solid and soft and there was nothing about that hand that didn't seem utterly real. "I know some very smart people. Don't give up."

She also seemed fascinated by the hand that held hers. "You'll help me? You don't mind, then? Me being here?"

He smiled quickly and released her. "I'm always up for an adventure," he said. "So let's get busy and get you home again."

"What are we going to do?"

"First, a little clean up and intel gathering. I like to keep things tidy." He avoided glancing into the cluttered cabin behind him when he said this. "My DNA is all over that officer. Unfortunately, it's also all over Air Command files. They'll be looking for me. I know someone who can call them off. He won't like it, but he'll do it."

"For someone who's not a rebel you're awfully shy of Air Command."

"We've had disagreements. We'll head to Feyd. I do a little work for someone there."

"But not a rebel?"

"Hardly. My boss is Baroch."

"Baroch? Delphian. Factor. One of the ten governors of the whole entire Commonwealth?"

"The same. He's my source of Union intel and clearance, which is useful. He can find out what Air Command has to do with your people being stolen."

"And you think he'll get them to stop chasing you for killing the officer?"

"I hope so. As far as the Commonwealth sees things, you either follow their rules or you're a rebel. An outlaw. If Baroch says I'm not an outlaw, Air Command they will accept that."

Chris Reher

"Then it's lucky you're friends with someone powerful like that."

"It's been helpful," he agreed, surprised by her comment and relieved to have avoided an ethics debate about getting away with murder. "Sometimes things are dealt with... carefully. Out of sight. Most of the Union governors are civilians. They can't always use Air Command to... proxy for them. So most of them have their own staff."

"Spies. Agents," she said, pointing at him. "Assassins."

"You read too much. Few people know what I do. Or for whom. Most think I'm a mercenary or smuggler or something. You can't get far into rebel territory if you're flying a Union flag. So I keep my hands dirty."

She frowned. "That's a lonely way to live. And dangerous."

He shrugged. "Kind of profitable, too."

She browsed through his archive and brought an image of Factor Baroch onto the screen. Severe features scowled down on them, not softened by the slate blue hair so tightly pulled back into the traditional Delphian braid that the skin of his forehead seemed stretched. "And you think he'll help?"

"I'm not much good to him in prison. He'll make it go away. Also, he's Delphian, as you can see. His people don't really care much about Commonwealth expanding into places they shouldn't be. I can trust him to keep news about you quiet until we know more. You'd be of great interest to Air Command."

"Me?"

He nodded. "They'll want to... meet you."

She tilted her head. "Stop treating me like a newborn, Sethran, even if that's what I am. You think they'll hurt me, don't you. Because they'll want to know what I am. Or..." She chewed on her lip in a way that seemed Human. "Or because of what happened. What I did back there."

"Let's not find out. Baroch lives on Feyd when he's not on Commonwealth business, so you'll jump us there. I want him to get us in touch with one of their Shantirs."

"The Delphian priests? Why?"

"They're not even remotely priests although that's the story. Officially. Not so official is that they can hack into my brain as easily as you can. Baroch can find us a Shantir without drawing attention."

"And a Shantir will help us?"

"I think so. They don't care about the Commonwealth at all. But they care about other species. And they're a curious bunch. I have a feeling they've heard of your people by now. They've been poking around subspace more than any of us have."

She seemed unconvinced, still focused on the image on the screen. "I don't know if I want one of them... umm, in here with us."

"In my head, you mean?"

"Yeah."

"It appears that I have a lot of empty space in here." Seth relayed the information she had stolen on the Eagle from his data sleeve to the main screens before them. "We have some time before we get to that keyhole. Let's see if we can get anything useful from what those officers had."

"They didn't know where those smugglers were going."

"I don't think they were going anywhere. I think those people were just collecting for someone else and Air Command walked in before they handed the goods over. Pirates, smugglers, even most rebel bands don't have spanners that can use keyholes. That sort of navigator is just too rare. Anyone like that would have more interesting jobs than flying around places like Rishabel." He let a long row of symbols and images scroll over the monitors. "Whoever is after your people owns some pretty powerful talent. And the attack back there was precisely executed. They didn't even loot the bodies. That's telling us something."

They combed through the files, finding references to the trip to Rishabel, some discussion about Delphi, a message to someone's friend on Targon. Seth happily tucked a few unrelated morsels away for future reference but his main interest was the incident with the people that had taken the subspace entity.

"They don't like Rishabel any more than you do," Khoe said after a while. "What's wrong with the place?"

"Kinda ugly, don't you think?"

"I haven't been anywhere else. There, I think I found a message from their colonel." She transferred the file to the main screen. It had been a while since Seth had seen the officer but it was unmistakably Colonel Carras, the commander of Air Command's Vanguard squadron.

"We read your report with interest, Captain Rephan," the Centauri colonel said in his usual, slow drawl. "Good work. Go ahead and head over to Rishabel. The rebel we picked up is barely coherent but Targon wants it checked out, anyway. The objective will be a metal wheel, fairly heavy, trading hands out there. On a Fleetfoot tagged *Haygen*. Secure and return without delay to Targon for quarantine. Project is classified as *Sius Red* under General Dmitra. His people are tracking the other incursions."

Seth paused the display. "Other incursions?" He glanced over to Khoe, who had decided to perch on the main console in front of him. "You shouldn't sit on that."

"You only *think* I'm sitting on it." She slid off the board. "I didn't want to frighten you again."

"I was startled back there," he amended. "That's not the same thing. Any idea what he meant by 'other incursions'?"

"None." She tapped the screen where the colonel's image was frozen into a still frame. "It's not an incursion. We didn't mean to come here."

"*You* did."

"We are expanding the operation," Colonel Carras continued when Seth resumed the message. "Your priority will be to secure the mechanism being used to harvest the pathogen. Vanguard Seven's heading for Delphi to make inquiries there. Good luck with retrieving the storage unit. I'll be tied up with the Shaddallam event for a while yet. Carras out."

"Harvest." Khoe grimaced. "That sounds evil."

"Pathogen," Seth pondered. "Doesn't sound like he thinks your people are sentient. It also sounds like they think you might be dangerous to our species. If someone's collecting your kind Air Command is going to pay very close attention. And they'd want to know how it's done."

"So do I," she said. "If we can find out how it's done, we can maybe find a way to avoid it. Your Air Command people are going to try that 'harvest' for themselves, aren't they? Your people are a curious species. Collectively speaking." She considered this for a moment. "Would they, though, if they knew that we're not some pathogen? That we're sentient?"

Seth nodded slowly. "The Commonwealth grows by including other worlds peacefully. Mostly for profit. But not if they think you're dangerous. Doesn't sound like Air Command thinks you're harmless. And today we've given them another reason." He looked over the screen showing the message packet code. "What he said about consulting Delphi is interesting. Guess I'm right about checking this out with Baroch. I'm surprised this message wasn't sent more securely."

"It was," she said. "Took me a while to get through the encryption. The tab on it was coded with a symbol like a hand."

He raised his eyebrows. "A hand? Are you sure?"

"Yes."

He whistled appreciatively. "You've got talent, lady. You might want to encrypt it again. Do you still have the code?"

She tapped her forehead. "What goes in there stays in there." She pointed at his head. "Actually, in there."

"I'm going to start charging you rent, I think. Speaking of which..." he peered at one of the maintenance monitors on the console. "We might want to pick up more thorium. You're an expensive house guest."

"Pardon? I wasn't listening, being so busy decoding your

secret messages."

"Your secret messages, darling. If not for you, I'd be on my way to Aram for a payday."

THREE

The creature, dark and insectile, had barely moved during the endless hours since the last jump. After their ship emerged from subspace, the pain in Liron Deve's head felt like someone was pulling his brain out of his eye sockets. He'd passed out; the only way his commander would let him get away with remaining in his bunk while the others went to meet their contacts over Rishabel. The headache stopped soon enough and then the madness began.

The thing crouching in the middle of the cabin shifted now and again, sometimes spoke in languages Deve didn't recognize, and ignored Deve unless Deve tried to leave. Or speak. Or call for help. At those times it lashed out with *something* that caused such intense pain that he soon learned to cower on his bunk and keep his mouth shut. Where were the others? It had been hours since they left to deliver the disks.

The thing was some sort of alien, that much was clear. Deve had never bothered to learn much about the non-Prime species of Trans-Targon but when he tried to capture an image of it to feed into his data sleeve, he'd gotten some more of that pain.

Something was going on with the unit on his wrist. The com was busy, and the indicators on the flexible screen showed constant activity. He wondered if a systems diagnostic was being run aboard the ship while docked on the orbiter.

He flinched when the creature moved across the floor. Its primitive extremities reshaped into something vaguely mammalian, grew in size, changed in color, and sprouted dense, horse-like hair, patterned in blond and brown whorls like those of a Caspian.

Deve, himself Human like most of this crew, stared in mute incomprehension as its hands grew an extra thumb and then fierce claws appeared on the oversized feet. Like those of all Caspians, its reproductive organs were internal but the shape of its elongated head along with powerful shoulders identified it as a male.

The yellow eyes turned to Deve. After a long silence, the alien shifted again to thicken his waist, a weak point of the Caspian body, and changed his rich caramel color to dark gray with black patterns over his back and thighs. For some bizarrely whimsical reason he reshaped his head to look almost Human. "That'll do, I think," he said finally in a voice that sounded as if it came from the next room.

Deve cringed back against the wall by his bunk in an attempt to make himself as small as possible – a difficult feat for a man of his size. Expecting another surge of pain for his impertinence, he said, "What... who are you? What do you want?"

The alien considered the question for a while. "Looking for someone," he said. "You're going to help me."

"What? Not likely! You'd better get off this ship before the boss gets back here. He won't tolerate stowaways aboard."

"There is not much he can do about that," the alien said. He turned slowly in front of Deve. "Only you can see me. That's a pity, don't you think? Should I add a tail?"

"Tail? What..." Deve frowned, overwhelmed by all of this.

"I'll take a Caspian name. Call me Lep Ako." The alien

sat down on Deve's bed, companionably close. Deve tried to shrink back and found himself out of room. "Grow a spine, Pirate," Lep Ako said, using words and an accent that had never crossed a Caspian's lips. "I've just spent a long time trying to figure this place out and you people are so irrational it's making my brain hurt. Your brain." He pointed to Deve's data sleeve. "Nothing useful on that, but I got to the ship's data bank. And from there I grabbed anything I wanted on this orbiter. It's been enlightening. We better leave."

Deve blinked. "Huh?"

"Leave. As in: go away. I might have tripped something so some folks are getting nosy out there."

"You didn't! Boss'll tear my head off if we ruin things with Rishabel. You don't mess with the locals."

Lep Ako nodded. "I know that now. Come, let's leave before your master returns."

"He's not my master."

A slow grin pulled on Lep Ako's features. "That's true. I am."

"You are nothing! I'm imagining this whole thing. I've heard about people coming out of that jumpsite with their brains scrambled. What I need is a doctor."

"What you need is a little discipline."

Deve's eyes widened when the alien raised his hand toward him. He launched himself from his cot to race for the door. But Lep Ako slapped his shoulder in mid-leap, almost playfully, and some tremendous electrical shock flowed from the alien's hand into his body. Deve stumbled over his own feet and slammed to the floor where he lay twitching and unable to move.

Lep Ako loomed over him. "Now look at the pain you've caused yourself. Lucky for both of us you're a healthy specimen. I'd love to see your face right now. This didn't bother me one bit, thank you for asking, unlike that hole you tried to punch into the wall earlier today to find out if you were dreaming." He cocked his head. "You're not the brightest among these Humans, are you? Don't worry about it. I'll do the thinking for both of us. You just keep your gun loaded and follow my lead and we'll work out just fine."

"Leave me alone," Deve moaned.

"That, unfortunately, I have no control over. I think we need to come to an understanding, Liron Deve, so you can stay healthy. About what is acceptable behavior. About who's in charge and what needs doing around here. Seems to me what you need is to stay pain-free, no?" Lep Ako waited until, finally, Deve nodded.

"There's our first understanding. Believe me, it's all for the best. You don't want to bust heads for your chief for the rest of your undoubtedly short life, do you? You can do something far better with your time."

Deve pulled himself up and leaned against the wall, not yet trusting his legs. "Like what," he said sullenly.

Lep Ako pulled back to walk across the room. Something about his feet seemed to bother him and he reshaped them at little. "Those claws are fearsome," he commented. "I have no idea how these creatures manage to walk with feet like this." He faced Deve again. "I just sucked up every last bit of data from every storage system on this station and you ask me 'like what'? Are you that stupid? We're going to have us a great adventure, you and I."

"What are you? Please just tell me."

"Time for that later. Get up. We need to go."

"We're not alone here. They won't want you on board."

"They won't know if you keep your mouth shut about me. And you will. Doing anything else will just get you dead."

Deve scrambled to his feet, rotating a shoulder still vibrating with whatever Lep Ako had done to it. "They'd think I've lost my mind, anyway," he muttered.

He left his cabin, aware of the alien moving along beside him. He paused in the narrow corridor leading to the ship's airlock. There were voices ahead. He glanced at Lep Ako, wondering if, truly, he was invisible to all but him. Could he warn the others before it harmed him? Perhaps he could pass some subtle signal. Surely, this creature was a danger to them all.

"Deve!"

Before Deve could duck out of the way, Sybelle, the captain's ever-present, silver-haired mistress, stood in his way. Wife, he reminded himself. It's what she liked to call herself. Whatever she was, the boss doted on her, leaving her the run of the ship until she had even replaced his second in command.

"Finally got your ass out of bed, I see," she said, daring him to make another excuse for doing nothing while the others worked. He glanced at Lep Ako hovering in the air beside him, not quite vertical, making no impression on the woman at all.

"Head hurts something awful," Deve said to her, knowing better than to show the disrespect this harpy deserved. Last time he ended up swamping the hygiene closets.

"Sure it does." Her eyes moved from his broad face down along his well-maintained body. He cringed inwardly, also remembering when he had mistaken her cruel teasing for an invitation to touch. The beating he received from the captain served as a warning to the rest of the male crewmembers. She pointed to the rear of the ship. "How about you get yourself some fresh air and help get those supplies on board. Boss'll want to take off the moment they get back here. They're way overdue as it is."

"Sure," he said. She made no effort to get out of his way. He felt her brush against his arm as he sidled around her to make his escape.

Deve could almost hear Lep Ako snigger spitefully in his ear but the alien made no comment. Somehow, this seemed more disconcerting than his ridicule would have been. But would he have mocked him for meekly taking orders from his master's bed-mate or for not alerting his crew to the alien among them?

He owed them for nothing. Nothing but years of living

rough aboard this tin bucket and ducking out of the way of Air Command patrols. He thought about what Lep Ako said earlier. Had the creature really circumvented the orbiter's security systems? If so, of what else was it capable? He envisioned simply slipping into some secure facility to make off with untold wealth. Taking any ship he fancied. Becoming someone to be reckoned with among his fellow thieves. After the servitude he endured aboard the *Haygen*, wielding the power this alien had shown him exceeded his imagination.

Wait and see, he told himself and strolled to the exit ramp, wrinkling his nose at the fetid air that greeted him. The expletives peppering his compatriots' language wasn't any less foul but he joined in as they brought the delivered supplies aboard and installed replacement coolant tubes.

"It's here," Lep Ako said. "Or it was. Not long ago. I can feel it."

"Feel what?"

"What I've come for." Lep Ako stabbed a finger against the side of Deve's head. "Just use your interface to talk to me, like you send commands to your data unit. No need to talk so people can hear you."

What did you come for?

"You won't understand. We need to get to the shops on the far side of the shipping docks."

I can't leave here. Things will go bad for me if I'm not here when the boss wants to leave. They'll be back soon. He'll want to leave this place at once.

"He'll leave without you. Your work here is done." Lep Ako leaned far too close to Deve, daring him to protest.

Cowed, Deve heaved another crate into the cargo bay. His *work* here, as smuggler and occasionally as pirate, meant risking his thick neck to protect his leader and whatever unexplained schemes he carried out in the name of profit and sometimes the Shri-Lan. Calling himself a rebel when it served his purpose only added a thin veneer of justification for what amounted to murder and theft in the name of a cause he didn't really understand anyway. Maybe it was time to move on.

He loaded his last crate and waved to his crew mates. "Taking a piss," he said and sauntered away from the docking platform to the service area. There were few people about and the loudest sound was the whistling of the breeze responding to the unevenly pressurized components of the station.

"From over there," Lep Ako said and the urgency in his voice made Deve walk more quickly. "I feel it. Get an air car."

"I have no currency for this place. I'm not even supposed to be off the ship. If the boss finds me out here he'll—" Deve yelped loudly when a pain rammed through his insides as if impaled on something sharp and unpleasant. He bent over, thinking he might vomit.

Lep Ako waited patiently until he straightened up again, pale and trembling. "Let that be the last bit of whining I hear from you, pirate," he said. "See that Human over there? Take his currency. Hurry."

Deve nodded and lurched along the concourse to follow his target into a poorly lit part of the service area. Like much of the place, it was deserted by anyone with more pleasant things to do elsewhere. It took only a few well-placed strikes with his large fists before the man fell to the ground, leaving his possessions for the taking.

"Not much here," Deve said. "It'll get me a car, though."

"So what are you waiting for."

They soon headed toward the orbiter's hub, guided by some beacon only Lep Ako perceived. Their route zigzagged as if following a moving target and Deve felt a growing agitation that wasn't his. His own had settled into a steady state of apprehension. What he perceived from this creature was anger and something akin to panic.

"What's wrong?" he dared to ask when they threaded their way through a crowded commercial quarter.

"It's not here anymore. The signal is static now, decaying."

Some residue left here. I need to find it. Turn left."

"Residue? What is it you're looking for? I can understand if you speak plainly."

"The sire. It's here, dragged out of subspace by your people's incompetence. I've been sent to find it. Return it."

"Sire? You mean like your father?"

The yellow eyes narrowed. "Do I look like I have a father? Don't try to think, Deve. It'll just hurt your brain."

"You don't have to be nasty," Deve said. "I get that you're in my head somehow. That means you need me to drag *you* around. I'm stuck with that, I guess, but I won't be your mule if you're going to make my life miserable. I'm not that attached to it, if you know what I mean."

The creature regarded him for a long moment and Deve prepared himself for another blast of pain. It didn't happen, perhaps because he was currently speeding through some very narrow gaps between buildings. "That's kind of sad," Lep Ako said. "Or it would be if I cared enough about your pathetic life. If you jump ship I'll find someone else. Do not threaten me."

Deve steeled himself. "What is this sire?"

"The beginning of all of us. Without it, we can't be. It draws us together, we join and grow into something that thinks and understands."

"There's only one of those sire-things?"

"Yes. Maybe it's a new beginning for our kind. Maybe it was all an accident. Just one more particle in a chain, maybe one change in the resonance, and something happened to make us into more than what we were."

"And it's out here now? In one of those disks we're delivering to the Shri-Lan?"

Lep Ako nodded. "I think that's what happened. Your people took it, took the sire, and some of us followed to get it back. Your ship passed by and I came along."

Deve furrowed his scarred brow. "Didn't think anything lives in subspace. It's just space in-between stuff. It's not really a place at all."

"Guess you're wrong about that, Human. Just as we were wrong about here. After all, it's possible for us to exist here." He considered for a moment. "Even if it means being tied to one such as you."

"You can find yourself someone else. I won't mind."

A cruel grin reshaped the alien's lips. "I may. Let's see how useful you can be. Your fists work. Your legs work. That's all I need." Lep Ako suddenly raised his hand, making Deve flinch. "Stop."

They did, hovering above a crowd of revelers making their way from one tavern to another. One of them walked into the sled's turbulence and shouted at Deve. Receiving no response, he hurled a bag which burst as it hit the sled's side, adding the smell of rough alcohol to the air.

"Here," Lep Ako said. "Stop in here."

Deve lowered the skimmer to the ground and then followed Lep Ako's directions to a shop wedged between a few others that didn't look any less dusty or dilapidated. The door yielded to his touch when Lep Ako obliterated the lock's circuits. His perimeter scan told him that no one occupied this thin slice of stacked crates pretending to be a building, but the alien nesting in his head demanded caution.

The carnage on the second floor made even him blanch. He walked past the bodies of Humans, Centauri and a Feydan, recognizing his crew mates, three civilians in suspiciously expensive clothes and armor, and a few strangers. "That's my boss," he said wincing. "Used to be my boss. What a mess."

He crouched beside a Human and, after a brief search, enriched himself with a fine rail gun and a large sum of currency accepted on a number of planets, if you shopped in the right places. "This one's rich."

"Vanguard," Lep Ako said.

Deve recoiled. "You could have said something before I touched him."

"Another over there. The female."

Reluctantly, Deve walked to the fallen Centauri Vanguard

officer. He saw no blood, no burns, nothing that showed how she had died.

"It was here," Lep Ako said. "The sire. Trapped inside the thing we felt when it was taken from us. But there is more. There was another here. Another like me. This female was killed by that other. See if she has a bio scanner."

"We need to get out of here," Deve said. "Someone's going to come for the officers." When Lep Ako only glared at him, he bent to search the dead woman's equipment. "Yeah, here." He waved the scanner inexpertly along the body. "What's it say?"

"Her heart stopped. Exploded, actually. Interesting. Four hours ago. Scan for DNA."

Deve fumbled with the settings and soon came up green. "Just two people on her. Males. And some *tappit* on the sleeve. Maybe a pet drooled on her."

"Centauri," Lep Ako said thoughtfully, studying the scanner's returns. "Both of them."

"Why do you need this?"

"If there are more of my kind out here I want to find them. The sire was here. Maybe this Centauri has it or maybe he knows where it is. What I do know is that the sire isn't on this orbiter any more. Let's head back to the docks."

Deve shrugged, quite happy to get away from this slaughter. His foot slipped in a smear of blood and he took a moment to obscure his boot marks before remembering that his DNA, too, was now deposited on two of the bodies. "What do you want there?"

"I want to leave this place, what else?"

Deve trudged back down into the shop and out to the street, barely clear of the building when three expensive air cars pulled up in front of it. Uniformed officers and Air Command soldiers poured out of them. All but one guard rushed into the building. The soldier glared at Deve but stopped short of ordering him away.

"Get back to the skimmer," Lep Ako said. "But don't leave."

Why do you want to hang around here? They'll round everybody up when they see that mess up there.

"Just do it!"

Deve climbed into his rental and puttered around with the mapper while Lep Ako used his data sleeve to hone in on the com traffic in the area. He shared none of that with the Human who amused himself by watching the growing crowd of onlookers. Hookers and their customers this time of the night, Deve assumed, wondering what Lep Ako would have to say if he approached one of these women. Did Caspians even mate outside their species? It wasn't even clear to him how they mated *within* their species. Of course, Lep Ako wasn't even a real Caspian.

"What's so damn funny?"

"Huh? Nothing."

"Get back to the docks. Hurry before the soldiers return. We've got a few things to do before we can get off this station."

Deve obeyed by lifting the car above the pedestrians and then merged with other traffic into the main traffic lane. "We'll need more cash if you're looking for passage."

"I don't think so. Turn here."

Deve followed Lep Ako's directions to the vast service hangars belonging to the orbiter's administration. Here the components keeping the platform functioning and its population alive received maintenance and crew bosses dispatched repair gangs for work shifts. The plant made up one of the arms reaching out from the central hub, allowing crews to work in reduced gravity. The noise from machinery and the metal it worked upon obscured all other sound.

He hurried across an echoing atrium, dodging trolleys and cranes, to reach a staff area directing workers to showers and change rooms, a med station and a food dispensary. No one paid much attention to the burly Human pulling work clothes from a shelf to change into coveralls in place of his shabby combat gear.

Lep Ako absorbed himself with accessing the

administrative information system, paying no attention when the smuggler broke into a few private bins to look for valuables. Deve filled his pockets with currency, some tools that caught his interest, and a nice little packet of *mince* to enjoy later. It occurred to him that the alien would probably not tolerate anything that would affect his brain and, reluctantly, he tossed the drug aside.

"What are you doing?" Someone had walked around the end of the row of lockers he was exploring and spoke before considering Deve's size and questionable activity. Another mechanic came in behind her.

Deve lashed out and gripped the woman's neck. A blow with his other fist broke it. He turned to grasp the other intruder when a peculiar, painful contact materialized between them. He watched, dumbfounded, as the man convulsed before dropping to the floor. That was unexpected. Deve examined his hand, wondering what had happened.

"You're not totally useless," Lep Ako said, as surprised as Deve by this. "Maybe I'll keep you after all."

"What… what happened to that one?" Deve's foot nudged the dead man on the floor. "I barely touched him."

"You did more than that, my friend. Get one of their sleeves and her badges. Then we better leave. The Air Command ship is leaving soon."

Deve blinked, startled from his contemplation. "So?"

"Just do exactly as I tell you. I want to find out what Air Command knows about the sire. Why they sent Vanguard agents and not just some patrol. From what I understand, they don't bother with smugglers like you unless there's something important involved."

Deve made his way back to the docking ports where the Air Command transport had commandeered much of the space. Guards paced about but no local officials had appeared, making it clear that the military enjoyed no special status here. He had to take several deep breaths before he dared to approach the entrance ramp of the sleek transport.

The *Kimura*'s three decks loomed above them and he saw fighter plane gates through the bleary observation windows of the concourse. Lep Ako prodded him along with cruel little jabs that irritated as much as they motivated.

A husky soldier barred his way when Deve's identification was not recognized by the sentinel parked near the air lock's entrance. "Restricted," he said, using Union mainvoice.

Deve feigned surprise and waved his wrist at the sensors again. "I have orders to report here," he said, coached by Lep Ako. "This is the *Kimura*, isn't it?"

"It is."

"Then I need to be on this ship. I was told to be here."

"Calm down," Lep Ako warned. "I'm almost in."

"You can check with the CO," Deve said to the soldier, battling with the tremor in his voice. The last time he'd stood this close to a Union soldier had been the day he'd left that jail on Feron. "I've got a job waiting on Targon and the boss arranged for my trip there with you."

The guard shrugged and forwarded Deve's data to someone inside the ship. "Do we have clearance for this brownshoe?" he asked, appraising Deve with a critical gaze that included the stolen service badges. "Engineer going to Targon, he says."

Deve wished himself far away from here, maybe back with his smuggler crew running dope out of Pelion. *I don't know anything about ships like these*, he sent to Lep Ako. *They'll toss me out the air lock when they find that out.*

"Leave that to me," Lep Ako replied. "Just don't wet your pants."

Deve put on his most belligerent scowl and tried to look like he wasn't worried about his imminent arrest while they waited for a response.

Finally, a lazy drawl issued from the security sentinel's speaker. "Yah, that's confirmed. Deal was made with port management two days ago. Must be some talent if Targon wants him. Tell him to report to Stubbs and make himself useful. We're shoving off in a couple of hours."

How did you do that? Deve sent when he was given directions and waved through the checkpoint. He gaped wide-eyed at the Air Command ship's expensive interior. The air even smelled good in here. The floor wasn't caked with whatever had stuck to everyone's boots, the wall seams fit perfectly, and the engines were unheard up here. Officers moved through the corridors with crisply-uniformed efficiency, paying no attention to the man in the engineer's coveralls, and the grunts didn't even seem allowed on the main deck.

"Air Command encryptions aren't much harder to crack than the others here. This is going to be much easier than I thought." Lep Ako already pored undetected through the *Kimura*'s data banks. "Black sky ops. Crew of twenty. Carrying thirty troops, including four Kite fighter planes. Interesting. There's also a Ghoster off-planet, carrying another fifty troops. Must have been on some kind of mission when this went down here."

So much for getting to Targon.

"All of these eventually end up there. Have patience. We're here to get information. Don't interact with anyone, don't talk to people, keep out of everyone's way and we'll be fine. I'll show you what you need to know to look busy."

I'm hungry.

"The mess is one deck down. Don't distract me."

What are you looking for?

"The Centauri. The man who took the sire. His DNA is all over Air Command files. I have a name already."

Deve skipped the elevator and, like a proper engineer, descended a ladder through a conduit to the lower floor. His nose led him to a small dining hall. *So who is it?*

"Minor sympathizer named Sethran Kada. They think he might have some Arawaj affiliation but he's done work for the Shri-Lan in the past. Smuggler who looks like he gets results."

Guess he's with the Shri-Lan now, if he's collecting those disks for them. Deve chortled with delight when the available meals also turned out to be of far greater quality than the grub he was used to. He didn't really give a damn if Lep Ako found this magical sire of his. If stowing away on the Union ship meant eating like this, he'd be happy to be aboard for months.

"And he's long gone. I can't feel the sire at all now."

He might not even have it any more.

"Maybe. We'll let Air Command do our work for us. He's wanted now because of that dead officer. They'll find him, I'm sure. And then we'll find out where they're taking those disks. Stop eating now. You better get to work."

Deve managed a few more mouthfuls of real rice and fake meat and then stuffed a bag of sweet pricklebean curds into his pocket. He found his way to engineering where, after another inspection of his brand new credentials, he was given a job with the ship's air and heat exchange crew. He actually knew a little about such systems and, guided by Lep Ako and using his considerable skill for slacking on the job, managed to stay outside everyone's attention range for the next few hours.

Lep Ako continued to comb through the ship's data, concentrating on communications between the ships that worked this sub-sector. Information that would take a physical being days to decipher, organize, and interpret passed through his mind in minutes. Still, the *Kimura* had cast off and headed toward the jumpsite again before patterns emerged, names stood out among the chatter, and orders given by Union and rebel leaders started to make sense. He spent some time learning an obscure Caspian language but that, too, was worth the trouble. Little was being discussed about subspace entities, but that something unusual was being organized out here was clear.

"Bringing my kind out of subspace is no easy job," he said to Deve at last, startling the Human into dropping his tools. "People are dying. I and the other out there, with Kada, might actually be very rare."

"Your sire should be easy to find then, eh? You'll be

home in no time."

Lep Ako shimmered into view. It wasn't a pleasant view, given the sneer on his face, but Deve felt better having a person to talk to than the voice in his head. "Perhaps."

"You're going to take them all back, aren't you? Your... your people? Out of those disk things?"

The alien inspected himself through Deve's eyes, studying his six-fingered hands as he turned them slowly. "I think maybe not."

"Huh?"

Lep Ako spread his arms wide. "I like this place. This physical space. It's small and limited but it's filled with... with things! You would not believe the intel I'm finding in this database. What more is out there, I wonder." He perceived Deve's confusion. "Don't you get it? This place, this real-space, is where my people belong. I know that now. I can bring them here. It's been done at least twice. It can be done again. For all I know, someone's already doing it."

"With those disks."

"Right. Someone out here knows about us. Maybe they're looking for a way to keep us here. Maybe they're looking for damn pets, who knows. They'll find out soon enough who we are. There is only one thing that can stop us."

Deve swallowed hard when Lep Ako glared at him, waiting for him to respond. "Your... your sire?" he ventured.

"Yes! As long as it is out here, we can be here, too. It calls, it points the way, and we just need a passing ship to leave subspace. We only need a host to..." he amended whatever he was going to say. "To befriend. To join with us as a new life form. To give us shape in exchange for some very useful abilities. They *are* useful, wouldn't you say?"

Deve recalled the incomparable surge of power when he murdered that mechanic on Rishabel. Not just the painful bolt of energy he channeled into him, but the thought that a simple touch from his hand could do so much damage filled him with awe. "Yes," he whispered.

"Once I have the sire we'll create a small team to infiltrate places we'll need to establish ourselves. Hopefully I won't have to go through too many duds till I have enough matches. I'm going to have to learn more about real-space physics. It's so different from what we understand."

"I think my people feel the same way about your home," Deve said. He returned to his assignment and knocked a heat sensor out of the way to install a new circuit. "Is this the relay I'm looking for?"

"Yes," Lep Ako said absently. "We can get that Sethran Kada to join us. He might have access to the sort of people we can use. Important rebels, people with the planes and equipment we'll need. Men who aren't afraid to try new things."

Deve busied himself with his tools, knowing too well that Lep Ako spoke of people who were nothing like him. His presence here was merely an accident. With every moment that passed, he felt the alien's disapproval of him, perhaps even outright dislike. As much as he wanted to be rid of this frightening presence in his head, the thought that he only served until something better came along filled him with misery.

"Targon is a good place to begin with," Lep Ako said, oblivious to the Human's dejection. "Imagine the fun to be had there." He considered for a moment. "It's got some awfully dense security but I can do it if I get near the mainframe."

"The Shri-Lan have been trying that for a hundred years."

"Longer than that. But they didn't have me. That's all changed now."

FOUR

Even in the shade, the temperatures of Feyd were no more pleasant for the average Centauri than they were for other Prime species. Except, of course, Feydans. The natives seemed to make a point of walking about thickly dressed while people like Seth stripped down to their undershirts. Perhaps it amused them.

Seth slumped on a ledge against someone's garden wall, watching a woman and her children make their way toward the Union-operated commerce center to the north. Like most of her people, her smooth brown skin was tattooed with patterns and symbols that told the stories of her ancestors. He had studied some of that but meaningful interpretation of these markings took more than casual interest.

"Do you like that?"

Seth tipped his head back against the wall. The heat of the day seemed doubled by Feyd's high gravity and he wanted to sleep. Somewhere behind him water gurgled into a pool and he wished himself already within Baroch's private compound, cooled by such water and served a long, cold drink.

"That woman?" he said without looking at Khoe who had come to sit beside him.

"Yes. With those lines drawn all over her."

He shrugged. "She's pretty." He watched Khoe turn her arm in front of his face to study her Centauri-pale skin. "You don't need tattoos. You'll just end up writing something rude on your forehead or something."

She squinted at him. "I can read. Besides, you have a tattoo."

He turned his arm out to peer at the detailed drawing of an ocean-going vessel with massive sails just above the inside of his elbow. It disguised the slightly raised edges of the emergency com unit embedded under his skin. "The Flying Dutchman," he said, running his finger over it.

"What's that? Other than your ship, I mean."

"Some old Human legend I read long ago. A ghost ship that sails around forever."

"Like you?"

"Yeah." He found his eyes traveling past his arm to the gauzy swath of fabric she had chosen to wear, simulating the fashions worn here. It displayed a rather spectacular neckline. "Do you feel this heat?"

"Yes, like you do. It's not pleasant. It makes you sluggish."

He moved his hand closer to her and poked her thigh. "You don't feel that?"

"I told you. I feel you feeling me."

"Because you're in my head."

"Right."

He pulled his hand back and smiled broadly at an elder passing by with a suspicious look on his face. *I really shouldn't sit here talking to Miss Invisible*, he projected.

"Or feeling her up," she added. "So where is this driver your boss is sending for you? You sent that message hours ago."

Late, I guess. Baroch won't be happy about that. Delphians are very punctual.

61

"Why do you need a driver? Are you important?"

He looked beyond her and jerked his chin toward an approaching skimmer. *There he is now.*

The air car slowed down as it approached the appointed meeting place and the canopy retracted. A Human woman inspected Seth with a critical eye. "Kada?" she said.

"I was expecting Vydian."

She climbed out of the skimmer and handed him a uniform jacket after passing a wand over his eyes. Matching his retina information against her data display, she shrugged. "He's busy." She watched Seth dress in the coat that would identify him as a member of Baroch's personal staff. "He's at the stables. Get going."

"*I* was here on time," Seth said as he took her place in the vehicle.

"You don't like that one very much," Khoe observed. "Because she's not pretty?"

Because she's rude. He pulled a water bottle from a compartment and drank a good portion of it before handing it to the woman. "Have a nice walk."

"That was also rude," Khoe said when they had left the driver behind.

"Yeah, it was." Seth grinned, starting to feel better. He left the skimmer's canopy down and sighed happily when the breeze cooled the sweat on his body. The vehicle turned away from the town where he had parked the *Dutchman* and headed into the lush countryside. No air scenter available to spacefaring crews matched the live, ever-changing smell of green things growing. "She started it. Since when are you an expert on manners?"

"Things are fitting together," she said earnestly. "It's thrilling. I scan through your database and I find... themes. Concepts that don't seem to belong together somehow do. Some agree with others, and then some things just come up as such wonderful mysteries. It's starting to feel like I just know things without even meaning to."

Seth glanced at her intent, excited expression. The joyful

smile was utterly contagious. "I noticed that, too. Look at your face."

"I don't even have to think about some things any more. Non-verbal communication, for example. Happening on its own. Of course, there's just you to try that out on."

He laughed. "Bored with me already?"

She quickly put her hand on his arm. "I didn't mean that! I like being here with you. I'm so grateful for your help. You don't have to do this."

"Yeah, I do," he said. "I love a mystery." He let his eyes roam across the charming landscape to give her a good view of what Feyd had to offer. The rolling hills produced some of the best food in this sub-sector and he made a mental note to pick up fresh supplies before he left this place. *Arooja* berries, which yielded a delicious sweet-bitter juice even if they did tend to stain one's teeth for hours afterward, were at the top of his list.

Trees closed in when they passed into a valley and finally reached the Factor's estate. Seth passed through a security check at the gate and then took the vehicle beyond the main building to the stables a little further along the road.

The stables were a rare indulgence for the Delphian leader. His people did not keep pets and these animals, descended from a mammal brought here by Humans and bred for riding, served little practical purpose. Seth had once joined Baroch on a ride through the valley's meadows and looked forward to another such outing. He smiled when he imagined Khoe's reaction. Of course, taking horses into the fields also meant an opportunity for a private meeting with his employer.

He parked the skimmer near the entrance to the stables beside a few others undoubtedly belonging to Baroch's ever-present security detail. Baroch's personal shuttle, gleaming and well-appointed, seemed out of place here.

By the Factor's own strict directive, he left his weapons in the vehicle. The service entry yielded to his hand print and he entered the cool, quiet stable redolent with the scent of horse, wood and hay. His scanner showed a few people near a paddock at the other side where Baroch would be waiting for him. He stopped near an enclosure to let Khoe take a look at one of the animals but it was skittish and refused to come closer.

Something not right here, he projected. The silence seemed more like that of a tomb than a drowsy summer's day. He noted tension, like being surrounded by people holding their breath in anxious anticipation.

"What do you mean?"

Not sure. Where is everybody? Not even a stable hand worked among the animals today. No voices, no sound of water running or harness clanking. He turned back to the front entrance, pretending interest in one of the horses there.

"Check your perimeter," Khoe said urgently.

He did and counted several bodies rapidly moving around to the front of the barn. Despite its bucolic appeal, this place was as tightly sealed as any secure facility and he doubted that the door to the corral was currently unlocked. He stepped into the brilliant sunlight to face the muzzles of a half dozen guns. *Damn.*

"I don't see your boss," Khoe said.

Seth felt someone take position behind him. "Good morning," he said cautiously.

"Sethran Kada, I'm guessing?" a lieutenant said from a calculated distance. None of the guards looked like mere grunts; he felt himself measured and judged down to every atom of his instinctively battle-ready body.

"I expected to meet with Lord Baroch. Privately." Seth looked past the soldiers and saw none of the estate's own staff out here, either. "He's not the warmest Delphian I've ever met but his welcome doesn't involve guns."

"I am Lieutenant Soogan," the officer said. He gestured to the vehicles in front of the stable. "Please join us in the Factor's shuttle."

"It is empty," Seth said. He walked reluctantly back to the parking area. "Where is he?"

"Is this bad?" Khoe asked. "They seem very grim."

Yes, this is bad. This is Air Command. Not his own security. They have no business out here unless there is some emergency. Baroch would not meet me here if the place was crawling with cops. He doesn't exactly want to be seen with me.

Seth had little choice but to accept the lieutenant's invitation to enter Baroch's shuttle. A floating lounge for someone of high esteem, it was furnished in gleaming wood and rich fabrics, the usual accessories for one of the ten absolute leaders of the Commonwealth. Even with the other soldiers in here, the vehicle did not seem crowded. All of them knew that it also made a very secure prison.

Soogan gestured to one of Baroch's well-cushioned chairs in a way that suggested a refusal on Seth's part would be poor manners, indeed. "Let's have a sit-down. Targon asked us to head out here to take a look when you landed. Xenoscience Div. Isn't that interesting? I'm afraid we have bad news."

Seth's eyes took a quick tour around the shuttle, noting windows and doors and the chances of making it to any of them before he was taken down. Unlike the research being done by Targon's excellent ethnology departments and an expert staff of exobiologists, *xenoscience* was a polite Air Command term for keeping tabs on non-Union species. Perhaps on species like Khoe's. "Has something happened?" He sat on the edge of the chair, his body coiled for flight. *Can you get into the shuttle's system without them noticing?* He folded his arms to hide activity on his data sleeve from the watchful eyes around him.

"I'll try," Khoe replied. "You seem tense."

Soogan leaned toward Seth. "You traveled out here for nothing, I'm afraid. Factor Baroch was killed in the line of duty."

Seth blinked, utterly unprepared for this. Baroch dead? He cursed inwardly, calculating the loss of his benefactor but also oddly upset by the news. He had always held a fair measure of respect for the leader. This did explain Air

Command presence here now. All of the governor's matters, official or private, would now be under intense scrutiny before being passed on to his successor. And that included unexpected visitors landing here with very little notice to request an audience. "Baroch? How? When?"

"That's classified. It does leave you in an awkward position."

Seth shrugged carelessly. "Leaves me unemployed. Please give my condolences to his wife. She's a kind lady."

"Stay a while." Soogan raised his hand when Seth made to get up. "We have some questions. What brings you to Feyd? To the Factor's private home?"

I don't like this one bit. How are you doing?

"Still decoding," Khoe said. "I will get through."

Seth reached for one of several cover stories. "There's nothing to be asking about. I run a few errands for the Factor now and again. He's not the first official to have a fondness for things that aren't... well, appropriate. I doubt Air Command is interested in how he relaxes at the end of the day."

Soogan smirked at one of his men. "So the honorable Factor liked a little taste of *mince*, did he? Anything stronger?"

"I do not gossip. So, unless you have a replacement for Lord Baroch already looking to interview delivery people, we're done here." Seth stood up and noted the immediate tension among the guards. "Time to start a new job search, I guess."

"I don't think a job search is in your future, given your talents. Let's get on with things, Kada. How about you fill us in on what happened on Rishabel?" The genial tone seemed flushed from the lieutenant's voice.

"I'm in," Khoe announced. "What am I looking for?"

Locks, lights, alarms. Turn off cameras in here. Scan everything. Seth turned his attention back to Soogan. "Just some brawl. The usual toss between outlaws and you fine folks. I happened to be nearby. I have nothing to add to that."

"You killed an officer."

"Did I?"

"Why were you seen with rebels?"

"What rebels?"

Soogan checked his wrist unit. "Man name Gage saw you. Identified you. Owns a shop where the shooting happened. Said you were there to meet up with some Shri-Lan."

"You're not accusing me of murder, are you? I have no reason to take out Vanguard agents."

"What seems to interest Targon is your reason for immediately heading for a Factor's residence after killing a Union officer." Soogan nodded to a civilian in the room who circled around Seth, sensor wand in hand.

"Please stand up, Mister Kada," she said.

Seth watched her move the scanner over his body. "That's kind of intrusive, isn't it?"

"Yes," she said, straight-faced. "You might feel a pinch."

Seth smiled. "Be gentle with me." He faced Soogan again. "What do you want?"

"A little cooperation would be nice."

"What sort of cooperation?" *That word is never a good sign when it comes out of an officer's mouth*, Seth sent to Khoe. *I'd like to get out of here before they get serious.*

"You don't think they could help us find the disk?"

They're not here to help you, Khoe. If they really thought you were some sort of pathogen they'd be walking around in hazmat suits. I have the feeling Targon already knows about you.

"Doctor?" the lieutenant said to the civilian.

"DNA match," she reported. "I'm also seeing very unusual brain activity. Could be hallucinations taking place. His physiology is unaltered and healthy, which is baffling, given his current epinephrine levels. It's like he's using it up as fast as it appears."

Is that you doing that?

"Yeah. Can we leave now? That man is making me nervous." Khoe waved her invisible hand around the officer's face. "I drained their guns, too. Girl's got to eat!"

You are brilliant, Seth replied, struggling to keep a grin from his lips.

"I think it may be best if you accompanied us back to town, Kada," Soogan said. "Those readings match the pattern Targon sent for comparison."

Seth pretended to think about that. "As much as I appreciate your concern for my health, I have to be somewhere." He winked at the doctor. "I can come by afterwards, though, if you're so worried about a little adrenaline rush. I'm sure you know how to burn that off."

Soogan exhaled sharply. "Cut the games, Kada. You're wanted by Targon and you damn well know that's not a polite invitation."

"Are you arresting me?"

"We feel that you are safest in our custody until we have determined the nature of your condition," Soogan said. "But, yeah, we are. You killed an officer. As far as I'm concerned, you're a traitor, maybe even Shri-Lan."

If I get out of this shuttle, lock them in here and disable all com channels in and out. They'll have to shout if they want help.

"Got it," Khoe said. "Won't they just break the door?"

This little bus is about as secure as you can get. The Factor is well protected. Was, anyway.

"What are you going to do?"

Get off this damn planet. Don't let anyone get in my way. Do what you have to.

"You can't mean that. I don't want to kill anybody else. Besides, they're upset enough over just one officer."

Can't you just zap them a little?

"Yes, let me wave a magic wand, Kada!"

Now you're thinking.

She grimaced at him. "Don't worry about the guns. But those men look awfully big."

And I'm awfully fast.

Seth took a step toward the door. "After giving this careful thought, I've decided to pass up on your hospitality." He half-turned to the guard behind him. "I don't suggest you try to stop me."

The soldier raised his weapon, his opinion on the matter made plain.

Seth sent a silent signal to Khoe. He slapped his flat hand onto the guard's armored chest and felt a prickle of *something*, not nearly as painful as it had been on Rishabel. The man froze, staring in numb incomprehension until Seth pulled away. Everyone watched him drop to the floor, stunned.

"Anyone else?" Seth said, surprised by a flood of new energy coursing through his body. But the shock received was milder, almost exhilarating, than the one that killed the agent on Rishabel.

"Take him down!" Soogan shouted.

Some of the guards fired their weapons and found them useless. Another lunged toward Seth and met the same fate as his mate.

"Come no closer," Seth warned the others. "You have no idea what I can do." He didn't, either, but this wasn't the time to admit that fact. "I will destroy any ship that comes after us."

"Us?" Soogan said. "Kada, stand down. You're not getting out of this."

Do I have to touch them?

"No," Khoe replied. "The floor is conductive enough. Barely, though."

Seth smiled at the lieutenant. "Consider this my termination notice."

"Kada—" the officer began before he shuddered and fell to the ground along with the others, senseless.

The door behind Seth opened as if by its own will and he leaped to the ground to drop another guard before she could raise the alarm. This time, the energy drain was palpable. Gasping, Seth pulled her into the shuttle and then the doors slid shut, locked down by Khoe.

"They're not dead!" Khoe exclaimed. "I did it."

"I'm not doing so well," he replied, racing back to his skimmer to retrieve his guns. Feyd's gravity dragged on his legs as if attempting to hinder his escape. "I'll take some of that adrenaline if you can squeeze some out of me." He took a deep breath when a little energy returned to his depleted limbs almost immediately.

"That won't last," Khoe said. "I'm getting tired, too. Weaker, I mean."

"I'll treat you to some fantastic thorium when we get back to the *Dutchman*."

Seth climbed into one of the vehicles used by security after briefly touching his own and the others to be disabled by Khoe. He passed the Factor's mansion like a man on his appointed rounds and, once out of sight, ramped up to race back to his ship.

It seemed to take forever before he was given his take-off clearance and he paced nervously as he waited, certain that every last Air Command soldier was converging on the air field. He considered just taking the *Dutchman* up without permit but, while he had certainly severed his ties with the Union today, he was not willing to jeopardize his welcome on this planet.

Finally, flight control cleared him and he lifted off, aware that Khoe was using up as much of his fuel as the ship did while she restored herself.

"Where are we going?" she wanted to know, curled up on his copilot bench.

"Keyhole not far from here." He tapped one of the ship's indicators as if that would improve the coolant levels. Then he displayed a holographic map to point out their options. "They'll expect us to head for that jumpsite. It's a busy gate and the relay station is fully manned. We'll never get past there. We'll take this keyhole instead, which they won't expect, seeing how I'm just a chartjumper and they think I'm alone. Once we're through it'll take them a while to track us down. Did I mention how amazingly handy it is to have you aboard? It would take me weeks to make that trip on my own." He adjusted the *Dutchman*'s scanners to cast wide for any pursuing cruisers. "I wonder if they're still asleep back there."

"What if I hurt them? That's not going to help things," she said with a very small voice inside his head. "You can't go home again, can you? Because of me. They'll hunt you. Even if you get off, they'll never trust you again."

He shrugged and got up to leave the cockpit. "I don't have a home."

"Don't pretend. You know what I mean."

He pulled his shirt over his head, feeling the need for a quick decon and a whole lot of sleep. "We were never exactly on good terms, anyway. Most probably think I'm a smuggler and a petty criminal. The few that do know don't like me working for Baroch. They prefer the Factors to use Air Command and not run their own agents."

"What happens now? Without Baroch?"

"They'll have to elect another Delphian. The Union needs Delphi's cooperation far more than Delphi needs the Union. Most top level spanners are Delphian. Without that sort of navigator, Air Command would have to rely on simple charthumpers like me to get around, instead of using the keyholes. So the Delphians insist on having one of their own among the governors. Delphi is against Union expansion as much as the rebels are but they prefer to oppose from within. The Commonwealth is all about trade. Wealth. Power. Someone like Baroch makes sure that things don't speed out of control."

"And getting through subspace is dangerous enough. They don't want to worry about picking up alien invaders now, too."

He nodded. "The Commonwealth companies won't be too concerned about being polite to some energy entities floating around subspace."

"Not if they think we're dangerous."

"You *are* dangerous." Seth raised his hands and stared at them thoughtfully. "That's some powerful mojo you're capable of." He looked into her unhappy face, remembering the incredible feeling surging through him when he took those soldiers down. He was an expert close combat fighter as well as marksman but harming others was something he did out of necessity, something that had been too often a part of his life for years. This, however, felt extraordinarily *good* while it lasted. The rush of energy had been nothing short of physical pleasure.

"I just hope it's not hurting you," she said. "I'm becoming troublesome."

He sighed, pained to see her upset. "I'm fine," he said. "Just tired. Don't worry so. Once we know you're safe I'll report the whole thing to Air Command. It'll end up classified and everyone'll pretend this never happened." Without really thinking about it, he stepped closer to her and pulled her into his arms. She flinched, startled by his touch, but then relaxed against him to return the comfort of his embrace. He closed his eyes, again amazed by the absolute reality of her presence. The soft curves against his own body felt right, as did the arms now wrapped around his middle. He could even feel her soft breath against his bare skin when she spoke.

"So this is what a hug feels like," she said.

"Yeah."

"Can I sleep with you?"

He released her abruptly. "Huh?"

She nodded toward his lounger. "You said you were tired. If you don't mind."

"Well, no. If you wish." He nodded toward the cockpit. "After we jump."

"Where are we jumping to?"

"We're going to find us another Delphian."

FIVE

"Another one? Are you sure?" Colonel Celois barely glanced at the display screen his aide held out to him. They had arrived at Targon's sprawling research center after news of the fiasco on Feyd convinced him to leave the nearby military base and take a closer look at the victims for himself.

"Yes," Lieutenant Lanyu struggled to keep up with the colonel's long strides. "One of ours this time. Patrol ship cruising near Aikhor. The pilot is dead."

"Same indicators?" Celois slowed for one of several security checks on their way to a facility deep below Targon's largely uninhabitable surface. The wide hallways, following the planet's natural tunnel system, made up for the lack of daylight with brilliant, color-balanced illumination.

The ability to burrow easily into Targon's porous crust along with its strategic position within the sector's jumpsite network made this planet a perfect location for Air Command's military headquarters. The massive base, in turn, protected valuable installations, among them this vast, interspecies medical research center.

"Yes, cortical lesions and intracranial hemorrhage. We've got one witness to the pilot's hallucinations, incoherent speech, convulsions, death." The lieutenant scanned through more of the message. "She's on her way here with the body, quarantined. The patrol ship is on the Magra base. They're awaiting orders."

"Have them send any on-board audio and video along with the systems security data here and then seal the ship." The door before them yielded to their hand and retinal scans but a guard on the other side scrutinized their cards and insignia before permitting them into the secured section of the facility's exobiology wing.

Most of the new species studied here did not require diplomatic or even military interaction. Contact with sentient populations took place long before they arrived here, which of course happened eventually if a willing test subject could be found. Over the past three hundred years of Union expansion into this crowded, diverse sector of their galaxy, the occasional patient here had been less than willing, he knew. But these days most research delved into plant, animal and microscopic life forms found elsewhere. The study of ethnology was left to the sociologists on the upper floor.

Until recently, anyway. Celois and his lieutenant entered another locked sector and then a lab area where they would meet with Doctor Patman and her team. He had met Patman during the initial meeting between Air Command and Xenoscience Div when this situation first came to light.

He walked into her division where technicians worked on their monitors or near the project screen taking up the entire far wall. This was a dry lab and no one asked them to change into protective gear. Still, the others wore the white coveralls used in this wing, emblazoned by the badges proclaiming their specialty. He noted that a fair number of them belonged to Neuroscience. What looked like small hospital rooms, each with a mirrored window allowing a view of those inside, lined two sides of the open central space.

Someone he did not expect to see down here, deep in conversation with the doctor, was General Tanvin Dmitra, the commanding officer of Targon's main military base.

Things had indeed escalated if the general himself took an interest. The doctor, a diminutive Human, noticed him by the door and she and Dmitra left their spot by an observation window to meet him.

Celois saluted his superior, a Feydan whose angular features could be mistaken for those of a Delphian if not for the bronze, intricately tattooed skin stretching over sharp cheekbones and hairless skull. "General. I expected to meet you upstairs later."

The nod he received from Dmitra was on the frosty side. "I decided to see for myself. We'll meet with security down here. Doctor Patman was about to brief me on the latest cases."

Celois peered over her head into the room behind her. A Caspian sat on the floor there with his arms wrapped around his knees. His people bore a richly patterned hide which they rarely covered with clothing and he had been allowed to discard his hospital garb. The yellow raptor eyes stared listlessly at nothing, oblivious to the people on the other side of the window. A medic sat on the floor beside him, propped against the wall in what seemed to be a mixture of patience and boredom.

"This is Ras Ceta, our first victim," Patman explained.

Celois remembered the name from their earlier meeting. This was the Caspian rebel that had led the Vanguard agents to Rishabel. He'd been found wandering near the docks and his peculiar ramblings had worried the local security force to contact Targon's specialists. If not for several ships in the area turning up with dead pilots, his tales of people living in his head would not have caught Air Command's attention. But the claim that the voices originated in subspace were uncomfortably reminiscent of several recent distress calls. All six ships with such occurrence had recently traveled through subspace. "Your diagnosis?"

"Still too soon to tell. This is not a mental illness found among Caspians. There is something foreign inhabiting his system, but it's not organic, nor caused by any mechanical means. Even so, it caused the formation of a separate neural circuit sharing this man's nervous system. If you want me to throw an analogy in the air, I'd say he's two people in one body. Or was. The alien neural activity has ceased now. He claims that his… passenger has died. It seems to have caused his current state which is very much symptomatic of depression."

Celois sighed. If this followed the same process exhibited by another pilot, the Caspian himself would not live much longer, either. "A non-organic parasite? Is that even possible?"

"You'll have to consult your physicists, Colonel. Subspace is not my area of expertise. It's certainly nothing we've ever encountered in real-space. So far."

She gestured for them to move along. The door to the next room was open and a Centauri woman, reclining on a tilted chair and apparently unconscious, served as the center of attention for several technicians. Celois winced when he took in the array of diagnostic equipment connected to her remotely or by wire. One of her elbows twitched rhythmically in response to some stimulus.

They continued to yet another exam room. "This is the patient you'll want to speak with," Patman said.

A Centauri sat stiffly on the edge of his bed, also staring into space, but looking far less dejected than his neighbor. Whatever he was undergoing right now was not distressing to him and a small smile played over his lips.

"He's coherent?" Dmitra asked.

"Quite. He's a communications officer on a freighter heading to Pelion. Your people checked that ship out. No special cargo, no smuggling, no rebel affiliations. Just a transport. No one else aboard was affected. When he started to talk about a voice in his head they isolated him in their med station and contacted Targon." Doctor Patman checked her data unit. "He goes by name of Orajah. Besides the two patients you've already seen, he's the only one to survive the infection."

"Wasn't there another one? The Union pilot?"

"Unfortunately, when we tried to scan more precisely to see if we can separate the second set of neural tissue from the Human victim, she died without apparent cause. I agree with your theory that we are dealing with sentient beings."

"Murderous ones," Celois muttered.

"Perhaps. The pilot was not very… cooperative with our efforts to remove the parasite. Maybe we triggered some self-defense mechanism. If so, it was at the cost of its own life. We did not detect any energy transfer upon death."

"So not likely contagious. Or replicating."

"Not in any organic way that we can determine."

"I'd like to speak with the Centauri," Celois said.

Doctor Patman ran her hand over a sensor and the door before them opened to allow the colonel to enter. He handed his sidearm to his aide and gestured for her to wait in the lab with the general.

Orajah looked up at the colonel but remained seated and silent. Celois stepped awkwardly past the bed and took a chair placed beside it. "Evening," he said cheerfully.

The Centauri nodded. "More questions?"

"No, I just wanted to chat," Celois replied. "I'm sure you're tired of the doctors by now."

"Yes. But the food here is good, so that's something." Orajah shifted his gaze beyond the colonel and then back again. "I suppose you want to know about Oss."

"Oss? Your… guest has a name?"

"No. I call it that. I had an invisible friend when I was a boy. It seemed fitting. I think it likes having a name."

"You can talk to it?"

"Of course. In a way. It doesn't really understand what we are. It made a shape for me, so I can see it. It's right over there, behind you."

Celois turned abruptly and saw nothing but a tray of food not yet cleared from the bedside shelf. Still, the thought that Orajah saw something there made the closely-cropped hair at his nape bristle. "What does it look like?"

The Centauri sighed. "I answered all that already. Several times. I'm sure it's in a report somewhere. I thought you didn't have any questions."

"You can imagine our curiosity, I'm sure," Celois replied. As a civilian, this man did not owe him the rank and file subordination that he was used to but even civilians tended to exhibit respect for Air Command. Without the Union's military, few freighters would make it far without paying tribute to pirates and rebels. Orajah did not seem to care who had come to interview him.

"I can. You've locked me in here and I'm sure it'll be a long while before I'm let out again. I understand why that is. It makes me wish I had not told anyone about Oss."

"You don't mind it being here with you?"

The Centauri shrugged. "It's soothing. I don't really know what it wants. It talks sometimes but I'm not sure it knows the difference between us and that chair. I think maybe it's damaged. It's hurt or sad or something. It looks like a small Prime species now, but it keeps changing. Sometimes it's just *there*, without any real shape."

Celois glanced at the mirrored window where he knew the doctor stood by to observe. "Do you think it's dying? Leaving again?"

"No. It wants to know us." Orajah leaned forward and stretched his arm toward the colonel. "It needs that," he said and covered the input panel of the colonel's data sleeve with his hand.

Celois pulled away before remembering that only his own touch and code allowed access to Targon's highly secured network. Orajah tried to grip his arm again, leaping from his bed at the officer. Like most Centauri, he loomed over his smaller Human cousin. Celois, seated in his chair at a disadvantage, struggled to reach for a gun that wasn't there.

The Centauri released him and turned to the door just as two medics rushed into the room. He pushed them aside and one of them yelped in pain when she was thrown back and then crumpled to the ground.

"Security!" Lieutenant Lanyu shouted, drawing her gun to stop the Centauri.

"Don't shoot!" Celois shouted at the same time that Doctor Patman did. Somewhere an alarm rang. They heard doors slamming as the facility was locked down. Orajah looked wildly around the clinic and then rushed to an interface screen that took up most of the wall beside the workstations. He thrust both hands against the glass and remained there until two guards tackled him to the floor. He gave up without struggle and allowed them to restrain him.

Celois stood over them, still gasping for breath after the attack. "What the hell was that?"

"I'm sorry," Orajah said calmly and not especially apologetically. The guards yanked him onto his feet and he did not resist when they secured his hands behind his back. "Oss wants to learn more about here. Real-space here, I mean. So it looked. It learned from our ship's database but it's not interested in charts and cargo lists. You have more."

Alarmed, Celois inspected his data unit. His security code had not been entered, and access to the network had not been breached. He hoped. Cursing, he entered the necessary code to have his clearance reset. "So what did it get?"

The Centauri said nothing for a while. "Not very much. There was no time to look and your system is well partitioned. It doesn't like you, I think, but it can speak better now. At least I can understand more. It knows what this place is now. It wants to leave."

"We are not going to harm it. We need to know more about it. Attacking us is really not a good idea. Maybe you can convey that to your friend."

"You don't understand, Major. It doesn't care what happens to it. Or me. Or at least it doesn't worry about it. It doesn't care what we learn about it. It just needs to get to the others of its kind."

"Oh? What others? Where are they? How many are there?"

Orajah shrugged. "It doesn't know."

Celois turned when someone arrived with a stretcher to take the injured medic away. The woman was conscious but unable to stand and didn't seem to recognize any of them. "What did you do to her?"

"I don't know. We did not mean to hurt her. I'm sorry about that. I hope she'll be all right. She was very pleasant with us, earlier."

Celois watched as Orajah was returned to his room. "I want him sedated and the other victims isolated. Disable all electronic devices in this room and install a manual lock. Bring in a security detail and remove all access to the external network. For everyone." He looked around to find the general in the bustle of guards and personnel rushing to follow his orders.

Some of them had hustled Dmitra into the next room, partitioned from this one by a transparent wall, where he conversed with a uniformed officer on a screen, apparently not bothered by the commotion. He activated a com panel. "Colonel Celois, I think we've seen enough here. Doctor Patman, if you would join us, please." He exited the clinic, leaving the others to hurry after him into the adjoining meeting room.

Celois was not surprised to see Captain Bayla, an expert in electronic security systems, waiting for them. The captain was poring over a large sheet spread out over the table, moving data from one section to another, some of which was displayed on a wall monitor, while speaking in low tones with someone over his com band. Another specialist sat before another display, studying replays of the surveillance video of the incident in the lab. Both men looked up when the others entered, then straightened to salute the senior officers.

"What do you have for us," General Dmitra said curtly but not unfriendly.

Bayla disabled his com link and indicated his project sheet. "We've completed our assessment of the reports from Feyd," he said without preamble, no more interested in formality than their commanding officer. "What you've just witnessed in the clinic is not an isolated phenomenon any more than the fatal incident with the Vanguard team on Rishabel."

Celois groaned. "Kada?"

"Kada. We were able to reconstruct some of what happened on the Factor's estate. We've concluded that Sethran Kada may, indeed, be infected and pose a considerable threat." He paused before adding, "of course, we have no way to confirm that since Kada declined our invitation to join us here."

The colonel scowled. "They sent six men to collect him."

"What do we know about him?" Dmitra said.

"Wouldn't quite call him a pirate but he's not above helping himself to what he needs. Has the ear of some fairly high-powered Shri-Lan and not a few Arawaj. Does work for them, although mostly for himself. Slippery. Tends to turn up exactly where we don't want him. We never end up with quite enough reason to take him down."

"Until now."

"Yes, sir. He was trained by Air Command until he decided he'd rather play by his own rules. Top tier pilot. Language expert. Fully trained in special ops. And what we didn't teach him, the Shri-Lan did. He's been on his own for over ten years and doing quite well. UCB Feyd should have known better than to send a bunch of grunts to arrest him."

"I'm more impressed by how he got onto the governor's grounds than how he escaped again. And what interests me the most is why he was there after just murdering an Air Command officer." Dmitra nodded to the security specialist. "What happened on Feyd?"

Captain Bayla consulted his sheet. He circled a part of it with his finger to send it to the vertical screen on the wall. A Centauri with thick black hair curling around his neck gazed back at them with just a hint of a smirk. Beside him appeared an image of the Factor's armored ground vehicle. "He was being interviewed in there, according to the recordings made by your people. The situation was not especially confrontational. Then all recordings stopped. All weapons were disabled at precisely the same moment. The squad and the doctor you sent woke up with a big headache hours after Kada left the planet. They are largely unharmed, thankfully."

"You think Kada did that?"

"Not a single gun was fired. In fact, Kada wasn't even visibly armed when the recordings stopped. We compared the doctor's scans of Kada's brain to the Centauri patient in the clinic. The activity, mostly involving the auditory and visual cortex, is very similar." He looked to Patman for confirmation.

The doctor nodded. "Not only that, the residual radiation detected on the deceased officer on Rishabel is identical to that collected on Feyd. There is little doubt that, whatever weapon he is using, it was the same. And if this was not some new mechanical weapon, this parasite is not only intelligent enough to communicate with its host, it is capable of tremendous energy conversions." She nodded in the direction of the lab. "I'll expect we'll find the same radiation on Milena after what we saw just now."

"If Sethran Kada is hosting one of them, he's not showing any ill effects," the general said. "In fact, he seems to be working in tandem with it, or vice versa. From our perspective, not a good development. Perhaps he's only one of many and the few we've found are only those who, for some reason, weren't compatible and are washing up on the shore."

Celois stared moodily at the display wall where Seth seemed to mock them with his smile. "And if that's the case, we could have a whole lot more of them out there, ones that haven't spun out, who are as opposed to joining us here as he is."

"A reasonable assumption," Patman said. "The victims we have been able to interview aren't unhappy about being possessed by the aliens once they get over the surprise. Having conversations with them. Giving them names.

Avoiding capture. Perhaps these visitors have a way of convincing their hosts that their presence is desirable somehow. Plenty of parasites, even some viruses, exhibit such behavior. If the host is unaware of them, or benefits from their presence, he's unlikely to want to remove it."

"All the while being used to infiltrate our ranks," Dmitra said. "And not just ours."

"You're anticipating some sort of invasion? By subspace entities?" Celois asked the general.

"Dismissing that possibility is a dangerous gamble. I don't have to tell you that whatever method Kada is using to evade capture has my attention. I'm sure Doctor Patman is also eager to get a look inside his head. So let's come up with something workable to bring him in alive, shall we?"

Celois pretended that the general's last sentence hadn't been aimed squarely at his head. "I'm troubled by what we just witnessed with that Centauri victim. His ability to interface with our systems would indicate that these entities can enter and scan our networks for information rather than learn from their hosts. Orajah mentioned that, just in those few seconds, his parasite improved its language skills."

"This is something we suspected," Bayla said. "These entities can invade our electronic systems but they require living hosts to get around, perhaps even as a source of sustenance. This would mean they can't simply hijack our equipment, a rather reassuring thought, I may add."

Celois did not share the captain's elation. "But their living host found a convenient way to enter Factor Baroch's home. Who knows what other opportunities they'll have through Sethran Kada. The man knows as much about Air Command as he does about the Shri-Lan. He's not someone we want controlled by some alien."

"It'll be a chore to find him," Bayla said. "After fleeing Feyd he keyholed and disappeared."

"He's a spanner?" Dmitra asked.

"No," Celois said. "But he suddenly seems to have picked up the talent. Another point of interest. He was frisked at

Aram Gate, alone, and then showed up at Rishabel not ten hours later. That's a four-week trip via three charted sites for someone like him."

Dmitra turned to Patman. "I want your entire team on the thing inside this Orajah's head. If they are sentient, we need to communicate. If we can't, we need to control them, eradicate them if necessary. Advise all stations to be alert to reports of any unusual mental aberrations among our flight crews. But for now the matter is classified."

Colonel Celois addressed the general. "Sir, we should consider closing the gate at Rishabel. And increase patrols at other sites. If we can intercept these beings before they disperse—"

"Out of the question. Closing any site is going to have the entire trade sector pounding on the Factors' doors. I don't want to have to explain why we decided to block their transports. And if we had the means to frisk every ship that uses the sites we wouldn't have a rebel problem in Trans-Targon."

"Then we should at least restrict subspace travel by those with top level clearance. We can't risk someone with that sort of access becoming infected. Or at least issue a directive to avoid engaging their neural interface during the traverse."

Dmitra shook his head. "Order increased security for the Factors. We'll assume them to be a target. But I don't want to escalate this just yet. We're missing too many answers. You'll direct Intelligence to determine if there is reason to believe we're looking at an actual incursion or if this is just some sort of anomaly."

Celois nodded, grudgingly. This wasn't the first time that his instincts and the general's adherence to policy had clashed. Then again, he didn't have to deal with civilians whose political interests wouldn't let them admit to a threat until someone was lobbing missiles into their streets. "Major Terwood is already in position and equipped to track Kada. By now Kada will have scrubbed his ship, wherever it is. But he'll turn up sooner or later." He gestured to the woman at the table. "Doctor Patman, please prepare a protocol that'll let the governors' security teams add a brain scan to their routine processes. Nothing too overt. See if we can add it to the retinal scans."

Bayla raised his hand. "Sirs, we still have that mystery with the disk," he reminded them.

"What disk?" Celois said, wondering how much other information wasn't being shared here today.

"There appears to be a device being used to bring material out of subspace," Bayla said. "The Caspian said they were hired to deploy it during the jump and then deliver it to someone on Rishabel. That's when he became infected and was abandoned by his cohorts. The Vanguard agents went to intercept a subsequent delivery, with catastrophic results."

"Do we know the reason for this collection?"

Bayla shook his head. "Until we know more we can't even guess at a reason. Our worst fear is that, while they are bringing the entities out of subspace, some of them have escaped, or were released, with the outcomes we've seen."

"If they are able to invade our people's minds as well as our electronic systems, we could be looking at an invasion that might be orchestrated right here in real-space. Someone is bringing them here to gain an advantage. Which leaves us with Shri-Lan, of course. Perhaps also the Arawaj rebel faction."

"Rebels?" Dmitra said. "You think they can orchestrate something like this?"

"The Arawaj faction has some very fine minds among them, if not the funds to do much with them," Celois reminded him.

"Speaking of fine minds," Doctor Patman interrupted. "I'd like to request more staff. Specifically, I could use a telepath."

Dmitra grunted noncommittally. "You mean a Delphian?"

"Yes. Shan Chion is here at the facility. Given this case, I'm sure we can persuade her to join our team on this project."

"Very well. Move your patient, the coherent one, to the upper floor. I don't want a Delphian civilian down here." He ran both of his hands over his hairless, tattooed head. "Let's be clear. I appreciate the research opportunities these aliens present. But if someone is deliberately bringing them here, our first priority is to find out what their intentions are. Structure your interviews accordingly."

"Yes, sir."

Dmitra sighed. "If Kada is being controlled by an alien entity, a great many of our operations are compromised. Find him. Contain him. Get a grip on that thing in his head. Bring in those who are behind this collection project. Send whatever support Major Terwood needs without drawing too much attention. I want this thing contained before it spreads." He watched Bayla pull the data sheet off the table and sling it over his shoulder. None of the others moved. His eyes shifted to Celois. "By any means necessary."

SIX

"That is a research lab?" Khoe followed Seth's eyes as he craned his neck to find the tower perched on a cliff jutting out from the mountain before them. From here it looked like it wouldn't take much of an earthquake or rockslide to tumble it off the edge.

The *Dutchman* had brought them to Magra, one of the more contested planets of Trans-Targon. Magra Torley, the smaller of two continents, offered services for people, like Seth, looking for a thorough scrubbing. His favorite outfit would ensure that the *Dutchman*'s identifying signals were replaced and screen it from tail to tip for any Air Command tracking devices he might have picked up on Feyd.

A commercial flight then took them to Magra Alaric on the opposite side of the planet. Aligned with the Commonwealth, this continent remained largely unmolested by rebel activity while Air Command forces staffed a number of bases there, both on the ground and in the sky. It was a pretty place to live and work, with a temperate climate and a mix of modern, sociable populations.

The Delphians had found a perfect location for their research center here, in the military's protective shadow but free of the social strictures imposed by their own government. Unlike those on their homeworld, this facility welcomed visitors and colleagues of many origins to collaborate and share their knowledge.

Seth paid the shuttle operator and leaped to the ground. "Delphians are secretly very dramatic. They love an impressive edifice." He started up a small skimmer provided to bring visitors from the drop-off to the main building. The ground rose sharply from here to the foot of the tower, built for some long-ago purpose and adapted by the Delphians for their research station. It blended into the craggy mountains that surrounded them with a stone façade covered in clinging plant life. Only the transmitter array on the rooftop suggested something other than ancient battles taking place here. Unseen, a sophisticated deep-space telescope traveled above it in geosynchronous orbit.

He breathed deeply of the clear highland air, as always happy to inhale something other than the canned gas aboard the *Dutchman*. A broad valley below them reached for the distant sea with a network of rivers and he let Khoe have her wide-eyed fill of the spectacular scenery. She exclaimed in amazement when a flock of long-legged shore birds swooped overhead on their way down the mountain. He obliged her by slowing the air car when she insisted that he touch the pink and purple seed fluff on one of the evergreens that grew up here. The trip to the tower had seemed far too short and he resolved to show her more of the planet on the way back.

"Doesn't look like anybody is home," Khoe said when they approached a door set deep into the stone wall.

"I'm just hoping Caelyn is here. It's been a while." Seth placed his hand onto the door's com panel to request entry. He had not dared to call ahead, fearing Air Command eyes on this place like they had eyes everywhere. But even if his friend was away on one of his frequent missions into whatever unknown fascinated these people so much, he hoped for a relatively friendly welcome here.

"Have you known him for long?"

"Some years. He helped us save a bunch of cephalopods in the badlands when we needed a spanner to get us out there. We've been friends since."

"Squid? Isn't that what people here eat for dinner?"

"They were special squid."

The door slid aside to show a towering Delphian woman dressed in crisp blouse and sarong. She inspected Seth with calm indifference. "Welcome," she said without inflection.

"Thank you, Elder Sister," Seth replied, using a Delphian dialect although she had addressed him in Union mainvoice.

Khoe peered at her with interest. Like most Delphians, she was hatchet-faced with cold sapphire eyes in a pale, unsmiling face. Her silvery hair hung straight to her shoulders, much shorter than was customary among the males of her species. "She doesn't sound very friendly."

For a Delphian, that was a loving embrace, Seth replied when he was waved inside.

"What has brought you to us?" the woman asked, allowing him no further than the small vestibule from which two interior doors led elsewhere.

"My name is Sethran. I am here to see my friend Caelyn," Seth said. "I have not seen my Elder Brother in many months."

She regarded him silently for a long moment. "I will ask him if he wishes to see you," she said finally and turned to a door which opened only after a hand and retinal scan.

Don't touch that, Seth told Khoe when he felt her reaching for the access panel. *We have nothing to fear here. Let's not annoy them by poking into things we shouldn't.*

"You didn't think you had anything to fear on Feyd, either."

He reached out to pinch her for that but then considered the cameras that were surely observing him closely. It would probably not do to have him seen groping through thin air down here.

They did not wait long before the door opened again and another Delphian arrived. This one was dressed as casually as

Seth and his straight blue hair hung loose over his back. "Centauri," he greeted him. "What trouble brings you to my door this time?"

Seth grinned. "I'm happy to see you, too, Delphi."

Caelyn beckoned him to follow into the tower's interior. Seth almost expected damp stone walls and musty dungeons but walked instead through a bright open space where only support pillars remained of the walls. "You're lucky to find me here. I'm leaving in a few days for Callas. You should have let me know you were coming."

Seth shrugged. "Too many ears listening in. I took a chance." He stopped to peer curiously at a complex diagram floating above a holo emitter. A few people, not all of them Delphian, sat around it in murmured discussion. In another part of the workspace, a Caspian blessed with a beautifully spotted blond hide lectured in front of a disassembled mechanism. Neither group seemed to be disturbing the other. Seth had not visited before but it was generally assumed that the researchers here concentrated their efforts on astrophysics. Hopefully, he thought, the sort of physics that explained Khoe's existence and the events that brought her here.

"Of course you did," Caelyn sighed.

They took a small lift, little more than an open metal cage, to one of the upper floors of the tower. A window set into the deep, curved wall seemed to wrap almost entirely around the comfortable lounge, flooding it with sunlight. Caelyn ushered him to a lounging area and went immediately into a service alcove. "You still drink that vile charwood tea?"

"All the finest people drink that these days," Seth said, looking out of the concave window and over the valley below. He drew Khoe's attention to the side of a steep embankment where long ago people had carved homes into the soft rock. Colonies of birds now roosted in them and the cave openings were a riot of brilliant plumage. "This place is terrific."

"Isn't it? I've been here a while now, off and on. We're doing some wonderful work with the signals from the outer badlands. Time to head out again, though. My feet itch."

"What's wrong with his feet?" Khoe asked.

He's an explorer. And a top level spanner. He's happiest out there. I've seen him crack the tightest of keyholes and come out laughing.

"Didn't think Delphians laugh."

Not in public.

"What's that?" Caelyn, bearing two cups, came to where Seth stood.

Seth blinked. "What?"

"I thought you said something."

Seth sipped his tea. "I did. But not to you."

The Delphian's steel-blue eyes regarded his friend with curiosity. "To the point, then. Why are you here?"

Seth considered how to approach this. "I met someone," he said finally. "Might be first contact, for all I know."

Caelyn's eyebrows rose. "Where? When? Do you have recordings?"

Seth glanced at Khoe. "More than that."

"Are you going to share that? I'm assuming that's why you came out here. What does Targon have to say?"

"Targon isn't sociable about the whole thing."

"Why not? They're much better equipped for xenology than we are. Delphians aren't exactly experts on other species."

"To say the least." Although Delphi had communities of xenobiologists working off-planet, it was no secret that they, as a society, viewed outsiders with suspicion and even disdain. Few off-worlders were allowed to set foot upon Delphi's well-protected surface. "But I think your people might actually be better suited for this than Targon." He perched on the deep stone sill and waited for Caelyn to do the same. "Found something in subspace. Someone."

The Delphian's cup paused on its way to his lips. "Did you just say subspace?"

"Did." Seth studied Caelyn's expression before his friend

shuttered it behind that sometimes irritatingly bland expression Delphians wore to hide their thoughts. It was not as surprised as he would have expected.

Caelyn leaned back into the curve of the window and drew his long legs up onto the sill. "Tell all," he said.

"Something came aboard my ship during a jump. Charted site, easy span. But I emerged way out by Rishabel. It... She says she originates in subspace. Someone out here is harming them. Taking some of their people out. I've seen evidence that she might well be right about that. Unfortunately, it seems to involve pirates and Air Command by now. Maybe rebels."

"She?"

Seth smiled. "Want to meet?"

"Yes! Where is this creature?"

Seth tapped his forehead. "Right in here. Small enough to ride a com link into my brain. Communicating, even manifesting." He grasped Khoe's wrist to tug her closer to himself. "You'd be looking at her right now if you could see her."

Caelyn cocked his head to the side. "You do know that extended periods of time alone in deep-space can have some unpleasant side effects, right?"

"I'm sincere. Her name is Khoe."

Caelyn put his cup down on the sill and raised a hand, a question on his face. Seth nodded and leaned forward. After a moment's hesitation, Caelyn touched the neural interface at Seth's temple and briefly closed his eyes to establish the *khamal*, a mental connection usually made only between Delphians. But being off-world and restricted by fewer rules, along with the advent of the neural implant, led some Delphians to extend the privilege to other species.

Caelyn dropped his hand and turned his head to see Khoe standing beside them. She took a step back when she felt his presence.

"Hello," Caelyn said gently.

She looked over to Seth. "He can see me?"

"I can," Caelyn replied. "Through Sethran."

"I don't know if I like that."

Seth took her hand in both of his. "Just let him take a look. There's so much we don't know."

Caelyn's eyes took on a faraway look as he tried to reach out to Khoe. But after a moment he frowned and returned his attention to them. "Nothing. Only what you see and hear." He looked at their hands. "And feel. That part is interesting. This is far beyond mere hallucination." He held his hand out until she moved closer to allow him touch her arm. "You would be a fascinating study. You manifest perfectly. How did you assimilate so much? How long have you been here?"

"Not very. Would be..." she calculated silently. "Would be about sixty hours on the *Dutchman*."

"Targon-time," Seth confirmed. "She's been scanning my on-board archives and I've downloaded some things from Feyd when they weren't looking. Well, she did. She is able to breach anything, it seems. Including Air Command encryptions."

"Electronic systems?" Caelyn said. "I can see why Air Command wouldn't want you running around loose out here." He nodded to Seth. "And with that I mean you. You're not exactly a favorite son among them."

"They're already trying to get their hands on her."

"Why are you here?" Caelyn asked Khoe. "Some explorer from the Big Empty, here to learn about us mortals?"

She shook her head, too unfamiliar with Delphians' austere features to see the humor brightening Caelyn's eyes. "They... somebody has taken some of my people. One of them is most important to us. I have to find out how they did that. To... to stop it. We don't know why that is happening."

"On purpose, you think?"

"I was kinda hoping you could help us figure that out," Seth said. "If someone is taking her people, we need to know why. What's so valuable?"

"I can see how breaking into secure systems might be valuable," Caelyn said. "Do you have any other talents?"

Khoe glanced at Seth, looking guilty.

"We've observed some energy transfer," Seth said. "She's using thorium and a bit of me but I've been able to crank out a lot of punch. That sort of conversion would be worth quite a bit, too." He winced. "Some folks might have gotten in the way of that."

"Dead?"

Seth nodded. "Vanguard. But she's able to control it now."

Caelyn exhaled sharply. "I think you need more expert advice than what I have for you."

"What do you mean?" Khoe said.

"He means a Shantir."

"There is one in the city," Caelyn said. "I could get him here by morning. And I want to talk to some of the others. Saias' team downstairs has been involved with subspace projects. We have some theories. Maybe they've heard of this."

Khoe took another step closer to Seth.

He slung an arm around her shoulder. "Don't worry so, Khoe. No one will hurt you here."

"The Centauri is right." Caelyn hopped off the sill. "We are able to learn from past mistakes." His sardonic look to Seth did not disguise his opinion of the Union's methods where exploration was concerned. He reached out to sever his mental link to Seth. "And now you look very peculiar doing that."

Seth dropped his arm. "Can I stay up here till your Shantir arrives? The *Dutchman*'s in the shop."

"Of course. We have some rooms upstairs. It's nearly time for dinner. But first I want to show you our new lab. I know how fascinating you find baryonic matter research." He smiled when Seth rolled his eyes. "We'll leave the actual quantum quandaries for tomorrow."

* * *

"Seth?"

Seth grumbled something that didn't sound like real words to himself any more than they did to Khoe and turned over to pull the blanket over his head. That of course didn't remove her persistent presence from his mind and he sighed when she continued to prod him.

"What?" he groaned finally, blinking into the early morning light peeking through the open window. How marvelous this soft, clean bed that was easily three times the size of the one he used aboard his ship and infinitely more comfortable. How wonderful the cool breeze flowing past his face, the only part of him not covered by this cozy blanket. He buried his face into the pillow and tried to doze off again.

"Seth, it's morning now."

"No, Khoe, it isn't."

"It's light out. I hear people across the hall."

"Delphians don't appreciate sleep," he opined. "Neither do you." When she said nothing more he opened his eyes to see her sitting stiffly on the edge of his bed, staring at nothing. "What's wrong?"

She lifted her shoulders. "Bored."

"Nonsense." Aboard the *Dutchman* she spent long hours with his archives while he slept, having developed a peculiar fondness for stories about mythical beasts and heroes. But she had also learned to withdraw into a silent resting state after learning that physical beings often required and valued times of solitude and privacy. It also meant less of a draw on his thorium inventory, for which he was grateful. "They must have something to entertain you here." He waved at a display platform in the corner of the room. "Look, 3-D even. Just don't hack into their system. They won't appreciate that."

She said nothing.

Seth sighed deeply and propped himself up on an elbow. "You're worried. I can feel that."

"Yes."

"Why?"

"I'm not sure. These people, these Delphians, have such purpose. All this machinery and all this knowledge they have. They *see* so much. I am scared what they'll find when they look at me."

He frowned. "You have too many thoughts. That's just the way they are. They are actually a very friendly bunch. It just takes a while to get close enough to see that."

"I know. I'm not scared of *them*. I'm scared of me."

"What? Why?"

She turned to look at him, which meant that she was looking at herself, through his eyes. He was still not used to the odd perspective that would present to her. Over these past few days she had sometimes asked him to stand before the reflective surface of his decon station so that she could see him, too. There she made him turn to show various angles and finally declared that she approved of what she saw. He smiled at the memory.

"Don't laugh at me," she said.

He tugged on her arm. "Come, lie down. I'm not laughing at you. Why are you scared?"

She stretched out beside him. "I don't really know. They're going to look at me and tell you that I'm just some unknown tiny clump of particles."

"Well, we know that. But I wouldn't say *just*. You're not *just* anything."

"Everything I am out here is because of you. What you see. How you see me. Without that I'm nothing at all."

"Stop that, Khoe. It's not true. You are what you made yourself to be. From what you've learned about us." He picked up one of her long, thin braids and tickled her nose with it. "No one can make that for you."

She said nothing for a while. Finally: "I don't know if I want to go back."

He blinked. "You don't?"

She shrugged. "The place where I come from is beautiful, in its own way. We're at peace, not like you out here. We play and we dream and we enjoy each other in ways you can't really understand. We can merge and come apart again and we can be anywhere."

"Sounds magical."

"Maybe. But there is so much to see out here. To feel. It's harsh and then it's hot and then cold and loud, but there is such variety of everything. I want to see more of that."

He smiled. "So don't go back. Not right away anyway."

She peered at him. "I can't keep taking up space in your head, Sethran. It's not fair."

"Am I complaining?"

"Well, not now. But you get impatient sometimes. I can tell."

"We all get impatient with each other sometimes. Caelyn thinks I'm the most annoying Centauri he's ever met. But we're good friends."

"You don't mind, then?"

"Not even a bit. We've got to figure out what's going on with your people. Maybe the Delphians can help; maybe we have to turn to Targon. Let's not worry about what comes later. Who knows, maybe you'll get tired of me by then."

She smiled slowly. "I'm so glad I found you."

"Yeah, I'm well-connected."

"That's not what I meant."

He looked into the deep violet eyes, suddenly very aware of her lying here next to him in his bed. She had done that before, but he felt ever more removed from the fact that she was merely a construct of their combined thought processes. Although she wore a loose-fitting tunic of vaguely Feydan design, it clung to her body in ways that made a man's mind wander too easily from the subject of conversation. He touched a hand to her cheek, feeling the smooth, warm skin beneath his fingers. "I'm glad you're here, too," he said, watching his fingers travel over her chin and then down along the graceful line of her neck.

She shivered.

"You can feel that?"

"I think I can. I know what this would feel like to you. I can take that from you."

His gaze traveled to the full lips, curled at the corners in that quirky, not-Centauri way that had caught his attention before. Without considering much further, he bent to touch those lips with his. Her quick intake of breath when he did this echoed the sudden rush of endorphins both of them felt. She returned his kiss, hesitantly at first but then with growing ardor and rarely had this felt so right inside his own head.

Or his body. When she reached up to pull him closer he drew back with a gasp, shocked by his sudden physical need for her. His last shred of conviction about her true form had flown out that open window when he kissed her, leaving only the woman here in his bed. He sat up and scrubbed his face with his hands. What was happening to him?

"Seth?"

He shook his head, unable to think, unwilling to look into her face. He felt her sudden apprehension as much as he heard it in her voice.

"Seth!" Someone banged on the door to his room with a striking lack of Delphian decorum. "Shan Quine has arrived. He'll take the meal with us if you get up now."

"Khoe," Seth began and turned to her but she had withdrawn. He was pretty sure it was not, as usual, to give him privacy during his morning ablutions. Angry with himself and still feeling the soft lips he had kissed, he showered, barely noting the soothing hot water for which he yearned during the long journeys aboard his ship, got dressed and heeded the call to breakfast.

The communal lounge, where only last night he had shared a meal and conversation with some of Caelyn's colleagues, was empty this morning except for Shantir Quine, a Delphian woman he had not seen before, and Caelyn. They looked up expectantly when Seth joined them at a table set carefully in deference to their esteemed visitor. Caelyn's hair was neatly braided and he wore a traditional blue vest looking oddly formal on his lanky frame.

"Seth," Caelyn called. "Come join us. This is Shan Quine and Shan Saias."

Seth gestured a respectful greeting to the Delphians before sitting. "I am honored."

Like many of his peers, the elder Shantir wore a knee-length blue tunic over loose pantaloons gathered at the ankle. The blue braid was nearly black, hinting at an advanced age that his unlined face did not. His rank did not require him to acknowledge lesser beings but he nodded graciously at the newcomer.

Are you going to appear? Seth sent to Khoe. *Shantirs don't talk to just anyone. This is about you, remember?*

She shimmered into view and hovered near Caelyn's shoulder.

None of them missed a sudden start from the Shantir when she did. He looked past Caelyn as if to find Khoe there.

"She's here, isn't she?" Saias said. Her severe features were softened by clever layers of blue curls and a smartly styled wrap around angular shoulders.

"Shan Saias leads our team here at the tower," Caelyn explained. "I've given them what you told me about Khoe. She has worked with us on many projects but subspace is her specialty."

"And that which is found within subspace," the woman said, still looking at the Shantir. "I have the feeling that some of our theories may be about to take a new turn?"

"Possibly, Elder Sister," Seth said. "Subspace physics is not my field."

"May we see… your visitor?" The scientist picked up a dough-wrapped breakfast portion and nibbled daintily.

"Of course. She's a little nervous. Tell me about your theory."

"There are several. But we have on many occasions detected quantum particles in subspace that defy current thoughts about what we can expect to find there. Simply put, we've found sudden restructuring of the way they connect into very complex patterns. We've suspected a certain resonance or other event to suddenly trigger this organization when certain conditions are met."

Seth looked up when Khoe gasped. "She's right."

Told you they were smart.

"We haven't been able to duplicate the effect in the lab. But we've started to replicate the resonance with the intent of trying this in subspace. If it works, it should cause a sort of tipping-point where these particles combine to create the patterns we've found."

"Are you sure no one is actually working on this now?" Seth asked. He watched Khoe sit on an empty chair beside the scientist and carefully match the woman's erect posture. He tried not to smile when Khoe lifted her chin and tried to stretch her neck to achieve the graceful tilt of the Delphian's head, perhaps forgetting that she could simply create any neck she wanted.

"We probably would have heard of that," Saias said, unaware that Khoe was copying the motion of her hand as she spoke. "Some of us have suggested that sentient life is possible outside our known physical system. If this is true, taking our experiments into subspace could have devastating effects. I have often wondered if our brutal tinkering with keyholes for the sake of traveling is disruptive to such life."

Khoe shook her head.

"She says 'no'," Seth translated.

The physicist looked at Seth as if surprised by his presence. "Oh," she said. "To be honest, I hadn't even expected so definite an answer." She pondered her biscuit. "We have so many questions."

"Aren't you going to eat?" Khoe said to Seth.

I'm not hungry. "From what she's told me, our traverse does not actually intersect the subspace matrix they inhabit."

"You're upset," Khoe said. "Because of earlier."

I'm not upset! Will you pay attention?

"Then how did she get aboard your ship?" Saias asked.

"That's what I hope you can tell us," Seth said to her.

"Have you detected this phenomenon via the Rishabel breach?"

She shook her head. "Keyholes, and the jumpsites we turn them into, exist of course only in real-space. So if there is a pattern, a contact between these particles, the dimension of space has nothing to do with it. Distance has no meaning. Location has no context. Once this trigger has joined them, these particles could be millions of light years apart and still work in perfect synchronization. It's doubtful that our kind will ever be able to truly understand subspace."

"And yet we exploit it as we see fit, using technology like a hammer," the Shantir said, reminding them of the once-habitable moon of Scorria whose orbit took it into the path of a keyhole. A single attempt to expand it from the surface had thrown the moon out of its orbit and destroyed all life there. Only two other keyholes had ever been identified within a planet's orbit and both were now tightly guarded by Air Command. "I'm not surprised that our intrusions now cause harm to others."

Seth inclined his head in acknowledgement, uneager to engage in a debate about Commonwealth expansion. "So we don't even know if this is happening only out by Rishabel. Khoe fears that this… harvest of her people will continue to the detriment of their species. A key member of their population was taken and that loss is now threatening everyone. Your trigger, maybe. We'd like to find out who is doing it and how. And why."

"Exploitation, perhaps," Caelyn said. "These entities may be useful to us out here."

"That would be a shame," the Shantir said. He pushed his chair back from the table. "Shan Sethran, I'm afraid my curiosity is overcoming my appetite. Please ask your visitor if I may meet her."

"Are they always so polite?" Khoe said.

They are Delphian. Are you ready?

She nodded, looking like she'd rather run from the room. Instead, she came to stand slightly behind him.

"Please proceed," Seth said.

The Shantir leaned over to him and, with the barest tap of his fingers on Seth's neural interface, established a link. His eyes traveled to Khoe at once to appraise her in silence.

Unable to disguise her impatience, Saias tugged on the Shantir's sleeve. "May we join you, Shan Quine?"

He nodded absently and reached over to touch her hand, then did the same to Caelyn's. Khoe shrank back when all four of them stared at her.

"What?" she said defiantly.

Seth took her hand. After only the briefest hesitation, she allowed this. "They're just bursting with curiosity, Khoe. You're a myth come to life."

"Barely even a myth," Saias said. "We've only begun to suspect. Scarcely a comment made here and there, quickly dismissed and filed away. We made a few findings available to our colleagues on Targon but I doubt anyone has taken them seriously. It's one of those things you mean to study when there is time for that. Even now, this is hard to fathom."

"I'm not lying," Khoe said.

Seth stood up and tugged her toward an empty chair. Like the others here, it was a paper-thin sheet with a graphene core, tastefully contoured to cradle a bi-ped in comfort. The others gasped in unison when she passed through it like a ghost while her hand in his remained perfectly solid. Everyone expected her to fall when she sat down on it. "Her interaction with solid objects is how, jointly, our minds decide it should be, led by her. She is real only to us."

"The manifestation of this entity is remarkable," Quine said. "I expect it's somehow seated in your thalamus, Shan Sethran, feeding directly into your cortex which, of course is accessed by our khamal via your interface taps. Very elegant. Almost by design."

"You're suggesting some purpose to this?" Saias said.

"I'm not sure. Could be simply opportunistic. All Prime species have more or less the same central nervous system configuration. This would be a very likely way to establish communication with the host." His gesture encompassed all of Khoe. "Shaped to elicit empathy, I suppose."

"What does that mean," Khoe said sharply. "I didn't even know what Seth was until I came aboard."

"Please, dear, we mean no insult," Saias said. "This is all very new to us."

"What I mean is that you could manifest as anything you like," Quine said. "Any species, some fantastic construct resembling nothing we've ever seen, or perhaps just remained invisible. You could be walking upside down on the ceiling for all the difference it would make to you. In a quest for power, you could have taken on godlike proportions, depending on our individual beliefs. But you chose something appealing to the Centauri, engaging his willingness to accept your presence as a peer. I doubt he'd be as easily swayed had you appeared as a Rhuwac."

Seth, who had only recently come to a similar conclusion, smiled grimly. "I never considered myself quite so easily manipulated but you're correct about the Rhuwac. She has been studying my data bank to create this projection."

"Which seems devoid of shoes," Caelyn interjected.

"I'm not interested in trying out new shapes," Khoe said. She looked directly at Seth. "I'm not here for your amusement."

"No one's expecting you to perform tricks," Caelyn said before Seth found some reply to that. "Your choices just seem very astute."

"And yet," Quine said, reaching for more warm berry juice, "she isn't merely the sum of pure data. She's able to reason, choose, feel and convey emotion. This may be learned from you, Shan Sethran. A reflection of your personality and another source of empathy between you."

"If so," Saias said. "Creating a Rhuwac or some other objectionable creature would probably not be possible."

"That, in itself, would make a fascinating study. These entities' ultimate appearance and personality would then depend entirely on their host and the information they are given at, well, I suppose 'birth' is as good a term as any. Attitudes, morals, emotional responses, all following existing neural connections."

"But, surely, from there they would be able to shape their own," Saias said, intrigued by the idea. "Even share them."

"Stop talking about me like I'm not here," Khoe interrupted. "My people are in danger because of you and you call me a parasite?"

The Shantir reached out to pat her arm. "Forgive us, Shan Khoe. The mind wanders when faced with such a fascinating new discovery. We shall call you a visitor and think of you as such." He sobered visibly. "I do have some concern about how your presence is affecting Sethran's physical well-being."

"How so?" Seth said.

Quine indicated Caelyn. "Shan Caelyn told us of some energy transfers taking place. I suspect that Khoe is able to manipulate electromagnetic radiation in some ways. Any such transition would take its toll on an organic host, no matter how efficient."

"I'm feeling a bit of a headache," Saias said. Caelyn nodded to confirm that he did, too.

"That's the result of our contact with the Centauri via his interface, not the alien. Forgive me, Shan Khoe. I meant 'our visitor'. I would expect far more extensive damage to Shan Sethran."

Seth frowned. "What are you saying?"

"I'd like to take a closer look, if you don't mind." The Shantir gestured toward Seth's interface node. "As a sort of diagnostic."

"That is a privilege, Elder Brother. Thank you."

Quine scraped his chair closer and placed two fingers over the thin metal implant at Seth's temple. He closed his eyes to concentrate on his task. "I can definitely detect a duality there," he said. "Although we don't have any descriptive language for this. Heightened activity where I'd expect to see that." A trace of a smile moved his thin, blue-tinted lips. "A female set of neural pathways in addition to your own within one nervous system. The distinction is quite obvious."

Caelyn looked at Khoe in wonder. "Were you even aware of race or gender before you met Seth?"

She shook her head, as fascinated by the Shantir's revelations as the others were. "It just seemed fitting. We just think of this as the physical world. We don't even distinguish between sentient and non-sentient. You are just moving shapes to us."

"Can you show us something of the nature that Caelyn described to me? Some energy conversion?"

"I don't know. That's a dangerous thing to try, I think."

Seth touched a finger to his bowl of tea. "Just a little."

She inhaled deeply and nodded. Before a second passed, the cup in front of Seth's hand slid across the table top and then careened across the room to shatter against the far wall. "Oops."

"It's all right," Quine said. He had not even flinched at the harsh sound of the breaking dish. "This had a marked effect on Sethran."

"A bad one?" she asked, looking worried.

Quine did not reply to that. "Do you have anything else?"

"Nothing safe," she said. "Except this, maybe."

Seth gasped when he felt a surge of adrenaline, like the one she had created back on Feyd when it was needed. "All right," he grunted. "Enough." He felt the Shantir's healing presence work to counter the effect of the substance and felt his heartbeat slow again and his breathing become more steady.

"I'm sorry. Did I hurt you?"

"No, don't worry." He gave her a reassuring smile as he exhaled shakily. "I'm fine."

Quine removed his hand from Seth's temple. "I'd need to review Centauri physiology and spend more time with you. I detect some chemical imbalances - the epinephrine surge you just experienced strained your heart and other systems - but your heart, your whole vascular system, can handle the strain better than your short-limbed cousins. I suggest you don't indulge in tossing tableware around if you can avoid it."

"That's a relief," Khoe said.

Caelyn was still appraising Quine's expression with a critical eye. "Shan Quine? There is something more?"

The Shantir nodded. "I am not certain, but I can't see any way that young Khoe can easily extricate herself from Sethran. Without extensive neuroimaging, which may have to involve our friends on Targon, I can't give a definite answer. I've tried to follow some pathways from your interface taps and am fairly certain that some of your axon terminals are actually fused. Others may simply share a synapse. I can only guess, but this may have happened during Khoe's... ah, creation."

"It can't be all that," Seth said. "If that were so, would we not also share moods, thoughts, even?"

"Indeed. You are quite distinct and separate. But your physical connection, at a cellular level, is detectable to me even here, observed over a cup of tea."

"You're thinking that separation might damage those axons?" Caelyn said. "Neurology is not something I understand in the least. But trying to separate them sounds dangerous."

"It would depend on how widespread those connections are. Some brain damage is inevitable. For either of them. Or both."

"That can't be right," Khoe said. "I can leave any time I want."

Caelyn cleared his throat and sat up straighter in his chair as if to prepare himself for what was to come. "Then let me volunteer. We are all linked. Transfer to me."

"Shan Caelyn, I cannot recommend that you attempt this," Quine objected.

"I agree," Saias said dryly. "We need you out on Callas before the quasar emits again."

"If Sethran is being harmed by this we don't have time

for drawn-out research," Caelyn said.

"Still, we should at least set up a safe and controlled environment," Quine countered. "I have a colleague on Targon who would come out here without needing to discuss this with Air Command."

"That would take days."

"I can't!" Khoe suddenly exclaimed.

They all turned to her, startled by the urgency in her voice.

"He's right. I can't... um, pull away from Seth to go to Caelyn. I can feel Caelyn, like I can access the *Dutchman*'s systems. But I can't just go there entirely. It just feels like we're all tangled up." She looked at Seth. "I'm so sorry, Seth!"

He took her hand again, stunned by this latest revelation. "Not your fault," he said automatically. "I know you didn't mean this."

"This could kill you! I can't just stay in your head forever."

Seth swallowed hard and looked to Quine as if for rescue. "I guess I'm lucky that she's not manifesting as a Rhuwac, then."

"This isn't funny," Khoe said.

Saias folded her arms on the table and leaned forward. "Khoe, did others like you also enter real-space? To join with physical beings like you did?"

Khoe's brows drew together as she considered the question. "I don't know. We don't... we don't talk about things like you do, sitting around for debate. We just know things. No words, no actions. I felt an imperative to latch onto Seth's ship to follow the path those smugglers took when they stole from us. It's possible that others did, too."

"We must assume that there are others like you, Khoe," Saias said. "Posing a danger to our people in this paired form. I suppose we can call you *dyads*. I wonder if there is a way to make inquiries with Targon."

"If Targon catches up with me I'll be locked up with a

probe in my head until they've cataloged every neuron," Seth said. "They've already tried once."

"We don't have time for that," Khoe said.

"Targon is not without scruples."

Seth smiled wistfully. "Perhaps it appears that way when they deal with Delphi, Shan Saias. But I am currently a fugitive. They have every excuse to detain me and no one would notice if I disappeared. I'm the perfect test subject."

"I thought you're a Union agent. Is that not so?"

"Not directly. I worked for Factor Baroch. Now that he's dead, I have few ties to Air Command."

Quine winced, a rare expression on any Delphian's face, when he was reminded of their leader. "A most valuable patron. For all of us."

The others nodded, momentarily silenced as they considered their loss. Even Caelyn showed not the slightest surprise and once again Seth was reminded that much went on among Delphians from which outsiders were excluded. He had searched through every possible resource on the way here to Magra and, although whispers had begun to trade rumors, nothing was yet made public about the Factor's death.

"What about that colonel that's bailed you out before?" Caelyn said at length. "Carras, is it? He knows about you, doesn't he?"

"He suspects. But I think I'll stay out of his way for a while. The officer we killed was one of his."

"He's probably not very fond of you right now, Centauri." His face brightened. "Then what about your friend Nova? Isn't she Air Command? Maybe she can help."

Seth shook his head. "Last I heard she joined the Vanguard squad not too long ago. So let's leave her out of this, please." He turned to Saias. "It's my hope that you will be able to help us, Elder Sister. If we can get our hands on one of their devices, those disks, perhaps your team can find a way to reverse the process."

"We will most certainly enjoy the opportunity."

"And you think the entities imprisoned in those disks can be returned to subspace?" Quine's question was for Khoe.

"I hope so, but what matters is the one I came here for. What you called the trigger entity. We must have that back. Maybe it's in one of those disks. Or maybe I can find a way to…" She threw a sidelong glance at Seth. "To take it myself. Take it with me back into subspace."

"In my head?" Seth said.

"It's very small."

"You have a peculiar sense of humor. How about we leave that as a last resort?" He turned back to the others. "If the bits got into those devices, they must surely come out again."

"Don't call us bits," Khoe said. She looked to Saias. "What did you call us earlier?"

"Dyads. A Dyad is really just a set of two. Paired in some way."

She nodded. "Sounds better than 'bits', I think."

"So that makes me a Dyad, then?" Seth asked.

Saias nodded, looking amused. "Since you are now a single physical being, I suppose you are, indeed, a whole new species."

Seth grinned. "Ought to be named after me."

"Except that you might not be the first or the only one," Caelyn said. "Considering this peculiar harvest that is happening."

"Don't ruin my joy. But I suppose you're right. We better get on our way."

"What do you have in mind?" Saias asked.

"Besides Khoe?" Seth winked at her and grinned when a deep shade of pink colored her pale cheeks. "I think I'm going to put on my pirate hat and see if I can get a delivery job. Someone is hiring those people to collect for them. I'm hoping it's the same someone that's got that trigger entity."

"Centauri…" Caelyn said thoughtfully, raising a slender hand.

Seth turned to him. "You're not going to suggest what I

think you are."

Caelyn gave him a benign smile. "You know it."

Quine looked from one to the other. "Something escapes me here."

Seth swiped a new glass for his tea from a nearby table. "Caelyn has dreams of becoming a spy. Occasionally, he likes to practice."

The elder Delphian blinked, momentarily taken aback. "Surely you don't intend to accompany Shan Sethran?"

"I am. He's going to need a spanner."

"I can make any jump," Khoe said.

"Maybe so," Seth said. "But you're sucking up thorium like cubes of sugar. I can only store so much without adding more shielding."

"You plan to take a Delphian into rebel territory," Saias said, incredulous. "If there is a bigger flag you can wave to draw attention, I don't know what is."

Seth grinned at Caelyn. Saias' point was well made. Delphians, seen off-world only when on their ambitious explorations or in service to the Commonwealth, would draw much attention where rebels congregated. "He shines up well with the proper disguise," he said. "Someday I may actually get him to cut his hair."

"Only if you cut off your head," Caelyn replied amiably. The length of his blue hair corresponded directly with the line of hair growing along his spine, considered a sign of virility on a Delphian's otherwise hairless body. Intellectually superior to most of the lesser-evolved Prime species of Trans-Targon, few Delphian males were willing to abandon this ancient affectation.

"That's probably not the best way to get Khoe out of my brain."

SEVEN

Reylan Tague stared moodily at the display screen in front of him, as undecided and distracted as he had been when he went to bed last night. Or what passed as night on this dismal planet where the Little Sun set only every six months, Targon-time, and darkness fell only when the other star aligned properly and one needed chronometers to know when it was damn well time to get some sleep.

Not that sleep had been much on his mind lately. Who had time for that when there was so much work to be done before one or the other of Tharron's sons prodded him for the results that just weren't coming together. It wasn't that he didn't have any results for them. The problem was that he had too many. The Shri-Lan rebels funded his research here in Suncion, tucked away among the lonely expanses of the northern grasslands of Csonne, but now he felt that he just might be grossly underpaid.

He had not heard from his employers in a while although funds and supplies continued to arrive. His deceptively modest lab required equipment and raw materials costing a small fortune to acquire and to ship out here. He paid a steep rent for this section of the rambling research center and yet more fees for the shared use of the orbiter and four satellites circling the planet. He didn't really need the satellites but, as long as the other teams here believed in his subspace research, they were worth the extra cost.

The rebel agents about to land out here would bring another shipment of raw materials but also came with new demands for faster results. What to tell them?

He looked past his screen at the samples encased in their protective housing. Of course there was nothing to see but a row of thick metal disks, shielded in every possibly way and plugged into a small power plant. Separate from the data grid, of course. He'd learned to make certain of that.

"Rey, they're here," a gentle voice behind him announced.

He turned to Isalia, his assistant and companion, standing at the door. She had not stepped into the lab since that frightful incident but now cast an anxious glance at the open door leading into the corridor. Down there the Feydan was still pacing about in her enclosure, talking and gesturing in some animated but one-sided debate. "Thanks, Isa. I'll come up in a moment."

"You don't want him down here?"

Tague stood up and stretched his cramped legs. Too much time spent in this lab, hunched over his calculations, experimenting with the material gathered in subspace, had taken its toll on him. The average Human just wasn't made for this, he thought. He'd gotten weak in the knees, round in the middle, and gray on his head on his quest for knowledge. That this quest involved experiments of the sort that few members of the Union Commonwealth would sanction was a small price to pay. Ethics and science had always been uneasy partners.

He had been fortunate to find a sponsor for his work among the Shri-Lan instead of having to find a likeminded partner among Commonwealth companies. As his work brought him ever closer to discovering the nature of the peculiar emissions first reported by the Delphians, he soon realized that there was something eerily aware, almost sentient, in the way the particles interacted. Disclosing that finding to the Union would mire it in policy and endless debate if not halt it entirely. Fortunately, the Shri-Lan asked no questions and looked only for outcomes.

He went to the door and shooed the woman up a narrow stairway. "Maybe later," he said. "Let's see who they sent this time."

The man waiting for him in the domed residential pod was probably the least welcome in his estimation. Tov Pald seemed to take up too much space in the tidy commons room as he stood stiffly, having removed neither his overcoat nor the respirator Caspians needed on this planet. Isalia's lips formed a thin line when she saw the claws of his three-toed feet scrape over the polished floor.

"Hello, Tov Pald." Tague forced a smile. The deliveries had so far been made by a couple of Centauri pilots who dropped off their cargo without even stopping to chat. This Caspian, however, ranked highly in the Shri-Lan hierarchy. He ran a gang of mercenaries without any apparent rebel affiliation who were loyal only to him. As far as loyalty among those ruffians went, anyway, Tague thought. "I hadn't expected you to make the trip out here yourself. A rare pleasure, indeed."

The yellow raptor eyes above the mask were cold when he set a large box onto the floor. "Your report is overdue. The Brothers are looking for news."

Tague peered into the crate. Delighted by the number of disks, he took two and hugged them possessively to his chest. "There have been some... developments."

"Surely you do not mean setbacks."

"No! On the contrary. I think you'll be pleased with my update."

"Let's hope the Brothers will be," Tov Pald responded. "They want to see progress. Air Command is getting curious about the operation. They tracked my crew to Rishabel; I have no idea how. They barely made it out with these."

"What happened?"

"Air Command sent Vanguard agents to intercept a delivery. Why they'd care about these is a mystery. Things went bad fast. Three officers dead. I lost two of my men." Tov Pald gestured at the disks. "One of these might have leaked. From what I heard, two Centauri went down without taking any fire. Not getting any radiation from it now, though. Made sure of that. I've shifted all drop offs to Belene-Noh now. Rishabel is far too hot."

Tague glanced down at the heavy containers he still clutched to his chest. "It would take a lot for these to lose containment. Are you sure?"

"Unless those people got struck by lightning, yes."

"Did you get any video of the situation?"

"No witnesses. And no video. Why?"

Tague chewed his lip, still not sure what to reveal to the Caspian rebel. Surely, there must be a way to leverage his new discovery in some way. Then again, just ensuring that the funding for his work continued might be enough. "I think I might have discovered a... a side-effect of this material."

"Like what?"

"Come downstairs with me. I'll show you." He picked the crate up and walked ahead of the Caspian into the research wing. The main space was another geodesic dome, cheerfully lit by triangular skylights. The entire compound consisted of clusters of such domes, easily transported and assembled, connected by short conduits as needed. From the air, the colony looked like some articulated creature sprawled out on the otherwise bleak plateau, following its contours as the terrain required. Several research agencies shared the facility, which included work and living spaces, support facilities, and even a small settlement of outsiders that came to hunt the native species roaming the moors. Tague's cluster, the Adrierra lab, sat apart from the others at the northernmost edge of the plateau.

The doctor led Tov Pald down a stairway into the

shielded lab. For a moment, the rebel's shadow loomed over him like a horrific storybook monster, made all the more frightening by the stalking gait of his oversized feet. He had now removed his respirator but that did not make him any less frightening to the Human. Knowing of what the rebel was capable only added to his sudden aversion to being alone with him down here.

Tague shrugged that eerie feeling off his shoulders as he entered the secured lab. Tov Pald had no reason to want to harm him or his staff. Their work on what may well be the most efficient and cheap power source to be developed outside the Commonwealth made him a valuable asset. Anything with such power also made for a vastly superior weapon.

No one currently worked in the brightly-lit space although several workstations faced the transparent wall of a clean room. In there a massive engineering marvel had grown in size and complexity over these past few weeks. A sealed door led outside through a narrow tunnel and a larger corridor opened to more lab space.

Tague rushed into the glassed-in room to insert the prongs protruding from each disk into the bottom of a cylinder. Tov Pald watched from outside as the indicators on the vertical pipes came to life, soon indicating a full charge. "No leaks," Tague reported, relieved. Obtaining the particles was costly, even though they employed traders already traveling through subspace to simply scoop them up.

A rapid ticking sound alerted him to a discrepancy in one of the cylinders. He adjusted the containment field but the sound only increased in frequency. "This is odd," he said, momentarily forgetting the rebel waiting for him. "A variance. This one resonates counter to the others. Interesting."

"So what can you report to the Brothers?" Tov Pald wanted to know. He looked at the lab's monitors which clearly told him nothing.

Tague emerged from the clean room to join him by the

work station. "Nothing you see here. We're able to use these transducers quite effectively. These particles can, indeed, be converted into vast quantities of electromagnetic radiation with very little loss. The main expense, of course, is simply procuring the raw material to begin with."

"I know all that."

Reylan Tague smiled, unable to contain himself. He had to share this with someone, even if that someone was a Caspian mercenary with a limited grasp of physics. How he wished for a colleague to revel in this new discovery. Of course, the shortage of available colleagues was part of his problem these days. He picked up a thin sheet that resembled the data sleeves all of them used and motioned for Tov Pald to follow him out of the containment lab and into a short corridor.

"Look." He stopped beside a door locked with a crude bolt but did not open it. Instead, he activated a screen that looked like it had only recently been affixed to the wall. A camera switched on and Tov Pald saw the interior of a small, mostly empty lab. Panels of pale green material similar to what he had seen in the main area covered the walls, hinting at heavy shielding against whatever the physicist found interesting. The floor on which they stood was also padded with it.

What seemed most out of place here was the folding cot along one wall and the presence of a young Feydan pacing about the space. She appeared to be talking to himself, complete with gestures and animated facial expressions.

"Who's that? Who is she talking to?" Tov Pald asked. Evidently, the woman was one of the lab's own staff, still in her protective coveralls.

Tague activated a speaker system near the screen. "Jael, how are things in there?"

The woman looked up and then rushed toward the camera, causing Tov Pald to take an involuntary step backward. "Rey! You've got to let me out. This is pointless. I need to leave."

"Because of your friend in there?"

"Yes, it can't be in here. You don't understand." The Feydan glanced to her left and bit her lower lip. "I… Please just let me out."

"Just try to relax a bit, Jael," Tague said. "We'll figure this out. You know I can't let you go just yet, don't you?"

"Come on, Doc. That wasn't my fault. We had no way to know it would react like this. I don't think it meant any harm."

"What is she shouting about?" Tov Pald said.

"I'm sure it didn't, Jael. Just try to keep calm. We'll know more soon. I'm working around the clock on this." Tague checked the data storage sheet in his hands before bending to slip it under the locked door. "This'll keep you both busy for a while. I'll see what else I can find later. How's that?" He closed the com system before the Feydan had time to reply. Something that might have been fists slammed against the door from the inside.

"Doctor…" Tov Pald said.

"She's agitated. I don't want to sedate her although I might have to slip something into her meal if she doesn't calm down. She was with us when we first isolated and captured the subspace particles discovered by the Delphians. Something happened to her. She was exposed." Tague nearly shivered with delight. "I have every reason to believe that she's been… inhabited by something sentient."

Tov Pald stared at him for a moment and then threw back his head to bellow harsh laughter. "Doctor, you've been out on this rock for far too long. You told us what we're collecting are just particle fragments. Now they're a whole new and invisible species and you have one in there talking to that Feydan?"

"No, not invisible. Not really. It communicates telepathically. It somehow affected that woman's brain. I am hoping to find out how. She was quite reasonable at first but then something upset her and she killed our assistant. Accidentally, I'm sure." He hesitated a moment. "Of course, research into this phenomenon will take time and funds. And more particles. For some reason, they have a far shorter half-life than expected. It's possibly even a self-destructive mechanism."

Tov Pald scowled at him, close to losing his patience. "So now your subspace spooks are suicidal? Perhaps you should build them a nicer habitat." He turned to walk back into the main lab. "I am damn sure the Brothers have no interest in your little zoo here. You said you can develop a decent source of power with this. One we can weaponize. If you lose a few people along the way, so be it. Don't waste our funds on this nonsense."

"You don't understand, Pald."

The Caspian turned, looking not at all pleased to be addressed by his given name. "What exactly am I not understanding?"

The doctor was undaunted by the man's sneer. "Once that being had a grip on Jael, it tapped into our data system. Got past our security like a neutrino through lead. I don't think it even slowed for a second. Jael tried to stop it from getting into our mainframe. When she couldn't we moved to isolate her. That's when she killed our colleague, Sanjay. She just touched him!"

Tov Pald regarded him thoughtfully. "It breached your system? We set that up ourselves. It's not something you can just hack into."

"Well, she did. Or, rather, *it* did." Tague gestured at the containment cylinders in the lab. "I think it needs a living host to survive in real-space. Imagine what that sort of ability could accomplish if one of your own agents were to be… inhabited by one of these beings. Yes, sure, you can use these to make weapons or power your ships. But if they are, indeed, sentient and able to cooperate, all of that is trivial. Imagine the possibilities! We'd have access to any Air Command system."

Tov Pald reached under his overcoat to scratch his finely-furred chest as he considered this, still gazing at the inscrutable machinery inside the lab. Tague hid a smile when he could almost see the figures coming together in this man's calculations. "Maybe one in ten trips actually comes up with one of these things. Some of the crews we sent ended up dead. One ship never even emerged again, as far as we know. Word is getting out. We have to pay more for each delivery."

"That's why you're using pirates and smugglers instead of your own crews."

"How much more do you need?"

Tague chewed his lip. "We can't develop this overnight. I'll need test subjects we can dispose of and of course more samples. More funds as well. This will require new security measures. I could also use an exobiologist, hopefully someone educated in neurology."

The Caspian's yellow eyes shifted to the physicist. "You're asking for much. What about Suncion?" he said, meaning the town that had sprung up around this cluster of research labs. "Recruit people from there to help you with your little project. I'm sure you can think up a story to have them join."

Tague nodded. "That would do. I kept the crew of the last water delivery. Two halfbreeds out of Pelion and a Magran. They, ah, didn't make it and I'd appreciate if you could, ah, dispose of them for me."

Tov Pald showed his sharp teeth. "Throw them in the swamp. Do not let me catch you experimenting with Caspians."

"No, of course not!" Tague had, in fact, considered just that. Despite their fearsome predator exterior, Caspians possessed superior mental capacities. But he was not about to risk the ire of this rebel whose loose trigger finger was legendary even out here. "This Feydan will do for now. The room you saw is shielded as tightly as the collectors. I've found a frequency that interferes with its ability to penetrate our electronic systems. But I've been, well I suppose *feeding* it data to help it understand our world."

"Feeding it what?"

"Languages, technology, ethnology and a history of our struggle against the Commonwealth, among other things. It's absorbing information at an astonishing rate. Unfortunately, it doesn't pass that knowledge on to Jael. The Feydan seems to exist as little more than a connection to our physical world. I hope to eventually be able to communicate with it directly." Tague pointed up at a blank monitor. "So far, it's shown no interest in using even written words to reach others."

"Be sure it doesn't get access to anything it shouldn't."

"Of course not," the doctor assured him, hoping that Tov Pald would dig no further. Clearly, the moment Jael was allowed to leave the lab area, the creature inside her head would have access to anything it wanted. "This lab is isolated. We continue to refine our processes but so far the success rate is not good. But what was done once can be done again. Imagine how much someone like that will be worth to the Brothers."

Tov Pald nodded. "I'll see what I can do to get you more to work with. Find out why people are dropping dead when they get exposed. I don't want more casualties out there. We need to keep this quiet."

"We're working on just that. I suspect a loss of linked particles during the merge. The entities are simply not complete by the time they are captured. I've been able to keep some of the other fusions alive, although their cognitive functions were damaged to some degree, unlike Jael's. They're over here if you'd care to—"

Tov Pald waved his hand in a dismissive gesture and turned away. "I'm not interested in your failures."

Tague walked ahead of Tov Pald into the upper lab. "Tell me more about those Centauri you saw going down on Rishabel. Did your people detect any energy discharge? Gamma radiation? Radon? Visible light?"

"Nothing. It was over in seconds. Messy. Vanguard neural taps send a distress signal the moment their brains stop ticking. My crew didn't stick around. No idea how much more Air Command scum is wandering around that station these days."

"Were both of them Vanguard?"

"Just the female. The other was with the smugglers, I guess."

"Hmm." Tague scratched his chin, finding several days' of growth there. When was the last time he had shaved? "Are you sure they're dead? Jael here didn't look all that well for a while after this happened."

"No, I'm not sure," Tov Pald said. "I wasn't there. You think they might have been exposed?"

"If they were exposed and survived they'd be very useful to me here. If they're dead, my Union counterparts will be suspecting something very unusual by now. We may not have a lot of time to take full advantage of this discovery."

"Alive or dead, they could be anywhere by now," Tov Pald said. "I'll have our people on Rishabel check it out. Meanwhile, the Brothers are going to be very interested in your discovery here. Make this thing work, and quickly, if you want to keep them happy." He checked his data sleeve. "It'll be dark in a few days, Targon-time, and I plan to come back for the hunt."

Tague winced. As much as he was glad for the extra armed mercenaries here when the suns set and Csonne's wildlife dared to encroach upon Suncion, the brutal murder of those beasts filled him with disgust. Caspians like Tov Pald, Humans and some Feydans prided themselves on their ability to face down the moor's ferocious reptiles armed with little more than knives.

"Be sure to have a few success stories by then. The Brothers won't tolerate anything less. You can figure out what that means."

EIGHT

"Is that an Aikhoran yast?" Khoe asked. "It's so huge!"

"It is," Seth said, touched by her excitement and even more amused by the way Caelyn was hiding his. Although she had studied the more common species of Trans-Targon found in his data bank, actually seeing them at such close range left her in awe.

The Delphian peered from under his hood at the lumbering beast being led down the narrow street, every bit as entertained as Khoe by the variety of people and species that converged in this Magran harbor town. Caelyn, too, had seen some of these only from a distance, if at all.

He stepped carefully around a pile of something left behind by the animal. "Why are we down this way," he said after a glance at his mapper. "The air field is to the east."

"Which is why we're over here," Seth said. "Smells like Air Command."

"Oh? Air Command on Magra Torley? And how do they smell?"

"To Khoe, like someone tied to the base station cruising around back there over Magra Alaric. She's been tracking some of their com signals since we left the tower." He tapped his data sleeve. "She's been able link through this."

They stood aside as a congregation of locals surged past them, dressed in somber robes that hid all but their eyes, on their way to whatever required such procession. Seth watched them move through the alley and out of sight. "Whoever they have poking around here will be suspecting rebels under every one of those cloaks. Very convenient. For us, anyway."

"They're just civilians," Caelyn pointed out.

"Armed like bandits, like everyone else is here. That sort of hardware will have our friends running in circles. Why do you think Torley is so popular among my supposed confederates?"

"I thought Air Command isn't welcome on this continent," Khoe said. She pointed at a towering metal structure from which small cable cars slid, soon disappearing beyond the rooftops into the direction of the shore. "Can we ride one of those? Those look like fun."

Seth looked up, thinking that the framework for the gondolas looked even more rickety than the last time he had seen it. "Expect agents in plain clothes," he said.

He led the way through a gate and into a cobbled courtyard walled off from the street. A portly Human sat on the ground before a grill upon which several shallow pans sizzled and steamed. From an open doorway behind him drifted the sound of a flute. The man kept time with the tongs he used to stir his concoctions.

"Kada!" He waved them closer when he finally noticed them.

"J'saa. Hello." Seth smiled when they approached.

"That's my second daughter playing like angels singing in the mists of Mount Avelar." The man named J'saa closed his eyes while they listened to a few more plaintive notes. "Have you ever heard such sweetness?"

"Not in recent memory," Seth said with a wink at Khoe. She was no doubt thinking of the long argument they fought to a draw aboard the *Dutchman* when she decided to study music. Clearly, they would never agree on that particular subject.

Caelyn peered at the grill. "Dinner?" he asked, although it was still morning on this side of the planet.

The Human squinted at the stranger. "You're keeping interesting company, Kada."

"New navigator," Seth explained. "I'm branching out. Doing some deep-space runs. I hear that's profitable these days."

"I'd say." J'saa pointed at his dishes. "You wouldn't like the taste of this, Delphian." Like a magician before his audience, he waved his tongs and then picked up a pan with dark red liquid. When he flung the content into a bowl of water it solidified at once into pearlescent beads. He picked out a few large specimens and scooped the remainder back into his pan. "See those? On Feron, that's currency. Here, all it takes are a few *tocla* beetle carapaces and my secret recipe."

"Impressive," Caelyn said to the forger. *Do any of your friends do an honest day's work?* he added for Seth.

He's more honest than most, Seth replied. *See anything around here?* he sent to Khoe, not wanting to risk their host's good will by checking his perimeter scanner himself.

"Nothing. Some children in that house. Two women. Nothing interesting on his com channels, either. No one's listening."

"Got my plane?" Seth said to J'saa.

"All ready to go. It's now registered to a Pelion outfit called Skykoro. Deloused down to the last circuit and detailed in a pretty shade of red. Coolant's topped up. You were covered in bugs. Thank you very much for bringing Air Command down on us. Why are they chasing you this time?" He fumbled through his caftan to fish a device from one of his numerous pockets.

Seth hunched down beside him to transfer the *Dutchman*'s new codes to his own system. "I have no idea," he said. "They often confuse me with someone else."

"Sure they do." J'saa took his code pad back along with a

packet of currency he didn't bother to count. "The *Dutchman*'s on Claude's east runway but you can bet the place is still crawling with cops trying to figure out which one is yours. Have fun trying to get back aboard."

Seth shrugged and stood up. "Guess you're the new captain, Delphi."

Caelyn nodded imperceptibly to Khoe. *I knew I'd be useful along the way.*

She scrunched up her nose at him which nearly made Seth laugh out loud. "We'll be on our way," he said to J'saa. "Kind of between jobs right now. Missed a pickup on Aram a while back. Who's got news?"

"Who do you think?"

Seth nodded and waved as he turned away to head back out onto the street.

"What did he mean by that?" Khoe said.

"I've got some contacts here." Seth turned to Caelyn. "Going to transfer command functions to your sleeve. Get to the *Dutchman* and look like you're getting ready to go. Maybe order some supplies. Don't make too much noise but make it convincing that the ship's yours. Air Command isn't likely to question a Delphian, even out here. But if they do, stick to the story about heading to Callas."

"I think I can manage that." Caelyn tapped Seth's interface node to sever their khamal and so his link to Khoe. "Let's hope no one wants to come aboard. Your sloppy housekeeping won't convince anyone that a Delphian owns that ship."

"Step easy around those soldiers. Try to keep a straight face."

Caelyn rolled his eyes and strode away to find a shuttle heading for the flight pads.

Seth turned the other way to stroll through increasingly shabby streets that continued to fascinate Khoe. He observed her expression as surreptitiously as he could, amazed by her unending willingness to be amazed by all she saw. She took in everything, judged nothing, and learned more than he could ever hope to remember.

"How do you find your way through this place without a mapper. It's a maze!" Khoe said when they turned down yet another alley. The shops crowded so tightly in the small space that their multi-colored awnings formed a roof over the street.

"I grew up here. I used to think that stall over there was the best one to steal cakes from until I realized that Lubetke and his wife looked the other way on purpose. They used to feed us like gutter birds." He smiled at the memory. "A nice change from getting beaten by some of the other merchants when we weren't quick enough."

Khoe peered into the stall where a young woman was tending a round hearth. The sweet smell of roasted sugar hung thick in the air.

"That's their granddaughter, I think," Seth said.

"Was it hard, growing up in a place like this? Having to steal food?" Khoe watched a couple of urchins slink past them. Seth's hand automatically moved to protect his gun from nimble fingers.

"Not for me. I lived up in the hills." He gestured to the north where the wealthier population lived high above the noise and smells of the harbor town. "I only hung around down here because that place was really very boring. Unfortunately, that eventually got me sent to the military academy on Magra Alaric."

"Where you became a pilot. And a soldier."

"Yes, I am a pilot," he said and then pointed to the end of the alley. "There we are."

The building he sought faced an open square populated mostly by eateries and taverns and the customers that frequented them. The rough slab of stonework made no attempt to look like anything but a jail. Khoe read the signage near the entrance, her brow furrowed. "Are you sure this is a good place for you?"

"The safest," he said. "Keep your eyes open."

"That's only possible if you keep yours open." She shifted

more of her focus to his scanners.

The clammy interior smelled of mildew and harsh cleaning chemicals. That, along with some rough cursing and shouts from other parts of the building, reminded him of past visits to places like these. Two guards, identically dressed in lightly armored chest guard over knee-length kaftan, sat near the door, chatting. They rose when Seth entered, their hands close to their weapons.

"Morning," Seth said lazily, using Union mainvoice.

The two, both native to Magra, waited silently for more than that.

"I'm here to see Master Faran. With Domeo's report from Aikhor."

The two exchanged glances and then one nodded to the other, who left the entranceway. Identified by his code words, Seth was waved through an open arch guarded by an electrified curtain of snag filaments. Khoe snorted with derision at such elementary fortification but Seth's respect for the barrier came through hard-earned experience. He waited patiently for the guard to disarm it and followed him into the interior and what seemed to be an administrative area. It smelled a little less like a prison here.

Once again using Seth's transmitters, Khoe tapped into the security system while he was made to wait for the guard to announce his arrival. She had no need to hurry; Master Faran measured his time carefully to ensure that everyone appreciated his importance.

"Only locals locked up here," she reported. "Thieves, mostly. A murderer." She dug a little deeper. "Awful lot of weapons being kept in a cellar. More than they need, even if everyone carried two of them."

"I know. They pay well for them, too."

"Extra income for you? Baroch didn't pay much?"

Seth sent a mental shrug. "Any idea how much a tube of coolant costs?"

"Of course I do."

The door finally opened and a Magran, also in

Chris Reher

embroidered robe and wearing a crossed weapons belt, stuck his head out to wave Seth inside the room.

"Camera facing this way," Khoe said. "What's that thing on his head?"

Seth walked ahead of the Magran and turned his back to the surveillance system. The lawman's heavy brow ridge and most of his sparsely-tufted scalp was covered with a painful-looking reddish scale. *He's a northerner. They end up with skin problems down here. That's a fungus, I'm guessing.*

"Let me see."

No, they don't smell so good, either.

"Really? Move closer."

No! Seth grimaced, wishing for the Delphians' knack for obscuring their reactions to things like this. "Master Faran, thank you for the audience."

"Leave the crap at the door, Kada." The Magran didn't pronounce his words so much as roll them around in his throat for a while and even Seth had to pay close attention to understand his accent. "You're not expected. Got anything for me?"

"No, unfortunately. Hoping you have something for me. Looking for some fast cash, actually."

The Magran pursed his fleshy lips. "Got a shipment of guns looking for transport out of Aikhor."

"Need something bigger than that. What's the deal out on Rishabel? Heard rebels are taking on extra crews."

Faran shook his head. "You don't want to get mixed up with that lot. Whatever they're smuggling is red hot. Dead people dropping into real-space and now Air Command is nosing around. Sent some sort of investigation to see what's going on by the jumpsite. They might block it altogether."

"For everyone's safety, of course," Seth added.

"That's the story. Shri-Lan shifted the drop to Belene-Noh. If you're interested I can send my regards. Personally, I wouldn't touch it."

"The Shri-Lan's running this?"

"Yeah. Hiring private charthumpers to run errands. The

goods go from there to who knows where. Not a lot of volunteers, from what I hear. You need a spanner to get to Belene, though. No open jumpsites going out that way."

"Good. Got me a crew," Seth said, looking past Faran at Khoe who was busily poking around the Magran's own data system.

"Business must be good if you can afford a spanner."

Seth shrugged. "Can always be better. Who do I see?"

"Put down near a charming place called Dead End. Pretty much the only settlement on the whole damn planet. There's a hangout there run by a Centauri named Tieko. He'll set you up. Don't drink the water."

* * *

In the years that Seth had plied his admittedly questionable trade among the far-flung worlds of Trans-Targon, he had never had reason to land on Belene-Noh. From what he had learned about it over time, most other people didn't either. It orbited its star at an uncomfortable distance but stubbornly insisted on putting forth scrubby life forms wherever the meager desert soil allowed. Without an indigenous sentient population, small but fiercely hostile wildlife thrived in endless battles for survival in the cold desert. Long ago a migrant ship crash-landed here after a disastrous subspace traverse, spilling its contents from a massive hull beyond repair. The surviving passengers, mostly Centauri settlers, made the most of a bad situation and clung to life until the first explorers arrived nearly forty years later.

Those who escaped Belene-Noh were soon replaced by others seeking any place with sufficient oxygen and gravity to settle far from the watchful eyes of the expanding Commonwealth and its military.

"I can only assume that your rebel friends have lotteries of some sort to decide on which of the most miserable wildernesses to settle," Caelyn commented during their approach. The Delphian slouched tiredly in his pilot bench, only marginally interested in whatever was going on down there. Any jump through an uncharted breach took its toll on navigator as well as machinery and even the Delphians, most suited for the task, required time to recover. At any other time, he would already be filling up Seth's data bank with whatever the *Dutchman*'s scanners found down there.

Seth switched the main screen to show a real-vid view of their destination. No town had ever been built on this planet. Instead, the ancient hulk of the crashed transport lay half-buried in the sand and rock, surrounded by a few decrepit outbuildings made of stone and salvage. Long fissures in the surface showed entrances to the below-ground caverns where most of the locals eked out a living. Smoke rose from a few of the gaps. "Not a lot going on down there," he said.

Indeed, only two cruiser-class ships parked near the wreck. They had detected a third leaving the planet but it vanished into the nearby keyhole before he was able to identify it. The *Dutchman*'s sensors reported perhaps two hundred people inside the hull and below ground; hardly a sustainable population. Like so many isolated colonies, this one had simply dissolved after much hardship and now only rebels, recluses and fugitives sought shelter here.

Seth came about for a landing near the other ships parked on relatively level ground. "Finding anything?" he asked Khoe.

She shook her head. As soon as Caelyn had completed the jump to this sub-sector she announced that the trigger entity they searched for was not here. They had expected this – likely, this outpost was merely a trading point to gather the disks for the trip to their final destination. Still, Khoe was disappointed when she perceived none of her kind out here.

"Get some sleep," Seth said to Caelyn. "We'll take a look around."

Caelyn disengaged his link to the ship and heaved himself out of his bench. He looked strangely alien with his hair temporarily dyed black and hanging loose over his shoulders. The Centauri disguise would work reasonably well at a distance; it wasn't likely that anyone out here had ever seen a

Delphian up close.

Khoe watched him leave for the crew cabin. "Should just let me jump," she said. "He's exhausted."

Seth nodded, concentrating on the landing. "You'll take the next one. I might need him on his feet."

Once the *Dutchman* had settled on the planet's surface, Khoe followed Seth into the ship's small cargo bay. "You'll want your heavy boots," she advised. "They have a pretty aggressive sort of land crab here."

"Yes, dear." He ran his hand longingly over the well-designed protective suit folded in its bin and then chose a rough desert robe instead. There was probably little point to looking like a dandy on this remote outpost and being robbed for it wasn't going to help his mission here. When he turned he saw that she, too, had added a similar outfit to herself. "The Delphian wants to be a spy and the Dyad wants to be a person. What a strange crew I've taken on."

She frowned. "You don't think I'm a person?"

He sighed, regretting his offhand remark. "That's not what I meant," he said. "Just that you don't need clothes at all."

"You're the one that made me wear them. So now I like them."

He grinned. "You're not just a person. You're a girl."

"Thank you," she said haughtily.

Seth fastened his boots and then chose a set of weapons, taking his time to make sure of their suitability for Belene's environment. He had been glad for Caelyn's presence aboard his ship during the days it took them to reach this planet. The Delphian's intellect and Khoe's capacity for combining pure data with an almost Human emotional range made for some energetic conversations. But he was also relieved to not have to grapple with that sweet moment at the Delphian research station which left him feeling a little awkward in Khoe's undeniably real presence.

Since she came aboard he, like most males of his species and many others, had taken the opportunity to cop an occasional look at her enticing curves. There had been little more to this than entertainment value. Now he wasn't so sure. Her physical appeal was undeniable and, considering her proximity, unavoidable. But she also had the intelligence and honesty he valued in any woman he had ever known for more than one night. As unpredictable and even eccentric as she was, he found himself drawn to her in ways he did not care to examine.

"What?"

He blinked, having been caught staring, and got busy holstering his guns. "Still no shoes?"

She followed his eyes downward. "I cannot make any sense at all of what sort of shoes are worn with what clothes. Doesn't matter; I don't see my feet very often."

They exited the ship, making sure to extend the *Dutchman*'s proximity alarm to his data sleeve. Even set to its loudest internal alert, it might not be enough to wake the Delphian, whose people found sleep in the deepest of khamals, another of their distinct states of consciousness, from which they were not easily roused.

He strolled past the other two cruisers parked out here, seeing nothing to identify them as anything but private ships; capable but hardly military grade. Khoe also found no indication of Air Command presence here, nor any unusual armament or electronic systems that would seem out of place in this isolated location. The single communications array was little more than a wind-battered antenna on a distant rise.

Night was approaching fast across the plains and the cold gusts soughing over the flat landscape soon made their way through the folds of his robe. He was glad when he ducked into the sheltered entrance of the one-time transport ship and found it pleasantly heated. This interior resembled a cave of decaying metal and warped plastics, perhaps once a cargo entrance, where a few people waited for the stranger in silence.

Seth directed a sunny smile of greeting at the most surly-looking of the locals. He counted three Centauri, a Human and a Feydan, both male and female and dressed in layers of clothes that ceased to be clean or fashionable a long time ago.

"The tall man in the back is holding a charged weapon," Khoe reported. "Rail gun."

"Hello," Seth said, looking at the Centauri she had pointed out. "I don't suppose you get a lot of visitors around here."

"Not until recently," a Feydan woman said. "Who sent you?"

"Master Faran on Magra Torley. Said this was a place to find a new commission. I'm looking for Tieko." He handed her a marker given to him by Faran.

She scanned the marker. The lines tattooed into the deep brown skin of her neck hinted that she belonged to a prominent family of a wealthy part of Feyd. He wondered what had led her to join the Shri-Lan. "He's down below. I'll take you," she said. Some of the others seemed to have lost interest and disappeared into the gloomy shadows of the hold.

Seth followed her back outside and around the wreck's repurposed cargo modules into which, over time, windows and doors had been cut to serve as habitats for those fortunate enough to claim them. They walked a short distance across an open space to the edge of a fissure. No attempt had been made to ensure someone wouldn't simply tumble into the opening. The Feydan led him to a crude ladder leaning against the edge of the crevice.

Once he negotiated the creaking scaffold, he saw that the bottom of the gap split into many directions, separated by paper-thin walls of delicate, chalk-like material. It seemed that just touching them would bring one of these partitions down upon them. The walls and the floor were coated in pale dust, much like the surface above.

They walked past alcoves set aside for sleeping or privacy, cisterns, storage areas, communal spaces where small fires burned, and the entrances of several darkened tunnels. As primitive as it seemed, the people here seemed comfortable and he heard calm voices and laughter. Two children ran across their path, giggling as they went.

"He's over there," the Feydan finally said and immediately left him to make his own introductions.

"Are these all rebels?" Khoe asked.

Mostly, I guess.

"They don't look very fierce. I thought rebels were dangerous and angry."

They are. But rebels have families, too. Seth approached a huddle of thickly-robed individuals seated around a fire. Here he saw clothing and weapons of more recent vintage on visitors from Pelion, Aikhor and Magra.

Deferentially, he went through the steps of identifying himself and his quest to find a new patron among them. A bearded Centauri gestured for him to sit with them.

"I'm Tieko," he said. "Faran's word is good enough for me. If he sent you, he must have reason."

Seth shrugged. "He has some concerns about all this."

Tieko chuckled. "Aye, but the money is good. Shri-Lan pays when due and they don't get pissy about it. At least if you make it back here."

"Fill me in." Seth accepted a cup from someone passing out drinks.

"What's that?" Khoe asked.

Kind of busy here, he replied but then relented and sniffed the offering. *Whatever it is, it's horribly fermented.*

"Try it!"

Not likely. Never had much interest in drink. Can you direct your maddening curiosity to that man's data system, please?

Tieko quaffed his drink with considerable enthusiasm. "Some experiment going on that the Commonwealth isn't to know about," he explained. "Shri-Lan is equipping pilots with a collector to take through subspace. That's all I know, really. Didn't think there was anything worth collecting in there."

"You have those devices?"

"No. We're waiting for someone to get here with them. Sounds like an easy job to me, but there've been accidents."

Seth shrugged. "There are always accidents. I've got a solid ship and a good navigator."

"That'll do it," Tieko said agreeably. "If you pass the muster, you're in."

"What muster?"

"Faran's endorsement is a good thing, but they'll want to know who you are. You'd better check out or your ship is going to be their ship before the end of tomorrow." He turned away to talk to another one of his compatriots.

"Was that a threat or a warning?" Khoe wanted to know.

Bit of both, I guess. Find anything?

"Those caves extend all the way to below that ruined ship. Full of stuff they're trading to rebels. Or storing here for them."

What stuff?

"Guns, machine parts, tubes, barrels of stuff."

Interesting. Seth's eyes moved over the crude accommodations around them. *And well-disguised.*

"Tieko's been here for about four years. Sort of a boss down here. He's recently had contact with someone named Tov Pald."

Seth winced.

"You know him?"

By reputation.

"Hey, this Tieko has three wives. I didn't think Centauri had families like that."

We don't. Things get blurry out here. We're a long way from home.

"Have you ever been in the Centauri system?"

Nope. Takes years to get out there. I've never been that curious. Plenty of Centauri here in Trans-Targon. We've been here almost three hundred years. Considering that we didn't originate here, there are more of us scattered around planets where we don't belong than any other species.

"I guess you stop being Centauri after a while," she

pondered, indicating their host. "You're probably a whole new race by now."

He sent a smile. *You would probably know more about that than me by now.*

"Aren't you curious?"

No. I was raised by Humans back there on Magra Torley. If there is a mongrel among us, it's me. Besides, I'm officially a Dyad now, remember?

"You look Centauri," she said. She touched a strand of his hair that was forever falling over his eyes. "But you're a lot more than that."

He was still searching for a reply to that when Tieko turned back to him. He held up a skewer bearing a half-roasted rodent. Seth accepted gamely and tasted the meat, more to give Khoe a new experience than to satisfy any real need for food.

"Better than the stuff on your ship," she commented. "But not as good as the Delphians had. That's a gonad you're about to eat. Your people don't like that."

Seth put the skewer down with a sigh. "When do you expect that delivery?" he asked Tieko.

"Should be here by morning. You're welcome to stay down here, if you like. Nice and warm."

"Five hours to dawn," Khoe supplied. "It's dark outside now."

"I think I'll head back to my ship." Seth came to his feet. "But thanks for the offer. I'll see you when the envoy gets here."

He made his way back to the ladder leading to the surface. "Did you find anything about how many other pilots have passed through here lately?"

"Now many yet," Khoe replied. "They just started to shift things from Rishabel to here. The smugglers drop the disks off here and the rebels take them elsewhere. Tieko is getting paid for putting them up while they wait."

"No wonder they're so friendly." Seth drew his cloak closer around himself when he started the walk back to the

Dutchman. A few locals were still about, moving from one shelter to another or standing around fire pits in quiet conversation. Although people had lived in this settlement for many years, something about this place seemed oddly transient, like a refugee camp where no one ever found their way home.

Someone waved to him as he passed. He slowed to see a Human woman sitting alone near her fire, gesturing to him. He nodded and accepted the offer, holding his hands to the flames. "A little cold out here," he said by way of conversation.

"It's my turn on the watch." She pushed her ragged fur hood from her head. "Only another hour."

"What are you watching out for? Doesn't seem possible to get near this place undetected."

"We have scanners for that. What we look out for are the four- and six-legged sort that'll creep into camp to make off with food stuffs. They've become bold lately. It's the season. They're desperate for food. They'll even take small children if we're not vigilant."

"It's a harsh place to live," he said. "Why are you out here?"

She looked into the flames as if debating her answer. "I was less free where I came from. I'll return some day, I'm sure."

"To where?" he asked. Humans had long ago joined the Centauri expansion into Trans-Targon and, although few in number, formed colonies on just about any habitable planet in this distant sector of their galaxy. This Human, more delicate and pale than the desert-dwellers, seemed out of place on this lonely outpost. He suspected that she had not been on Belene for very long.

"She's pretty," Khoe said, hunkering down on the woman's other side.

Yes.

"My home was Aikhor," the woman said. "But I think I have family on Pelion. I'd like to see them some day."

"Pilots come and go even out here. You're not stuck in this place. Just go."

She smiled wistfully and placed more fuel on the fire. "They all want payment," she said. "I don't have that. There is no work to be had on these small ships."

"There must be something you can trade," he said, then groaned inwardly at what surely sounded like a crass suggestion.

She did not seem to mind. "Yes, of course." She gazed at him and said nothing more.

"I think she's making you an offer," Khoe said.

I noticed.

"Are you going to take her up on it?"

What? No.

"Why not? She appeals to you."

She's probably made this same offer a few times today already. He exhaled impatiently. *Is that another new experience you're looking for?*

"Maybe," she replied after a moment. "I'll never know, will I?" She lifted a hand to the woman and watched with his eyes as it passed unnoticed through her shoulder. "How it feels to be touched, I mean. Really touched. You find the thought of touching me repulsive."

Seth frowned, ready with some denial or platitude or perhaps even rebuke but the look on her impish face was of such pain and sadness that he could not. *Gods, Khoe, is that what you think?*

"You made it clear. But if you take her, I'll know. Maybe that's all right, too."

That is not even a bit all right. Why are you talking like this?

She rubbed her hands, feeling the heat of the flames through his fingers. "I'm so worried about this. About you. If you can't get rid of me you'll start resenting me. You're never alone. At some point you'll want a real woman, won't you? I know how you look at me, sometimes, when you think I'm not paying attention. I know what it means." Khoe ran her hand through some of the braids of white hair hanging over her shoulders. "I should change how I look. I can be anything. I can just not appear at all, or maybe be a pet or something. That would make things easier for you, wouldn't it?"

The woman leaned closer to Seth and placed her hand on his forearm. "Hey," she said gently. "Are you in there, somewhere?"

He considered the invitation clearly written on the Human's face and then his eyes traveled back to Khoe. She was also intently studying the woman, but not with the vibrant curiosity she exhibited for all other things. Khoe was becoming as much of an enigma as most women were to him but what he saw on her face now was simply apprehension.

Seth stood up. "I can't help you," he said to the Human. "I'm not going back that way."

He walked with long strides back to the *Dutchman*, ignoring the few people he passed along the way. He slapped the ship's keyplate and stepped inside the cargo hold.

"You seem agitated."

He spun to face Khoe. "Do you really think I'd rather be with that camp follower than touch you?"

She lifted her shoulders. "I don't know. Having me in your head must be a bit creepy."

He frowned at her, uncharacteristically and overwhelmingly at a loss for words. She gazed back at him, waiting for, perhaps dreading, his reply without a clue on her face about her thoughts. Creepy? He saw only the strange beauty, the innocent wisdom, the shy courage with which she'd been turning his life upside down since she came aboard. With every day that passed she seemed more a part of his life, like someone who had always been there and always would be. Had he been so damn blind to something far more obvious because she did not belong in his world?

"How can you say that? You're anything but creepy."

She smiled thinly. "Just a little alien, then?"

"Stop that, Khoe. I don't resent you. And I'm not trying to get rid of you. I want to help you if I can and that means helping you get free and go home. That's not the same thing."

"Isn't it?"

"No!" he said immediately. "If you asked me before all this happened I would have said otherwise but now I'm a Dyad, whatever that means, and you belong exactly where you are." He struggled for words, not even sure what he meant to say to her. Finally he reached for her and held her pale face in his hands. "You *are* a real woman, Khoe. You feel so unbelievably good inside my head. Don't change how you look. You're beautiful and amazing and I'm sorry if I made you feel any other way."

"Beautiful?"

"Yeah."

She held his gaze for a long moment. "Then touch me now."

Even if she had not spoken, nothing would have stopped him from kissing her the way he should have on Magra, without second thought or hesitation. The body pressed to his felt as real as it had those few days ago and the hands that touched him now seemed on fire. He groaned when that magnificent sense of *rightness* suffused their minds and senses, this time fuelled by a need neither of them hid any longer. Her clothes melted away a layer at a time even as he fumbled through his own and it took just moments before he lifted her up, unwilling to wait another second to feel her body wrap around him. Neither noticed the cold wall against her back or the hum of the generators out here – nothing existed but the sensations their tangled minds created for each other. Both of them cried out when he found his release, sharing that exquisite moment as if they were one.

Countless moments passed before Seth caught his breath and felt his heart slow to something manageable, his head still lowered onto Khoe's shoulder. "Cazun…" he managed.

She disengaged herself gently and slipped from his embrace. He stumbled after her into the main cabin, numbly rearranging his clothing as she tugged him toward the lounger. He collapsed onto it with a grateful sigh and drew her into his arms.

"I see now," she said, smiling.

He swallowed hard around another gasp of air. "I don't know if you do," he said. "You feel what I do, right?"

"Yes."

"But not what you should?"

"I don't suppose so." She raised her head. "But maybe... Let me try something."

"What?"

"Close your eyes."

He did so but this did not shut out the world around him. He still saw her and this cabin and the exposed gas and circuitry lines running along the ceiling as though his eyes were still wide open. "What are you doing?"

She smiled and raised herself up to kiss him softly. "Now show me."

Seth reached for her and it seemed to him that something had changed inside his head, feeling almost like the close link of the Delphian khamal but, as she responded to his touch, far more intimate. He applied his hands and lips, teaching her, letting her teach him, and they soon came together again with as much fervor as before, followed by gentle bouts of playing games all lovers play. Hours passed in this way until, at last, he simply passed out in her arms.

* * *

"Centauri! Time for that ugly tea you like so much!"

Seth did not wake up so much as he regained consciousness from what felt like a drunken stupor. He blinked into the overhead lights, unsure of where he was and who was talking to him. He gasped when he realized that it was Caelyn who was cheerfully puttering around the small galley aboard his ship. In groping for his blankets he came to realize that, strangely, he was fully dressed, if disheveled, and that Khoe was nowhere in sight.

"Big cruiser just landed," Caelyn said. "I'm guessing Shri-

Lan, judging by some of the characters marching around out there. Why do their foot soldiers always look like they've gone a few rounds with a Rhuwac?"

"They probably have," Seth grumbled, running both hands through his hair. *Khoe?*

"Did you get anywhere with those people last night? I must have slept right through."

"We didn't wake you, did we? Khoe and me?"

Caelyn raised an eyebrow. "If you mean with your snoring, I'd say it takes more than that to wake a Delphian. You slept with your boots on, by the way. If I didn't know better I'd think you had a few cups last night."

Seth crawled from the lounger and into the decon chamber, dropping his clothes as he went. In there he braced his arms on either side of the mirror while he let steam roll over his body, still dazed by the previous night. Had he imagined all of it? Although tired, he did not feel the gloriously strenuous hours that had passed. He would have suspected a bruise or two, perhaps a scratch. There was nothing. He folded his arms against the wall and leaned his forehead against them.

"Seth?"

He pulled back to see Khoe beside him, impossibly contained by this small room barely large enough for one person. He looked into her curious and worried face for a long moment before returning his stare to the mirror. "I think I'm losing my mind," he said, barely audible.

"Why do you say that?"

He leaned against the door and tipped his head back, closing his eyes. "Because I am," he said with half a helpless laugh. "I'm walking around in a dream. I don't know where I end and you begin. That must mean I'm losing it."

She hovered closer to him and he felt her gentle hands move up along his arms, then her lips on the skin of his chest. "You still don't think I'm real? After last night?"

He took her face into his hands to kiss her gently. "Nothing unreal about you," he said, unwilling to admit to his own brain that he had not moved at all. "That's what scares me."

She nodded. "Me, too."

NINE

The morning outside was colder than the night had been and even the sun, hanging listless in a pink and hazy sky, seemed to have given up on the place. Seth stepped out of his plane, breathing deeply of the air that wanted to freeze him inside out. It felt great.

He had shaken off his odd mood during breakfast with Caelyn. Khoe joined them in the Delphian khamal to allow all three of them to share a conversation. This caused Caelyn a bit of a headache, as it had on Magra, but he was too fascinated by this alien being to let that deter him. She had found her way through his aloof exterior and even coaxed laughter from him with some well-placed quips about the planet of his birth. They decided that the recently arrived cruiser likely brought rebels who were more familiar with Delphians than the locals. Caelyn resigned himself to staying aboard while Seth and Khoe met their new employer.

Something had changed out here on Belene. Yesterday this had been a humble shanty town inhabited by people who were largely at peace with their lot, today the tension cut deeper than the harsh winds from the north. Few of the locals were about, none loitered around the sputtering fires, and armed rebel guards dispensed threatening glares to anyone daring to come too close to their ship.

Seth crossed the open space between the planes and the shelters and stepped into the entrance of the wrecked transport. He assumed Tov Pald to be holding court here, given the two massive Caspians guarding the entrance. He gave them a mock salute as he passed.

"Kada!" he was greeted by the Centauri leader of the colony. Tieko waved to him from the gloomy depths of this entranceway and through a door leading to the interior. Some of the rebels stood around a plastic crate being carefully unpacked. Seth recognized Tov Pald among them, looking more menacing than any image he had seen of him.

Grab what you can. Be careful!

"On it," Khoe replied.

Seth stumbled over a broken ramp, drawing everyone's attention while she tapped into the data sleeve of a nearby rebel. A light stripe blinked in mild protest and then forgot about her intrusion.

"Too much of the party juice for you, Kada?" Tieko said. "I'm hurt. I cooked that up myself."

Tov Pald looked up at the interruption. He watched Seth come closer, eyes glittering in the inadequate light. "I've heard about you, Kada. Fallen on hard times? Last I heard you had a nice little deal going on Aram."

Seth shrugged. "A couple of months in lockup and you're behind on the bills."

"You were in jail?" Khoe said.

No, he replied. *Well, not for months. Find anything?*

"Sure did," she replied, grinning. She placed her hand on his thigh. "What'll you give me for it?"

He bit his lip and concentrated on the rebel. "Still got my plane, though. Heard you're looking for pilots."

The Caspian nodded. "Pilots, yes. High risk, to be honest. You're probably overqualified."

"I'm broke. That makes me qualified."

Tov Pald picked up a thick metal disk from among

several on top of the crate. It had three prongs, like the one on Rishabel. He turned it thoughtfully in his hands. "Actually, you might be right. I have something a little extra for you."

"Do tell."

He waved at his men. "Out."

They complied without a hint of demur. Seth was impressed. Too many rebel leaders had trouble simply keeping their gangs moving in the same direction, never mind taking orders. Then again, Tov Pald wasn't known for kindhearted leadership.

The Caspian perched on the corner of the crate and studied Seth in silence. One of his feet swung loosely and his claws scraped over the metal floor with a sound that made even Khoe squirm. He tossed the disk at Seth without warning. "Good reflexes," he said. "I heard you're quick on your feet."

Seth let Khoe study the display panel on the edge of the disk. "Comes in handy," he said. "What is this thing?"

"Your new best friend. One of our lab rats figured out a way to collect some sort of particle in subspace. These disks attract them and lock them up. Those particles enhance your brain with a whole new set of talents."

"You're joking with me?" Seth said, sounding incredulous. "Like what?"

"EMR manipulation, from what I saw. Cutting through security systems. Power conversion, who knows. We can get past Air Command pretty much at will with these. So now we're looking for volunteers."

Seth raised his eyebrows. "Funny, I could have sworn you were looking at me when you said that word."

"Afraid?"

"Rumor says these aren't good for your health."

"Only if you get exposed out here. Our people can do this safely in the lab. Interested?"

"Of course." Seth turned the disk over for Khoe's inspection. "Walking through walls seems like a damn fine skill. What's the job worth?"

The rebel stood up. "Talented or not, you're a smuggler and a masterless mercenary. The question is: what are you worth to us?"

"I prefer 'privateer'. I get paid, you get what you want."

Tov Pald waved his six-fingered hand at the device. "With this, you'll never have to worry about anyone's security system again. So don't worry about money."

"Let me run this errand for you while I think about it."

The Caspian shrugged. "Don't think too long. Take this collector with you and go for a nice long jump through subspace. Just twist that band there when you enter. It'll do all the work. Return here. You'll get fifty doubles for it."

Seth whistled. "That's a pretty sum."

"If you catch one."

Seth glanced at Khoe. "What's been happening to those that don't?"

"As far as we can tell, those subspace particles get into the crews instead of the disks. It goes bad for some. Feydans and Centauri do okay."

"Delphians?"

"Don't be absurd, Kada." He walked to the door to gesture to his men. "Got anyone else for me?" he said to Tieko.

Seth tucked the disk under his robe. "I guess I'm done here."

"I'll expect you back within the next ten hours. Don't make me wait in this hellhole."

Seth nodded and stepped over the ramp to the exit. There was no one there now. "What do we have?" he whispered to Khoe as he fastened his robe on his way out and pulled a hood over his head.

"Why did he say that about the Delphians?"

He stepped outside the hull and started to walk back to the *Dutchman*. "Because there isn't a Delphian alive that would volunteer for this, even if the Union were doing the experimenting. But we have no way to know how this will affect Caelyn."

"Doesn't matter. We don't have to jump."

"Huh?"

"I can make it look like that thing has captured particles. You wouldn't know it's empty until you opened it, or whatever they do with them. Besides, I really don't want you to actually use one of these. It's what we're trying to stop from happening."

"That's true. We can just take off for a while and then return."

She grinned. "This is the part where you pay up, Kada."

He had to smile at the mischief on her face. The smile turned into a gasp when he felt her hand again, not on his thigh this time. "Back to the ship with you," he said.

"Caelyn is there. Not asleep."

"Did you just pout?"

"Did I get it right?"

"Yeah. Out with it. What else did you find?"

"We don't have to come back here, either. These disks are being collected for a lab on some planet called Csonne. Let's just go straight there."

"Csonne. Good hiding place. There are a few research stations out there. Privately owned. Astrophysics, if I recall. Something to do with the atmosphere there is good for that sort of thing. They'd blend in pretty well. No Air Command presence out there. Did you find out where on Csonne?"

"Got the coordinates for a place called Suncion," she said. "Right from that Caspian's system. Tov Pald got that project on Csonne prioritized with whoever he's working for. They're called The Brothers on his system. They're sending more supplies, equipment, ships. There was talk about more security, too."

"When?"

"Now. They use a lot of code to talk to each other but I think they've got some more volunteers 'safely infected'. I resent that word."

"I do, too," he said absently. "Sounds almost like they're

building an army. Or some sort of special ops team. Not a bad idea, actually. I can imagine the damage they could do with someone like you on their side."

"You're not saying that my people would be willing to go to war with you? We'd never agree to that."

"Unless it's fun? Khoe, you didn't even know what war is until you came here. Everything you know came from what's on my ship. And you believe it. How do you know what your people end up believing if they're on a Shri-Lan ship? Inside a Shri-Lan's head?"

"We're quite able to think for ourselves!" she said.

He stepped inside the *Dutchman* and shrugged out of his heavy robe. "I'm quite aware of that. Some of your thoughts are... delicious."

"Don't make light of this. I won't have our people used like this. Another weapon in your stupid, endless fighting out here. Turning us into tools for you to use. It's outrageous."

"The outrage started the moment one of you was taken from subspace. It doesn't matter why."

"Of course it does! I'd started to hope we could come out here, into this world, and learn and explore and maybe play. It would have been so wonderful to visit with your people, like this. Instead I end up tangled up with you beyond escape and now your people are using us to harm each other. That's just wrong, Seth."

He pulled her into his arms, surprised by her outburst. He kissed her face, expecting tears, but she just leaned against his chest as if intending to stay there for a while.

"Of course it's wrong," he said. "We'll go take a look at Csonne. If we have to we'll try to get some help from Targon."

"No! They'll want us for the same reason your rebel friends do."

Seth looked past her shoulder to see himself reflected vaguely in the cover of a storage bin along the wall. Alone. Standing in this cargo space as if lost in some thought, or like someone who had forgotten something but could not recall what. He looked back into Khoe's unhappy face. She had also seen the empty reflection and pulled away with a sigh.

"They're not my friends," Seth said and walked into the main cabin. "Caelyn? Time to fly."

"He's not here," she said after checking with the ship's system. "Left a little while ago."

"Without telling us?" Seth tapped his com band. "Caelyn? You out there?"

"Where else would I be?" came the calm reply over the speaker.

"What are you doing?"

"Relieving my boredom. I wasn't going to land on a whole new planet without taking a look around."

"Has anyone ever, just once, let you walk around a remote location without securing the area, first?"

"There is no one about. Don't worry; I'm well wrapped up pretending to be Centauri. Did you know that this entire valley used to be a lake? The fossils at the bottom are not to be believed. I'm trying to run some imaging but I just don't have the right equipment. We'll have to come back here."

"Later that. Can you come home now, please?" Seth sighed and closed the link. "I had to bring a scientist. To a rebel planet."

"Someone's coming," Khoe said at the same moment that the *Dutchman*'s systems voiced their agreement.

Seth rushed into the cockpit. "Damn." He punched up the sensor displays to see that three Air Command cruisers had dropped into Belene's airspace at maximum velocity. They punched through the atmosphere and swooped west, their destination clear. A glance at the *Dutchman*'s proximity monitors confirmed that the rebels outside had detected them, too, and with as much surprise. There was much rushing about, waving or arms and shouting as the mercenaries regrouped. Had no one been monitoring?

"Caelyn!"

"Yes?"

"Get back here. Air Command on its way down."

"Oh. That doesn't bode well for us."

"I'd like to get out of here before someone starts shooting. Hurry up."

"Surely they won't just open fire," Caelyn said. His voice sounded strained as he picked up his jog back to the settlement.

"Let's hope not," Seth said and began pre-flight procedures. Tov Pald's men seemed more disciplined than the usual rabble of thugs cruising the edges of Trans-Targon but the sight of Air Command would have them panicked by now. "Battlecruisers," he said to Khoe. "Not Vanguard. They'll be fully loaded."

Khoe swiveled the external cameras to look out over the plains. "Where is he?"

A crackling sound emitted from Seth's wrist unit. Someone was talking, but distantly. Seth relayed the transmission to the ship's sound system. "Can you fix that?"

She adjusted the quality until they made out separate voices.

"Those are plant samples," they heard Caelyn's measured tone. "Please handle them carefully."

"So why are you out here picking flowers?" a surly voice demanded, sounding Human. "Those are poison."

Seth cursed.

"What?" Khoe asked.

"Must have come across a patrol out there."

"Because they interest me," Caelyn said. "And they're not flowers but succulents. Given the environmental conditions, the flora on this planet is astounding."

"I think you're either a lunatic or you're lying," came the gruff reply. "We don't need either of those here."

"I assure you I am merely exploring. But this is your homeworld and I will abide by your wishes and return to my ship. We'll leave as soon as the captain returns."

"I think you ought to talk with ours, first."

Seth scooped up a flight jacket and gloves on his way to the *Dutchman's* exit. "I don't believe this," he grumbled.

"Delphians! More intellect than any known species and not a single brain cell wasted on common sense."

"Well, in terms of their evolution they never really needed—"

"Don't you start." Outside, he jogged around one of the ruined cargo modules where he had earlier seen a few dusty ground vehicles parked. Finding them locked down, he took a closer look at a skimmer leaning crookedly against the wall. Little more than a floating cargo box, it hummed to life when he touched it.

"What are you about?" a voice behind him said.

Seth spun and backhanded the watchman, then dropped him with two rapid blows. After a quick look around, he dragged him behind the air cars before returning to the hover. He crouched in it as low as possible, feeling weirdly like some ancient warrior in a horseless chariot. "You drive," he said after an obstacle on the ground confused the cart's sensors, nearly toppling it. He drew his pistol and adjusted its setting, ready for more people about to get in his way. "Do you see him?"

"Yes, his signal's over that rise." Khoe pointed past the jagged cave openings. "There are three others with him. They're coming this way."

"Hurry before he says something annoying."

She sped up, forcing him to grip the edge of the cart with his free hand. "Wait till they're behind that rock. Then you can jump out and punch them."

"Not going to punch them," he said.

"Because you remembered to draw your weapon before running into trouble this time?"

"You notice far too much. Go around to the left."

She swung aside just as a group of four rounded the boulders. By their clothing they were not Tov Pald's men. Caelyn, the tallest among them, wore the comfortable weather gear Seth had chosen not to use. A burnoose covered his head and most of his angular face. Two rifles jabbed into his midriff.

Seth raised himself up, keeping his gun out of sight, and waved to the group. "There you are!" he shouted to Caelyn.

The men stopped to watch him approach.

"Did you get those samples?" Seth said. "We're nearly done with the collection. Time to head back and get warmed up." He pretended surprise at seeing the others with him. "What's with the guns? Is there a problem?"

The Human wearing what might once have been a carpet exchanged knowing glances with one of his companions as some silent signal passed between them. One of the others, a Feydan, stepped aside to circle out of Seth's field of vision.

"Good," Caelyn said, rubbing his hands. "I could use a hot bowl of soup."

When he stepped toward the sled, one of the barrels moved up to point at his chin. "Not just yet," the bandit said. "Let's see what you've got on you other than… what did he say they were?"

"Flora," another said.

"He said succulents." Seth's hand lashed out to grasp the Feydan who had sidled close to his sled. Khoe unleashed a burst of energy from Seth into the man, throwing him back and off his feet, unconscious. Seth's gun dropped the one threatening Caelyn.

The Delphian jumped aside with surprising agility before the others reacted. Seth leaped from the cart, using its edge as a springboard to kick the Human's chest. The man went down, taking Seth with him as he fell. Seth twisted to fire at the one still standing. Another blow from Khoe silenced the chest-kicked robber.

"Damn, it's like you're reading my mind," Seth said aloud to Khoe.

"I'm clever," she said. "Although, to be honest, I can just tell which way you're going to move."

Caelyn still looked around himself in astonishment. "They were going to steal from me? You said these were friendly people."

"That doesn't mean you should turn your back on them.

Or wander off into the middle of some frozen desert by yourself. We're ready to go if you're done with your botany collection."

An ear-popping thrum filled the air, startling them. Two Air Command battlecruisers descended from the low-hanging clouds to land at the edge of the colony, uncomfortably close to the parked rebel ships. Seth sighed and gave up his plans for a quick exit from Belene.

"I know, I know, Centauri," Caelyn said, stepping onto the platform. "I have a lot to learn about being a spy."

"As long as we're clear on that," Seth grumbled. "You should at least take a weapon. That's often helpful."

"I'd likely just shoot myself in the foot. Did you get one of those disks?"

"Yes." Seth winced into the cold wind when the sled turned back to the colony. "And an offer to turn myself into a Dyad. I didn't mention I already joined that club."

"You know," Khoe said thoughtfully. "That gives me an idea."

"What does?"

"Caelyn shooting himself in the foot. I think I could diffuse a shot like that. Lasers, I mean, not bullets. Would take a lot of energy, though. Unless…" She nudged his hand. "Try it."

"Try what? Shoot myself in the foot?"

"Yes."

"And you don't think that's a really bad idea?"

"How else would we find out? You could be completely resistant to any sort of electromagnetic weapon."

"We'll discuss this later. Much later."

She shrugged. "Just being helpful."

Seth sighed and then noticed Caelyn's eyes on him. "She's being impossible," he explained. "I can't wait to get both of you off this planet."

"I'm not so sure we're going anywhere," Khoe said when the settlement came into view. Two of the Air Command cruisers had landed near the rebel ships and disgorged an unnerving number of Union soldiers. They stood in stiff formation, guns at their side. Some of them were inspecting the *Dutchman*.

Seth took control of the hover's navigation. "I wonder what brought this down on us way out here. Let's see if we can blend in."

They trundled back to the small motor pool as if they belonged there. Seth half expected to find a bruised and very angry mechanic waiting for them but the man was still tucked in his corner. They left the vehicle and circled their way around the confrontation taking place on the landing area.

An Air Command major stood in a central space cleared of both soldiers and civilians, speaking with Tov Pald, Tieko and another rebel. The troops on either side of the confrontation ringed the area uneasily, weapons holstered but ready for the draw.

"Khoe…" Seth began.

"Working on it," she said. "Something's blocking their system. Kind of like yours but they've added some nonsense that's hard to get through. A lot of them have cut their com links so I can't get in at all."

"That doesn't sound good. Could mean that they're here because of us, not just on some random rebel round-up mission. Guess they figured out that I'm able to breach their systems after what happened on Feyd. No wonder they're being careful."

"Three ships just for you?" Khoe said. "I'm impressed."

"Where is the third ship?"

She pointed up. "If it wasn't cloudy you'd see it from here."

"Strange," Caelyn mused. "I always assumed that everyone starts to shoot as soon as one of your people comes across one of theirs."

"They do," Seth replied, weaving through the throng of onlookers. "But Air Command has rules of engagement. There's no way to know which of these people are rebels and which are civilians."

"You people should just stop wearing uniforms," Khoe said. "Then the rebels have the same problem."

Seth smiled grimly. "That would be a good idea except that people like Tov Pald don't give a damn about civilians." He stepped up on a rock to get a better view of the discussion between the Caspian and the Air Command major. Looking beyond them, he counted a half dozen soldiers now gathered near the *Dutchman*.

Caelyn sighed when they saw a long blue braid trailing down the back of one of the men, identifying him as a Delphian. "I suppose you wish I had just taken that ship to Callas instead of tagging along with you. So much for my disguise."

"Are they going to let us go?" Khoe asked, sounding anxious.

"We're not prisoners. They've got no reason to stop anyone. Yet." Seth noticed the pilot emblem on the Delphian who was taking far too close a look at the *Dutchman*. He nudged Caelyn. "Don't let them try to intimidate you. Stick to your explorer story. Your kinsman over there will understand why you'd want to be disguised out here."

"I'm in!" Khoe said.

"Can you tell what's happening over there?"

"Yes. The officer is Major Terwood. He's trying to get answers from Tov Pald without actually accusing him of being a rebel. How very convoluted. We all know they are. They both sound awfully irritable. Tieko just sounds worried."

"Might be a good idea to power down the rebels' guns."

"Can't. Most of the rebels have ballistic weapons. I can take the rails out but the others are all just mechanical." She frowned. "The officer just asked about you."

Seth cursed and stepped down from his rock. "Well, now we know why they're here. I wonder how they tracked us. What did he say?"

"That you're a fugitive. A dangerous one. They want just

you, he said. Then they'll go. I don't think they believe him."

"I don't, either. Let's hope Tov Pald won't hand me over as long as I have one of his collectors. See if you can power down all crossdrives except for the *Dutchman*'s. Don't damage them. If you drain them it'll take a few hours to get them back up. We can make it to the keyhole by then." He nudged Caelyn. "Start heading to the plane around those sheds there."

They ambled through the crowd, keeping an eye on the discussion at the center of everyone's attention. He winced when he saw Tieko look intently around the wide circle of faces as if searching for him in the throng. He seemed about to give in to the pressure of whatever the major was threatening.

Indeed, the major took a step backward, gesturing for Tieko to follow. Deliberately turning his back on Tov Pald, he moved toward his own troops.

"Damn," Seth said, seeing the expression on the Caspian's face. "Move!"

The officer had underestimated the rebel leader. Tov Pald moved aside and signaled for the attack. The crowd surged back in fright when several of his men appeared from behind whatever cover was to be found, including the roof of the wrecked transport, to fire at the Union soldiers. Some of them fell to their aim before the others also sought shelter behind and inside their ships.

Seth shifted his eyes from the mayhem to keep Khoe's focus on her sabotage. Civilians scrambled for the caves, heedless to anything in their way. He heard shouts and curses and the sound of gunfire shattering the cold air. And then, thankfully, the whine of his own plane's thrusters preparing to lift off by Khoe's command.

Ahead of him, Caelyn suddenly wheeled around with a curse Seth had never heard a Delphian utter. He clutched his arm, staring in frozen horror at what remained of his hand. A bullet had torn through it and nearly severed it above his wrist. Blood spurted from the horrible wound.

Seth grasped the wide sleeve of Caelyn's weather gear and shoved him into the shelter of a metal bin. He clamped his hands around the torn arm to stem the bleeding. Another bullet whined over his head as it struck the edge of the bin. He peered over the top to see the fire fight concentrated on the larger of the two Union ships. "Come on, Delphi," he said, grinding his teeth when he saw the fear and pain on his friend's face. "On your feet. We can make it."

Caelyn shook his head but his eyes were on the shredded remains of his hand. "You get out of here," he grunted through clenched jaws. "I've done nothing but slow you down."

"Not giving up, are you?"

"They won't hurt me. Delphian, remember? If I let you patch me up I won't see the end of the day."

"Khoe can maybe…" Seth looked up to see her shaking her head.

"You've got nothing that'll show me how to fix this," she said.

"Go!" Caelyn said. "They'll have medics with them."

Seth bent protectively over Caelyn when something tore into their inadequate shelter and a piece of metal spun over their heads. "Khoe, when you get aboard, see if you can find the Delphian pilot we saw earlier. If you can tap his com, tell him who and where Caelyn is."

"Already looking," she said.

"She's on it," Seth translated as he used a strap from the enviro suit to tourniquet Caelyn's bleeding arm. He gripped his shoulder in a silent farewell and got up to race to the *Dutchman*. Khoe's dread was palpable as he ducked out of the line of fire, keeping low, circling the soldiers near his plane. The tracer of a laser gun crawled over his chest and he rolled under an abandoned tri-rider to return the fire. Two more soldiers spotted him and he shot them, too, wincing when one of them knocked her head painfully against his ship on the way down. He scurried to the next bit of shelter, now within steps of the *Dutchman*'s doors.

"Seth!" Khoe cried.

He spun to look for the threat and saw a soldier only steps away, pointing a gun at his head. The man shot without hesitation and then stared, flabbergasted, when Seth remained standing. Seth recovered first from the surprise and brought him down with his own gun.

"That worked!" Khoe said excitedly. "Did you see that?"

"See what?" Seth slapped the *Dutchman*'s keypad, grateful for his hunch to park the ship with its door facing away from the colony. He sealed it quickly and endured the endless seconds it took for the *Dutchman* to run its contaminant analysis and allow him inside.

"Like I told you. I was right. I diffused the output from his gun."

"Where did it go?"

"I scattered it. Pretty broadly. Using its own energy. You didn't even feel it, did you?"

He raced for the cockpit. "You said you were going to power the rail guns down, not test your theories on me."

"Well, I missed that one. Wasn't even a rail. Have a little faith."

Seth powered up and thrust away from the surface, leaving the waning battle behind. He kept his eyes on the real-video for as long as he could. It seemed that Air Command was starting to turn things in their favor.

Khoe drew his attention. "I found the Delphian. His name is Palas."

"How? A khamal?"

She grinned. "I'm still hacked into their com system. Typing out words to his sleeve. Their written language is remarkably efficient."

His knee had taken a knock somewhere and he winced as he rubbed it. "I just hope no one saw me get shot like that and walk away. That's all we need now. Dyads impervious to e-mag weaponry. Like we're not popular enough already."

"You sound a little cranky."

"Yeah. Worried about Caelyn." Seth read the single-word

affirmative returned by the officer, wondering what was going on down there. What had possessed him to let Caelyn join him out here? The Delphian's work and passion let him travel to the most remote regions of the sector but always within the relative safety of a scientific expedition. Valued by Air Command, equipped with high-end defensive systems, they were rarely bothered by rebels or pirates. But now, and not for the first time, Seth had dragged the gentle, unwary explorer into not only physical harm but most certainly difficulties with the Union. "I hate to leave him like that. He's hurt worse than it looked."

"He'll be all right, won't he?" She raised a hand to forestall his reply when another message arrived from the ground. "That Palas officer found him. He's going to help, but he's not happy about it. Caelyn's under arrest and they're taking him to a medic." She pointed at a monitor. "There's your third ship."

He looked up. The third Air Command cruiser, instead of aiding the battle on the ground, had changed course to pursue the *Dutchman*. "Take the helm," he snapped and shifted his attention to the weapons system. "Break out and head for the keyhole. I have the co-ords for Csonne in there somewhere."

She nodded, so intent on her task that she floated in mid-air. "It'll take two jumps to get there. You're not going to shoot them down, are you?"

"I'm outgunned. That's a Ghoster. But I can slow them till you get inside it."

"I have to do all the work around here!" she said, but her eyes gleamed with excitement when she pulled up the specs for that class of ship.

He shifted into an evasive maneuver when the battlecruiser opened fire. "They've sent a whole lot of fire power," he said and slipped his headset over his interface nodes to allow for greater precision. "Something must be worrying Air Command an awful lot about what's going on. They're not looking for us to surrender. They're out for the kill." He aimed his return fire across the Ghoster's bow and impacted a few missiles where they were unlikely to affect their shields.

"Breaking," she announced and he pushed back against his bench when they burst through Belene's atmosphere. The *Dutchman* took that in stride, as always, but shuddered when a well-placed missile slammed into the aft shield. He punched the autopilot, already set for their destination, to let her concentrate on their pursuer.

"Same additional configuration as the others," she said. "They have no imagination. What do you want me to do?"

"Lock the cruiser into diagnostic mode. It'll have to take the drives offline to do that. Then disengage the coolant conduit where they won't find it for a while."

"You're devious."

He twisted the *Dutchman* out of the way of another volley. Something scraped across the small observation bubble overhead but it had seen more direct hits than that and he hadn't needed to replace it since that unfortunate meteor shower some time ago. Still, he cast a nervous glance at the displays to check the hull's cohesion.

"There," she said with a measure of satisfaction. "I bet they're surprised."

He relaxed with a deep sigh and removed his headset when they left the cruiser far behind. Except for Caelyn's terrible injury, things were turning out rather nicely. He had the disk, a destination, and, if Air Command did its job, Tov Pald and his people would not be looking for him to return any time soon.

He climbed out of his couch and went into the main cabin to shrug out of his blood-soaked jacket and shirt. While the decon cycle took care of the gore on his hands and arms he wondered how the Delphian was faring back on Belene-Noh. Air Command would not harm him, that was true, but Caelyn was a long way from home and the protection of his people.

"I have the feeling you spend more energy trying *not* to

damage your enemies than if you just took them out," Khoe said.

"Yes, I try," he said. "It's not always possible."

"What do you mean?"

He shrugged. "Sometimes you have to act like a rebel to be thought of as one. How long to the keyhole?"

"Couple of hours. You've harmed people before? Your own, I mean?"

He waved the question away, recognizing it as one that just might lead to a conversation he really did not want. Sometimes, floating alone around in the middle of nowhere, uninvited memories and images haunted his thoughts when sleep wouldn't come. Leading his own private rebellion against a ruthless rebel force and the equally determined Commonwealth Union, the distinction between them faded at times and left him wondering about his place in this. Again and again he resolved to turn his back on it all, maybe join Caelyn on some extended trip to elsewhere, and forget about these never-ending clashes. And every time he did, he found himself drawn back into things, irked by the misery meted out by rebel and Union alike. But when self-reflection becomes too much, he told himself at those times, you put away the books, boost the music volume, and spend a few exhausting hours with the exercise equipment in the cargo bay. "Will you be able to connect to Csonne?"

"Hmm, yeah," she said. "Will take two days in real-space to the next keyhole."

He sat down on the lounger to remove his boots. A slow smile tugged on his lips. "Days, huh? Just you and me and the *Dutchman*?"

When he looked up she walked toward him, wearing only a whisper of fabric floating around her like mist. He exhaled audibly when he made out the gentle curves beneath. "Close your eyes," she whispered.

He did, half-afraid to lose the lovely vision before him, but she was still right there. He felt the gossamer cloth against his face and inhaled the bewitching scent she conjured up. When he reached for her she straddled his thighs, facing him. Her lips brushed over his. "Days," she promised. "Anything you want."

TEN

"Damn," Deve said when he jammed his elbow once again into the ridged edge of yet another conduit cap.

He supposed that Lep Ako's idea of making him an engineer aboard the Air Command transport ensured that he spent most of his time alone, away from curious questions of his crew mates and out of sight of the officers. The alien had little faith in his ability to keep his identity a secret. Deve suspected that he was probably right. And so he labored down here, directed by Lep Ako in whatever task he was assigned, working on things he had never seen before. For all he knew, what he did down here, in the bowels of the *Kimura*, was either making this ship fly or the toilets work properly.

Of course, it could have been worse. Lep Ako could have made him a soldier. Deve loved guns and uniforms and often wondered if joining Air Command might have been his true calling. But the *Kimura*'s grunts were made to pace around outside, freezing their tails here on Belene-Noh, a nothing-planet in a nothing-sector existing for no particular reason. The on-board crew had the better job today.

He slid a little further into the access conduit and stretched out on his back. Lep Ako, invisible, seemed distracted and had stopped showing him what he was supposed to be doing down here. It suited him fine. The entity in his head had little understanding of his need to eat or sleep and after days of this Deve felt exhausted and miserable. His head hurt all the time and he often fantasized about the food he'd eat if he ever got home again.

"Stay awake," Lep Ako snapped. "I can't concentrate when you're sleeping."

Deve scrubbed his eyes. "I need to sleep. Just an hour."

The answer was another vicious stab of pain somewhere in the back of his head where he expected it. He didn't even flinch this time.

"There's something going on in the officer's lounge," Lep Ako said, feeling his way through the ship's communications network. "A major is talking to that Delphian they arrested. He probably knows where Kada is going."

"The one that's got his hand shot off?"

"Yes."

"Can I see? I'm too bored to stay awake." Deve raised his arm to bring the display screen of his data sleeve up.

Lep Ako obliged him wordlessly. The ship's cameras, recording the interrogation, if that's what it was, sent their data without noticing the tap in the system. He saw a comfortable lounge furnished, he noticed enviously, with the sort of couches that would make for some truly remarkable naptime.

The major, Terwood, leaned against a bulkhead while the Delphian sat stiffly on a reclining chair. Even on the small screen wrapped around Deve's sleeve, the exasperation on the officer's face was unmistakable.

"How's the arm?" Terwood asked two decks above their heads.

The Delphian looked down at the bulky device supplying the end of his arm with what it needed to heal. "Missing a piece," he said. "But your medics are efficient. They've already received word from Delphi that our engineers are preparing a prosthetic hand for me."

"Surely, you'll reconsider next time you feel like taking up with renegades. These things never end well."

"Kada's credentials seemed appropriate," Caelyn responded. "We do not have an endless supply of ships. We must make use of able pilots when we have the opportunity."

"You're sticking with that story? You're out on this forsaken planet for research? What are you researching?"

"The colony. They have developed some remarkable survival mechanisms by simply regressing to a more primitive way of managing their collective. They are not completely isolated, yet they choose to remain here. It's an interesting study."

"They stay here because most of them are criminals, smugglers and outcasts. That can't be hard to figure out."

"Not at all. There is an entire new generation, with a third now coming of age. This sort of thing offers fascinating insight into isolated communities. As you know, Delphi also chooses to remain separate from the influence of outsiders."

"You're comparing this cesspit to Delphi?"

"Comparing what we know with what we don't understand is a sound basis for observation."

"Your little project almost cost you your life." Terwood gestured toward Caelyn's arm. "Was it worth it?"

"I'll remind you that neither I nor Sethran Kada provoked the attack that took place here yesterday. You showed your back to a Caspian. One apparently known to have an unstable disposition. Cesspit or not, this colony was at peace before you came."

"Crawling with Shri-Lan."

"I'm an explorer, Major. Your political problems impact the worlds we study, but we do not involve ourselves with them. I do appreciate your offer to return me to Delphi as your unexpected arrival caused my pilot to leave me behind."

"Your safety is of great concern to us," Terwood said, with only the slightest edge of sarcasm in his tone.

"Thank you. My people will appreciate Air Command's attention to my well-being."

Deve shifted uncomfortably on the floor. "What kind of interrogation is that?" he scoffed. "He'll get nowhere with that Delphian. They're treating him like some guest they're having for tea and cake."

Indeed, the Delphian looked as composed as Delphians always did. Deve had caught a glimpse of him during the short but fierce battle yesterday, looking disheveled and in a great deal of pain. But now he was dressed in crisp coveralls in place of his bloodied clothes and someone had brushed the black coloring from his hair and tied it neatly his nape. His gaunt face, of course, was utterly expressionless now.

"That Delphian is having himself a good time," Lep Ako said. "You can tell by the color of his eyes. He knows the major can't do a thing to him."

"Why not? If he's hanging out with Shri-Lan he should be locked up with the rest of them."

"They wouldn't lock up a Delphian." Lep Ako had spent his time since leaving Rishabel in browsing undetected through the *Kimura*'s data system, absorbing every bit of information stored there. The ship's library, not even tied to Targon's massive mainframe, filled in the countless blank spaces that his forays on Rishabel had left in his knowledge. "The Union needs Delphi in a good mood if they want to keep the supply of decent navigators coming. All the really good jumpers are Delphian. Something about their heads. I'd love to get into one of them."

Deve scowled and returned his attention to his screen when the major spoke again.

"We'll leave for Targon as soon as the medics stabilize the last of the casualties," Terwood said, looking as though his patience wouldn't hold out much longer. "Frankly, we've gotten no useful information from any of the captives and their leader isn't in any shape to talk. Are you sure you don't have something to add here? Did Kada say where he was going?"

"No."

"Was there something... unusual about him? About his

behavior?"

"Such as...?"

The major shrugged. "Tics, talking to himself."

"He did not talk to himself."

"Did he tell you that he murdered an Air Command officer just days ago?"

"We did not trade much personal information."

Terwood pushed away from the wall, perhaps to seem a little more intimidating. He looked like someone ready to raise his voice a few notches. "Maybe you should take a greater interest. People are dying and they're not all just rebels. And I'm fairly certain you know exactly why we're here. If you know where these aliens are gathering, now is the time to share the news."

In the aft section of the *Kimura*, Deve frowned when he heard the sound of a door opening up there, and he had to strain to make out the voice of the new arrival. "Major, there is someone to see you. We're not sure what to do with her."

Terwood looked up with a scowl. "This can't wait? I'm almost done with the... with Shan Caelyn."

"I think you want to see her."

The major waved his hand in resignation. "All right then."

Before the officer even turned back into the corridor, a Human woman came into the lounge. Her layers of ragged clothing identified her as one of the local civilians. She had arranged them rather provocatively and it was not hard to guess how she made her living here on Belene. She shrugged off the hand of the guard and marched directly to Major Terwood. "You the major in charge here?"

He glared past her to his officers with an unspoken promise to reprimand them later. "I am Major Nevon Terwood, stationed on Targon."

"My name is Chann. I have something for you, if you're interested," she said. "I think you will be." She looked around the room and then blinked in surprise when she saw the Delphian sitting nearby.

"You can be sure I'm not looking for company right now," Terwood said.

"I'm not sure if you're a bit daft or just rude, Major. I'm not here to give your no doubt magnificent equipment a workout."

The major's eyes snapped to Caelyn whose face remained immobile as he busied himself with the sling holding his arm in place. "What do you want," he said tersely.

"I've got information for you. About the rebels."

"My people will get the results we need with their interviews," Terwood said.

"I doubt it. Guy who told me has a bullet in his head right now."

"What have you heard?"

"It's going to cost you," she said.

"Of course." The major sighed. "If I think it's worth something."

Chann crossed her arms and regarded him fearlessly. "Subspace monsters and someone experimenting on them. Do I have your attention?"

Terwood's jaded expression sharpened at once. He walked to the door and closed it after a quick glance into the corridor. "Let's have it," he said.

"Take me back with you. Out of this place. I don't care where."

"We're going back to Targon to deliver the prisoners."

"Fine. I can go anywhere from there. I want to make the trip on this ship, not with the prisoners."

Terwood nodded. "Agreed."

She turned to Caelyn. "You're a Delphian, right?"

"Yes."

"Your people don't hold with liars. You heard what he said, right? Promised me a lift to Targon in exchange for information."

"Indeed, that's what I heard."

Terwood's eyes narrowed. "Talk."

Chann sat down on a lounger next to Caelyn and winked

at him. "Is there something to drink?"

"Don't push your luck, woman," the major said.

"All right, no need to get impolite. I was with one of the men that came with the big Caspian. Before you got here. You know how men get to talking after they've had a good time of it."

"I'm sure I do not," Terwood said through gritted teeth.

She looked at him with concern. "Oh, I'm sorry to hear that. You just go down to Dalla's when you have a chance. She'll get that taken care of."

Caelyn lowered his head to rub his eyes as if afraid to lose what remained of his Delphian stoicism if he looked at the major again.

"Anyway," she continued. "He said they're collecting things from subspace that'll infect people out here. Gets into their heads and takes over. Centauri, Feydans, mostly, so you and me have nothing to worry about, Major." She looked apologetically at Caelyn. "Not sure about Delphians. He didn't mention those."

"I'm sure we're quite safe, Shan Chann." Caelyn leaned forward, carefully cradling his arm. "Do you know why they're doing this?"

She nodded. "Kind of scary. The guy running that project is making a whole army of spies or something for the Shri-Lan. Going to put the subspace things into their people and train them to do things that regular people can't. He didn't say what they can do, though. Whatever it is, it's important. He's got a whole lot of rebel mercenaries and their cruisers with him now for protection while they get all that ready."

"Did you get any names?"

"I have a pretty sharp memory. The person in charge of things is Tague. Used to be a Union guy."

Caelyn raised an eyebrow.

"You know him?" Terwood said.

"Yes. One of yours, if I'm thinking of the right man. Reylan Tague, Human. Once worked out of Targon. Nanotech. Disappeared a year or so ago, Targon-time.

Assumed lost in subspace. He worked with some of my colleagues for a while." Caelyn tugged thoughtfully on his lower lip. "Including subspace projects. I think you'll need Targon in on this."

"And I think you don't sound surprised by any of it." The major jerked his chin at the woman. "You're done here. Out."

She glared at him but then got up. "We have a deal?"

"Yes, yes. Ask the quartermaster to find you space somewhere. I'll have more questions for you later." He gripped her arm when she moved past him. "Did your *friend* mention where all of this is happening?"

"No, but something's happening soon. They're going to test something on a bunch of civilians as soon as he's gathered enough of them up. Take them through subspace for it."

"Civilians?" Caelyn asked. "Not rebels?"

"Civilians for now. Guess a lot of people are dying from this. Or ending up messed up. So they're using volunteers first, pretending to do some study. Expendable ones."

"Locals?" Caelyn said. "Did he mention at town, maybe?"

"No, nothing." She pulled her arm from Terwood's grip. "Sounds to me like you'll have a brand new sort of rebel on your hands, Major." She waved her fingers at Caelyn and left the lounge.

Far below them, Deve felt Lep Ako's fury and disappointment over the Delphian's revelation that Seth had eluded the major. The alien had become increasingly obsessed with this sire, whatever it was, to the point of spewing hours-long rants about his plans to colonize real-space interrupted only by threats to the elusive Sethran Kada. Deve was beginning to feel a little sorry for the man; apparently Lep Ako was going to either make him his commander of troops or rip his throat out for harboring the sire. Deve wasn't sure which would be the worse of these lots. But the trail was cold now and Air Command's only hope was to beg, beat or drug the information out of the rebels.

He didn't care anymore. This wasn't his chase and nothing here had anything to do with him. He was crawling around a cold, cramped conduit at the behest of this alien creature who treated him like an old pair of boots to get around. Except you didn't cause pain to your boots when they started to wear out. Through boredom or some weird alien perversity, Lep Ako had devised small tortures for Deve on the way out here. Just this morning, he did something to Deve's brain to blind him, letting him stumble around the generator shaft until Deve tumbled over a railing to the lower level. He closed his eyes, wishing to leave, to run away and hide from the thing in his head, or maybe just to sleep.

"What utter incompetence," Lep Ako hissed, shifting his focus to the *Kimura*'s main com system to see what message the major was about to send back to Targon. "Stay awake."

Deve cringed, expecting yet another mental slap. "Can't you at least show yourself?" he said. "You don't know how awful it is to hear you talking only in my head, hours at a time, and never see anyone. I'm tired of hiding. Tired of crawling around this damn machine. My back aches."

Lep Ako faded into view to glare at Deve with cold yellow eyes in his weirdly Human face. "Feeling lonely? You can sleep after we take off. If you hold together without crying I'll let you play with that whore. How's that?"

Deve sighed. He didn't want a woman. Not really. Although, he thought, by now a little company of someone who didn't take pleasure in torturing him sounded damn good. She looked like she might be fun. Had it been that long since anyone had had a kind word for him?

Another thought shaping vaguely in his mind was that the Delphian up there seemed like a kind fellow. If anyone could find a way to get Lep Ako out of his head, it would be him and his big-brained people. He tucked the thought away as soon as it occurred to him with an almost superstitious fear that the alien was somehow reading his mind.

* * *

Caelyn stood by the narrow slit of an observation window, looking out over the bleak landscape. Distantly, a few people scrounged around the fringes of the tundra where they scattered seeds in some agricultural effort. Closer to the colony itself soldiers paced among the ships, both Air Command and confiscated rebel vessels, but the locals had faded from view. Those who hadn't been arrested and were presumably being questioned wisely remained in their subterranean nests.

His com band chirped and he looked down, still unused to wearing it around his left arm. The sudden reminder of his injury sent a stab of pain to his wrist. He briefly closed his eyes to call upon the mental disciplines practiced by his people to compartmentalize the loss of his hand where it would remain tucked away until there was space to deal with it.

He used his lips to activate a message that someone at the *Kimura*'s com station relayed to him here. An image of Shan Quine appeared and the recording began.

"Shan Caelyn," Quine said. Caelyn saw fatigue darken the Shantir's eyes although nothing in his posture or expression gave that away. "I hope you receive this in good time. I'm currently on Targon, but Shan Saias kindly forwarded your message. The information about Reylan Tague is troubling. I've joined Shan Chion and some other colleagues to examine the unfortunates being housed here. It seems that very few Dyads result in compatible pairings like the one Sethran and Khoe enjoy. We suspect that, by the time the entities reach us out here, they have lost too much energy in some sort of quantum tunneling process. These individuals are truly remarkable and I wish we had a few years to study them. We do not."

Caelyn's eyebrow rose.

"What is of utmost concern to us now is the stolen entity we discussed on Magra as being some a kind of trigger. That individual that Khoe wanted to find. We believe that this trigger is actually a new compound particle appearing among her kind, maybe as random as any unexplained evolutionary catalyst. This could be the beginning of an entirely new species. To them, 'new' may mean a day or a million days. But this change is at a delicate stage, requiring this trigger to create more of their kind. If there is just one, as Khoe seems to think, its captivity out here in real-space may end this new species before it even begins."

Shan Quine's attention was drawn momentarily to someone nearby and he nodded to them before continuing. "We may well be looking at some hints about the very beginning of our own consciousness, mirrored in subspace. Shan Sethran's intent to return the entity to subspace is, indeed, of extreme importance. We must not interrupt the natural evolution of this new species with our never-ending quest for power. However, I'm afraid that once it has returned, any of the Dyads currently here with us will not be able to survive. Something connects them out here as much as it does in subspace. It might be as elementary a force as gravity is out here for us. Without that resonance, felt by all of them, they will decay and, from what we're seeing here, kill their host when they die."

Caelyn winced.

"We've been observing this in the victims brought to Targon. The weaker Dyad pairings don't survive very long. Once their visitor decays, the host succumbs within hours. We cannot know how many other Dyads exist, surviving more comfortably than these patients here on Targon. But if the trigger particle is returned to subspace they, too, will die. As will your friend Sethran." The Shantir paused to give Caelyn time to absorb this news. "In your message you mention some experiments taking place. If someone has discovered a way to manipulate these entities, perhaps we can find a way to separate the Dyads again. We *must* find a way although we may well be running out of time. But if we can mitigate the damage they cause us, future interactions with them will not be tainted by this tragedy."

Quine again shifted his attention to someone nearby. "Are you certain? The Centauri woman?" He nodded and then addressed the camera again. "A rebel pilot was recently brought in. She said that all of the entities are delivered to Csonne. That's a likely location. Someone like Reylan Tague would blend well into that facility without raising suspicion."

The recording ended after a few more polite words of greeting and concern from the elder. Caelyn's eyes remained fixed on the blank display for a while longer, going over this message in his mind. Finally, he left the lounge to find Major Terwood. It was a while before he met up with him and some of his people near the main entrance to the *Kimura*.

"Major Terwood," Caelyn said. "I just received word from Targon. The project is taking place on Csonne. I believe that is also where Sethran Kada is going at this moment."

Terwood frowned at him. "Csonne? How do you know?"

"The same way you knew to find us here." Caelyn glanced meaningfully at the officers nearby. "More… people are being found. They are able to talk."

The major nodded. "This is good news. We'll leave at once." He smirked. "Looks like you and your new lady friend will have to stay here a while."

"I need to come with you."

"I'm not taking you into another hostile encounter." Terwood tried to read Caelyn's expression. "If you're worried about those civilians, I'll assure you we'll try to avoid harm to them. That has always been our mandate." The major turned to his aide. "Kett, prepare for lift-off. All three ships. Let the rebels go but disable their planes. They can wait here for a ride back. Detain only the six we've got down in the brig."

"I'm sure you'll take every precaution," Caelyn said, watching the officer hurry away with the new orders. He was quite aware of Air Command's willingness to turn "avoiding harm" into collateral damage when necessary. "But I need to be there. Let me take one of the confiscated rebel ships as part of your fleet. I will stay out of any combat activity."

"You're out of your mind. This isn't some science mission. You may be an accomplished navigator but you're not a pilot. Those are not liftclass cruisers."

Caelyn followed the major toward the bridge of the *Kimura*. "Then give me a crew, Major. You probably suspect that Sethran Kada has one of the aliens. You are correct."

Terwood stopped in mid-stride. "You knew this? And you said nothing?"

"Major, what were your reasons for coming here to Belene? To capture Sethran Kada? With three fully-manned battleships? Was it to destroy these entities before they can launch some sort of invasion, or was it to obtain their abilities for your own purposes? Either of these strategies is unacceptable to us."

Terwood's eyes narrowed. "To you Delphians. But it's not you who ensure the safety of the entire sector. You leave that to the Union. You know as well as I do that Targon won't let these aliens spread out here, infecting our people, without taking control of that. And we're certainly not going to let the Shri-Lan get at them first."

"Sethran Kada is a friend. If negotiations between you and him become necessary, you will need me."

"So not only do you hire the services of known rebel sympathizers, you befriend them? Kind of unusual for a Delphian, isn't it?"

Caelyn did not reply.

The major seemed to mull over a few things and finally waved a hand in the air as if to give up on the argument. "Fine. I can use another spanner anyway." He activated his com band again. "Kett, have Lieutenant Palas prepare to take Tov Pald's ship with us. He'll need to find a few crew members familiar with that class."

"Thank you, Major," Caelyn said.

"Take no risks," Terwood warned him. "I am not going to spend the next six months explaining to Delphi how I lost one of their own. Understood?"

"Quite. I'm sure Lieutenant Palas is reasonably capable." Caelyn removed himself from Terwood's presence before the major could change his mind. He stopped by the *Kimura*'s med station to make sure that the sleeve protecting his injury would stand up to a longer delay and then headed for Tov Pald's vessel.

The rebel ship stood in readiness of departure by the time he arrived there, with a new crew busy with preparations for launch. The Delphian pilot, Palas, greeted Caelyn a little friendlier than the three others but Caelyn was used to that. Most outsiders viewed the aloof Delphians with disdain and, mainly because of unfounded rumors about their mental aptitudes, also with suspicion. The ship easily accommodated a crew of eleven but today they would only need the pilots, an engineer and the gunners. The engineer would also serve as com officer.

Caelyn nodded to the Human, wondering if he risked another message to Shan Quine on Targon. But there was little to say, other than to wish that the Shantir himself was here to accompany him.

"Did you want a packet, sir?" the engineer said. "We'll have com silence once we take the first jump to Csonne."

"No, thank you," Caelyn said. "I'll take one of the crew quarters. Please let me know when we approach the keyhole. I'll be assisting with the jump, uh, Airman…?"

The Human gave him a friendly smile. "Liron Deve," he said.

ELEVEN

Seth had hoped to survey Csonne a little before landing the *Dutchman*. The planet itself, as inhospitable as most, offered little but an opportunity for private research ventures to study well outside the radiation pollution that came with more populated regions. The binary star system and nearby keyhole made it an ideal place for developments in magnetic fields and research of dipole radiation on a grand scale.

The lush forests to the south teemed with wildlife so aggressive that no one bothered to even explore there any longer. In contrast, the slightly safer northern regions varied from vast tracts of treeless grasslands to gaseous moors no one ought to traverse on foot. The agencies clustered around a reliable source of water on a plateau rising above the swamps, companionably sharing their resources if not their research, to form a town they called Suncion.

This side of the planet had called it a night and the colony cluster stood out among the moors like a glimpse of stars in a cloudy sky. Khoe ran their real-vid scanners over the marshy flats to pick out ghostly flares of swamp gas, delighted when the bogs resembled a story she had recently found in the ship's library. Seth found himself drawn into her exploration when he tried to pick out the monsters said to roam these moors but he saw nothing.

Before they were able to take more than a cursory look at the colony itself, Seth answered a message from the surface demanding to know his reasons for approaching the coordinates Khoe had stolen from Tov Pald. It was not the usual welcome on a planet that rarely saw outsiders and where all visitors presented a most welcome distraction.

"Supply delivery," Seth told them, resisting an urge to point out that nothing in this solar system was anyone's personal fiefdom. He reminded himself that the Commonwealth, too, had competitors on worlds that chose not to join the Union. Unfortunately, rebel groups like the Shri-Lan took advantage of those without a military to guard their resources. "For Doctor Tague at the Adrierra lab."

Khoe perched tensely on the arm of the copilot bench, worried like Seth that, somehow, Tov Pald had eluded Air Command and changed his mind about Seth's trustworthiness. Men like that had no tolerance for those who fled combat.

"Tague, eh?" came the reply. "He's awfully popular lately. Stand by."

Moments later another voice, Human this time, cut into the transmission. "What cargo?"

"One shiny disk, sent by Tov Pald," Seth replied. "Want me to open it and tell you what's in it?"

There was a brief silence. "You got clearance. Land at the front of the north end compound."

Seth circled overhead, quickly mapping the network of domed modules scatted on the plateau. Short, covered walkways connected some of the units while others abutted without conduits. He was not surprised to find the doctor's compound a distance from the main cluster of the colony. An Explorer class spacefaring station had been put down beside it, outfitted with massive sensor arrays.

"That's unexpected," he said when they saw several private cruisers near their destination. "What's everyone doing all the way out here? How many of those disks are they gathering up?"

"Busy place," Khoe agreed. "Are those rebel ships?"

"Pretty sure the cruisers are," he said. "Nobody else's ship is that unmarked. Even the *Dutchman* shows as registered to a trade company. Currently, anyway. I sell it a lot."

"There are a lot of them down there."

He patted her knee. "We'll get along, don't worry."

She gazed at him, worried. "You keep saying that. And then people get killed. You don't have to keep downplaying the trouble I've gotten you into."

"Am I complaining?"

She started to say something but then turned her attention back to the sensors. "Just be careful," she said briskly. "I wonder why there are so many of them here."

"Probably heard about Air Command finding out about Belene. They'll have beefed up security. Likely been tracking us since we dropped into real-space." He landed the *Dutchman* as far from the other planes as he could without appearing overly cautious. The ship was still settling into standby mode when several people walked toward them, clearly armed although not especially battle-ready.

Seth slipped into his jacket and headed for the exit, the disk securely cradled in his arm. "I didn't expect this many guns. But the plan is the same. Find your trigger entity. Get into their files, download anything you can to the *Dutchman*. With luck, we'll be out of here pretty quick. With even more luck, the Delphians will figure out how to get you out of my head and your friend back into subspace."

"Are you trying to get rid of me, Kada?"

"Yeah." He smiled but her quip hadn't really sounded very funny to him. Neither of them had brought up what would happen if they found the answer to their problem, if one was to be found. Released from him, would she simply slip away? Would she cease to exist? He stayed awake last night after she had withdrawn, mulling over some fantastic scheme of asking the Delphians to try to transfer her to some sort of android, perhaps. Machines like that were in use on some worlds and, with a sufficiently shielded thorium reservoir, she could learn to operate it. Given her thirst for adventure, she would enjoy having a body that didn't require someone else to move around real-space. But then he thought about the smell of her hair, the taste of her skin and the sensation of pure pleasure inside his head that could never be replaced by someone not living within himself. She had become part of him in just a few short days.

"What?" She peered into his face, puzzled by his expression.

Seth gazed at her for a moment before realizing that this was neither the time nor the place to ask her what she thought about leaving him. Perhaps that moment had already passed. He shook his head and winked at her as he opened the *Dutchman*'s door. "Here we go. Act normal."

A Human stepped forward as soon as the ramp touched the ground. She pointed to Seth's thigh. "You can leave the weapons on your ship or turn them over to us. You won't need them here."

"Getting along, are you?" Khoe said.

Seth sighed and put both of his guns into a bin inside the cargo bay. "Not here to shoot anyone, darling," he said to the rebel.

She gestured toward an arched doorway leading into the largest of the modules. "That way." When Seth stepped past her she moved back, her eyes fixed on the disk as if it contained some sort of plague. The two Feydans with her did the same.

"Any chance of dinner?" he said conversationally as they walked toward the building. Clouds of what looked like large moths swarmed around the spotlights stabbing into the night. When they came closer he realized that these were winged animals, moving too quickly to identify. "Been a long trip. I'm right out of supplies."

"Learn to ration," she replied, oblivious to his charms.

They were startled by the sound of a gun, followed by harsh laughter. "Don't wander out here by yourself. You'll lose a leg."

Seth glanced around as if looking for the hunters, counting at least a dozen armed rebels or their hired mercenaries loitering within sight. "So what's going on way out here?" he tried. "Other than lizard stalking."

"I'll let Tague explain that to you, if he finds it necessary."

"I don't think she likes you," Khoe observed.

I think you're right.

"More for me."

He stifled a grin.

"I can feel them!" Khoe said suddenly. "Others of my kind. They're here."

Inside there?

"Yes!"

Seth loitered by the station's entrance before pressing his hand to the key panel. A quick look around revealed that the doors here were fortified and possibly even sealed. Whether to keep contaminants from leaking out or intruders from entering was unclear.

Only moments passed before one of the doors opened for a slender young man in a lab apron. Human, he wore his blond hair in curling ringlets around a delicate face. Like many who spent too much time on inhospitable planets, his skin was ghostly pale. He smiled at Seth in greeting. "Welcome. I am Avi Tashad. I work with Doctor Tague. May I?" He reached for the disk in Seth's hands.

"I was to deliver it personally to Tague," Seth objected.

"You will meet him shortly. Please." The youth continued to hold out his hands.

Reluctantly, Seth gave him the disk. Tashad inspected the display panel on its surface and entered something with a few taps. Khoe had tampered with the code to show that the disk was working as intended but neither knew what these people would be looking for. Whatever she had done passed the young man's scrutiny.

"Follow me. It is late but I will arrange accommodations for you. The doctor insists that we observe communal rest periods here. Our work shifts are long."

"No need," Seth said when they entered a short conduit to an adjoining module. "I'm comfortable on my ship."

"But you'll take a meal with us. We get few visitors." He laughed pleasantly. "Of the sort we appreciate, I mean. Those are some coarse characters out there."

"Why are they here?"

"I'm sorry... um, what is your name?"

"Sethran Kada."

"We have very strict directives regarding information, Mister Kada. I can't tell you much but those... guards were sent to make sure this facility is protected from... outsiders."

"Air Command, you mean?"

"Outsiders," he repeated and led Seth into a comfortably furnished room. Colorful blankets and cushions softened the stark design of the air-filled chairs and lounges. Someone had painted a marvelous landscape on a wall to enliven the otherwise drab panels. "Please, sit. Would you like something to eat? Drink?"

"Some tea would be nice," Seth said but remained standing. "Not too sweet."

The youth smiled shyly. "That is how I like it also, Mister Kada."

"All right," Khoe said. "I think I can tap into their grid. The network is shielded and the encryptions are a challenge. But I'm sure it can be done. The light by the door's going to respond."

Seth put his hand on the boy's shoulder to turn him slightly. "Call me Seth," he suggested softly. "No need to be formal. Did you paint that landscape? It reminds me of Zera."

"You've been to Zera?"

Khoe watched Tashad's cheeks blush softly pink. "He'll be knocking on your door later tonight," she predicted.

By then I hope to be far away from this place. Are you in?

"Give me some time. You're so impatient." She faded from view to give her full concentration to breaching the system.

Seth eyed the disk in Tashad's hands. "I hope that thing isn't leaking radiation," he said. "Maybe you should put it down."

Tashad looked up at Seth, eyes wide. "Um… yes. I mean, it's quite safe. The frequencies are keeping the particles inert. The shielding is a safety measure."

"Frequency?" Seth took the disk from his unresisting fingers. "What happens when you delete the frequency?"

"Mister… Seth, I mean. I should take this downstairs now."

"What about my tea?" Seth smiled warmly. "I'd love to hear about your work if you join me for a cup."

"You're having far too much fun," Khoe said.

If he doesn't start swooning on his own I'll have to disable him a little more painfully than with my irresistibly good looks. We can't lose sight of that disk. How are you progressing?

"Blocked at every turn but I've not been caught yet."

Don't say 'yet'. Hurry up.

Both men turned when the door opened to admit a Human whose lab coat, evenly creased, looked like it had just come out of its package. "Hello," he said. "You got here quickly."

Tashad, still blushing furiously, grabbed the disk from Seth and scooted around the new arrival to leave the room.

Damn, I almost had a date.

"I will assume you're Sethran Kada?" The man in the lab coat held his hand out in a quaint gesture of greeting, then withdrew it again to nervously wipe his lips. His skin seemed pasty, as if a thumb pressed to his cheek might leave a permanent dent.

"I am. You received word from Tov Pald?"

"Indeed. I had not expected you for a few more days. We're… we're not ready for you just yet. My name is Reylan Tague."

"He spoke well of you," Seth lied, and then lied some more. "I am a Level Three spanner and was able to get here fast. No doubt that is why he recommended me?"

"He did not mention that, but such talent is certainly of value. And vitally necessary for our work, isn't it? Tov Pald extolled your virtues as a field agent of some reputation among the Shri-Lan."

"I try to serve the cause," Seth said modestly.

"Actually, I expected him to accompany you back here. We must be careful to whom we reveal our location. And guard against too much traffic, of course. I've not heard anything from him since that last message."

"Mapping is complete," Khoe said. "There are just eight people inside this segment itself, but there seems to be a shielded space down below. What's odd is there are about fifty people on that Explorer parked outside."

That ship is designed to function as a self-contained lab when on the ground. Maybe they're using it for extra workspace. Or for radiation containment.

"Did Tov Pald explain the nature of our work here?" Tague continued, oblivious to their silent exchange.

"Not in detail. You've found a way to enhance mental capacities with some sort of subspace energy?"

Tague's smile was little more than an uneasy tic. "That Caspian doesn't waste words but, yes, that is basically the summary of the project. I'd originally examined the particles as a possible power source. But for our more immediate needs, using these entities in our struggles against our Union overlords is far more valuable."

"Absolutely!" Seth said with enthusiasm. *I'm guessing he hasn't actually met his Shri-Lan overlords yet*, he sent to Khoe.

"And the Brothers seem to agree, too. They've been showering me with anything I need to move the project forward." He waved a hand toward the exit. "A bit too much. They've sent far more security than I need out here. I think we've got five cruisers here now. Before they arrived we didn't even lock our doors at night. There are only the lizards to worry about. I'm afraid some of our neighbors are whispering among themselves."

"Security is a necessary evil," Seth said thoughtfully. He nodded toward the door through which his disk had disappeared. "Collecting these things must be tedious. And expensive."

The doctor's face brightened. "I think we're done with that. One of the entities turned out to be very special. We call it the Alpha entity. It's unique among the other samples we've collected. It exerts a force that excites the other subspace particles to create complex structures that can, under the right conditions, maintain that structure in real-space. The Alpha draws others near, like a magnet. As long as we have it, others will follow. So now I believe that, instead of bringing the particles out here to expose them to our people, we will enter subspace and meet them there."

"And you're looking for suitable carriers to create these Dyads?"

"Dyads?" The doctor's high forehead furrowed. "Dyads. I like that. A very apt descriptor. You are, indeed, resourceful. Yes, we are looking to find ways to create more... Dyads. We've completed the testing stages and have achieved several wonderfully successful fusions. Flawless! We're nearly ready to move ahead with actual agents loyal to the cause that can be deployed by the Shri-Lan as needed. I hope you will join the team. Obviously, Tov Pald thinks you're suited for this."

"Honestly, I'd like a little more information. How do you get rid of these things again?"

Tague looked perplexed. "We could well be looking at the next evolutionary rung in your particular ladder. You Centauri seem to be the most suited for this... composite. These are not hats you can simply remove."

"There must be a way. There could be, I don't know, incompatibilities. Illness. Accidents. Long-term effects you haven't discovered yet."

Tague nodded. "Yes, we have some challenges. But I've

been able to eliminate several threats and we've put our early setbacks behind us. Please be assured that you will receive continuous support from our team should the need arise. Agents like you take risks every day." He smiled thinly and turned to the door. "It's what you live for, isn't it? It's what makes you valuable."

"It does sound like an adventure," Seth allowed.

"Please join us for a meal. In nine hours we will travel to the keyhole and run one more experiment with a few volunteers already aboard my ship. If all goes well you will find yourself on the most exciting journey you've yet taken."

Seth remembered the last few days aboard the *Dutchman* with Khoe and silently agreed. What was less likely was allowing this Human to get close to his interface with his experiments. "Where have you found your volunteers?" he asked casually.

"Wherever I can!" Tague said brightly. "I sent around a request for volunteer testers to the other stations." He leaned toward Seth in an unpleasantly conspiratorial way. "They think we're studying brainwave activity during subspace transit. Easy money for the junior staff tired of compiling charts and monitoring the satellites. It's a wonderful change of pace for them. There is so little to do here on Csonne." He contemplated his own cleverness for a moment. "But in fact I'm going to allow the Alpha itself access to my ship's communications net during the traverse. It'll draw the entities directly to our subjects via their neural implants."

Seth smiled broadly to keep the look of disgust from his face. "Won't they be surprised."

"Indeed. I don't hold out too much hope for complete success. Some of these people have woefully outdated interface modules. But I suppose that'll give us another variable to consider. Is the quality of the nodes the key? We'll find out. This is an exciting time for us here. For now I just need a few viable Dyads, fully functioning, to show the Brothers what can be done."

I may have to punch him, Seth sent.

"He's experimenting with people who aren't even rebels?" Khoe said. "People who don't know what he's doing? Don't let him do this!"

He's rushing this just so he's got something interesting to show his money-people. I'm guessing those Shri-Lan outside are here to make sure nothing gets in the way of that. They'll be monitoring any outgoing message.

"What are we going to do?" she asked.

We need to stop tomorrow's experiment. We should be able to sabotage the Explorer out there if you can break into it. Then we can find a way to contact Air Command to take this place apart. But first we need his files. And the Alpha. I don't want some Union outfit to get their hands on them before the Delphians have taken a look.

"I can't reach the Alpha but I can feel it close by," she said. "Probably down in that closed-off lab. I can't get into that from here. That level even has a separate power supply. I'm finding a few things here and there, though. Downloading now. Mostly just early notes. I have the schematics for the collector."

If this guy is right, the collector disks won't matter. Is there nothing about that Alpha resonance he was talking about?

"Not yet. Oh."

What? Did you find something?

"Uh, no. Ramblings about brainwashing the Dyads when they first become aware. Making them hate the Commonwealth."

Keep pulling out what you can. Find out how your other pals are stored. Maybe we can cut them loose.

"You're going to steal them?"

If we can, yeah.

* * *

"Are you ready?" Seth whispered a few hours later.

The compound had settled into its rest period as decreed by the doctor. According to the scanners, the few people living inside had retired to their cabin-like rooms and only the low hum of power generators intruded upon the silence.

Before retreating to the *Dutchman*, they had endured a tedious evening with Tague and his colleagues, listening to several convoluted theories regarding dipoles that had even Khoe looking for diversion. The young assistant, Avi Tashad, added a few amusing things to the conversation but, annoyingly, was interrupted by his superiors just when it seemed that things might take a lighter turn. The single highlight came in the form of a surprisingly delicious dish of grilled reptile.

"Yes, this is very exciting," Khoe said, making no effort to get up from the lounger.

He played idly with a strand of her hair strewn over his chest. "What's going on outside?"

"Quiet. Some guards loitering around but a lot of them left for the marshes. There isn't anyone around for half a mark at least. Just those scaly eight-leggers. Lots of them."

He stood up, rearranging her as he did, and pretended impatience when she ducked through his arms to steal a kiss. "Let's do this," he said. "Time to find us an Alpha."

The *Dutchman*'s exit gate lowered soundlessly and he slipped around the ship, heading for the shadows to circle around the compound. His mapper had located an open skylight that might just allow him to enter undetected.

"Guard over there," Khoe said.

"I see him." Seth noticed another nearby, heading this way. "So much for sneaking off." He stepped away from the *Dutchman* and strolled toward the edge of the plateau.

"Up late?" the Human guard said when Seth reached him.

Seth shrugged. "Lagged," he said with a vague gesture to show that he didn't expect ground huggers like the scientists to understand space travel. "Thought I'd do a little hunting. That snake thing we had was tasty."

The mercenary smirked when he looked at the gun holstered at Seth's side. "We don't use guns for the hunt. No art to it. Knives and bare hands is how it's done. There's nothing poison about the lizards. Tracers spook the herd anyway." He motioned to the other guard to join them.

"Let's see how good you are, Centauri. I'll time you against Aliam. First one to get back here with a *greval* gets to watch the other skin it. And that, friend, is a nasty job."

The man called Aliam grinned. "Full grown one, too. And with none of your fingers missing."

"You're trying to scare me, aren't you?" Seth said, amused. "You've got a bet." He was less amused by having to leave his gun with the mercenary for the duration of the hunt.

They parted ways and Seth finally reached the moonless dark of the swamp. His boots sunk ankle-deep into the mire and he was glad for their waterproofing. "Keep your eye on the scanner," he whispered to Khoe. "I don't actually want to run into one of those things."

"No, you don't. They look pretty nasty."

He walked out from the parking area and began to circle back toward the north end of the compound. On this side it was only dimly lit as the boggy ground nearly reached to the foundation of the modules. Moving like what he hoped a hunter would appear on someone's scanner, he approached the side with the open skylight.

"Seth? That box there…" Khoe said.

What about it? Seth barely made out a large metal bin partly immersed in the soft soil.

"There are bodies in them. Two. Human-size, maybe Feydan."

Dead?

"Yes."

He spun when a cry rose into the air in the distance, startling both of them. The guttural sound was answered by another. He thought yet another exclamation sounded Human but none of the noise made clear who was preying upon whom.

"Behind you!"

He turned again to see a long, ridged body slide along the ground and then disappear in the murk. Only the dim light from the building showed its passage as a line of glistening scales. He crouched, his knife ready.

The animal switched back and reared up, towering over Seth who had no trouble making out rows of teeth snapping toward him. Several short limbs, more useful for moving the animal than grasping anything, waved in the air. He ducked under the whipping body and slashed at it, not particularly interested in harming the creature. Belatedly, he recalled Khoe's talent for dealing with opponents.

Could you do your zap thing, please?

"I thought you wanted to hunt?"

The greval's narrow head struck out toward him, hissing dangerously. He reached up and gripped its lower jaw to wrestle the creature to the ground before he felt Khoe's surge of energy move from him into the reptile. It jerked violently, throwing him down, before it lay still.

Thanks, he sent, frowning at Khoe as he came to his feet. His leather trousers dripped with swamp water. He shook greval drool from his hands. *If I ever had the urge to hunt for fun, this would not be the way I'd go about it.*

"Exciting, though. Did you see those teeth?"

He turned his attention to the building. The struts supporting the outer skin offered enough hand- and toe-holds for him to scale the short wall and reach the domed roof where he raised the skylight panel to slip inside. A quick glance around confirmed that this module served as a greenhouse, producing mainly vegetables but also a cheerful variety of flowers.

Got a grip on the motion detectors?

"Yes. They'll cascade as we go. Just move quickly."

He stepped into the darkened corridor. Not having a gun in his hand when sneaking through a night-silent building felt oddly like he'd forgotten something important, like his pants. Light panels glowed along the floor, making this place seem like they were aboard a transport ship. Khoe floated ahead of him, leading the way around a corner and into the first of the locks connecting the modules. The doors slid with barely a sound but Seth froze and strained to listen, anyway.

"Come on," Khoe urged.

He crossed into the adjoining segment, an octagonal lab space lined with workstations and equipment. A few dimmed light strips and some of the equipment cast feeble illumination to show him the way. Apparently, whatever work was done here did not require around-the-clock shifts. He found the short stairway that Khoe had discovered during her mapping exploration. Here, too, the motion and heat sensors remained silent at his passing.

"They're down there," Khoe said. "Hurry."

He followed her down and peered into the below-ground lab. It was brighter in here and he felt an odd, dead weight against his eardrums as if something dampened sound in this space. Before him a row of workstations with both flat screens and holo emitters faced a glass wall, likely also reinforced. Beyond that they saw a peculiar contraption with cylinders leading up to the ceiling. One of the familiar metal disks was attached at the bottom of each one.

Any idea how to get those off?

"I think so. They're just containment units."

We'll take a look. First see if there is any separate data storage. Just download everything and then wipe it all out.

She didn't seem to hear the request. Her attention was caught by the device holding the subspace entities hostage inside the clean room.

"It's not here," she said. "The Alpha. It isn't here!"

You said you could feel it.

"I can, but I thought it was down here. It's not. He must have it already on his ship, for tomorrow."

Seth pondered this revelation, switching gears, changing plans, weighing their options. *If it's on that Explorer we're not going to get near it. But we can probably disable the ship to stop the launch for now. It'll buy us time to get help.*

"What my people?" Her voice faded to a whisper. "Caught in this terrible machine. They're in pain."

Pain? How do they feel pain?

"Do I have to shoot you for you to feel pain? Or would

being stuck alone in a metal pipe be enough? They're so damn alone! We're never alone. And they're diminishing. Coming apart." She raised her hands toward the cylinder. "Oh, Seth, such misery! Help them."

How?

"Go in there."

Radiation?

"No, it's safe. Some traces of radon."

He let the door slide aside and stepped into the lab. The metal cylinders seemed to hum at several different frequencies, sounding almost like the distant notes of some stringed instrument. He examined the mechanism holding the disks in place. *How do we get that off?*

"Touch it."

What?

"Just touch it."

Mystified, he gripped one of the disks, prepared to wrench it out of its clamps or whatever held it in place. *Feels pretty solid. Maybe we can—*

A flare of heat, light, noise and pure fury blasted through his body, freezing it in place. It was carried by a wave of pain in his head and his chest that felt like his body was torn in two. He stared at his hands, unable to move, feeling bolt upon bolt of energy surge through him. He felt the skin of his fingers blister. The overhead lights dimmed and were immediately replaced by duller emergency panels.

A final blast of now-kinetic energy shoved him away from the container and he was thrown backward to collide forcefully against the glass wall behind him. He collapsed onto the floor and barely rolled aside when a rack of metal tubing crashed to the ground. "Gods, Khoe," he managed. "What happened?"

"Dead," she cried. "I had to. I couldn't stop!"

He rolled onto his hands and knees and then staggered upright, swaying. The violent hammering of his heart nearly obscured the ringing in his ears. There was blood on his hand when he wiped his mouth. "You killed them? Why?"

"They were dying. Such pain, Seth. I'm sorry if I hurt you."

"This isn't what we're here for. Now the whole place is awake." He lurched from the clean room, again acutely aware of his lack of firearm. His knees wobbled beneath him but he did not feel weak. He thought his heart might tear out of his chest if a massive embolism didn't do the job first. "We have to get out of here."

"There are people coming. Come this way," Khoe said, gesturing toward a door on his right. "There is a tunnel to the outside."

"The files." Seth coughed and waved at the workstations along the window. "Get the rest of the files. Seal the doors!"

"I'm locked out!" she said as soon as she touched the lab grid. "This entire space is shielded from the main system."

There were voices now, up in the main part of the compound. Seth checked the door at the end of the lab. "Sealed."

"You can break it," she said.

He put his hand on the door itself and a burst of energy leaped from him into the mechanism. The door slid aside.

Before he even stepped into the dark space beyond, an indistinct shape shifted in the gloom of the tunnel. He leaped back when the shape turned into five, moving rapidly toward him.

"Those are Dyads," Khoe cried out when she recognized the familiar presence within each of them. "They've got my people!"

Seth squinted at the tight knot of menace coming toward him. There was something odd about the bloodless, expressionless faces. The characteristic violet eyes of the three Centauri among them were pale disks looking at nothing. "What's wrong with them?"

Vacant or not, the Dyads' intention became very clear when the first dove at Seth with extended arms. By reflex that was more Khoe's doing than his own, he raised his hands and felt the immense buildup of energy flow from his hands into his attacker.

A massive thunderclap drummed through his chest, just as it had happened on Rishabel when he killed the Vanguard agent. The Centauri dropped and Seth reached for the next. Again and again, he grasped another of the men, discharging more of that energy, feeling it drain from him with each kill.

"Cazun…" he whispered when he stood alone among the fallen bodies. It had taken just seconds to take them all down. He was able to breathe normally again and that awful sensation of just too much adrenaline faded. His knees still trembled from the exertion. "What was that?"

"Are they dead?" she said, as stunned as he.

Seth crouched beside one of the bodies. "Yes, dead. Probably his experiments. Something must have gone wrong with them."

"You're right," a voice spoke behind them.

Seth spun around, ready to attack, only to find three mercenaries with their guns aimed at him. Two more stood on the stairs. All of them carried ballistic weapons.

Reylan Tague stepped in front of them. He glowered at the fallen men. "This was not necessary."

"Didn't seem that way to me," Seth said. "What did you do to them?"

"Nothing that didn't happen to you," Tague said. "Isn't that right? You've already been exposed. Although you seem to have a far better grasp on your alien than they did. I'm very interested in finding out why that is. As, I'm sure, will Shri-Lan command."

"How did you know?" Seth measured the distance to the armed guards blocking his way to the stairs. Their sneers almost begged him to try for escape.

"Besides you talking to yourself? We got word an hour ago that Tov Pald was captured on Belene-Noh. He did not send you to Csonne. Something tells me your reasons for coming here are not purely for profit. Probably a Union agent, am I right? I'm guessing that Air Command is eager to acquire the Alpha for their own use."

"I don't give a damn about Air Command," Seth said through clenched teeth. "These are living, sentient beings you're torturing."

"They are nothing until they use our neurons to create a presence. Don't mistake them for living organisms."

"Are you going to hit him?" Khoe said. "That's just rude."

"What do you want from me?" Seth said. Two of the guards searched him and shoved him back into the main lab. *I can barely stand up. Anything you can do?*

"No," Khoe said, sounding defeated. "I can't even get as far as out of this room. Not quickly, anyway. He's found some way to block me completely down here."

The doctor went to the glass wall and surveyed the destroyed containment system. "Despite what I told you earlier, every one of my attempts so far has ended in failure. Death, emotional collapse, brain damage. Even those that came through suffered injuries that make them no more useful than a Rhuwac foot soldier. You saw that for yourself. Perhaps it's the entities inside that have decided this. Perhaps that's all they understand."

"And you don't understand any of it."

Tague turned back to Seth. "True, so much is still a mystery. And Air Command is closing in, leaving us no time for research. The Brothers are becoming impatient. Taking the Alpha and the hosts into subspace is my last chance at making this happen."

"You won't ever get them to cooperate. They don't care about our Union or the Shri-Lan or our reasons for anything. They cannot be controlled. We are little more than life support systems for them."

Khoe scowled at him but said nothing.

"And yet you seem to get along just fine with yours," Tague said. "There is something different about your parasite, or perhaps in the way you have combined. I need to know what that is."

"Can't you see where this is going? These people don't

belong here."

Tague shook his head, impatient with this pupil who refused to see the larger lesson. "If we don't take control of them, the Union will. We are merely ahead of the competition. We've only seen the beginning of what can be done with them. We can lead the research, the development, the very evolution of the species. Your parasite is the key. It hasn't harmed you. You are what I've been striving to create. With just a few dozen like you, we will shift the balance between Shri-Lan and the Commonwealth."

"If you think I'm going to cooperate with this…"

"No need. Your Dyad is far too valuable to leave with Union spy. We'll find a more suitable host for it."

"You can get it out of my head?" Seth said. "How?"

Tague just smiled and motioned to his men. Seth's eyes widened when one of them turned his hand to reveal what looked like a small pistol, aimed at him. Then there was nothing.

TWELVE

"Don't move."

Seth fought weakly against the hands that restrained him. The blinding overhead light stabbed into his eyes and he moaned when the pain in his head grew unbearable. His chest still ached but not with the ferocity he felt earlier. Against the glare he was able to make out someone beside him. "Lights," he groaned and tried to shield his eyes with his arm.

A moment later the room dimmed. He blinked, grateful when the pain in his head subsided a little. This was some sort of clinic, he decided. Or perhaps another part of Tague's creepy research compound. He was stretched out on a metal table surrounded by cabinets and anxiety-inspiring gadgetry. Someone had removed his jacket and shirt and the surface beneath him felt like ice.

Avi Tashad returned to his side where he continued to bandage Seth's blistered fingers. Seth raised his other hand, finding it already wrapped in a clean layer of mesh.

That's when he perceived a peculiar void, like something very important that he might have forgotten or misplaced and now desperately needed.

"Khoe," he called out. His voice sounded hoarse. "Gods,

Khoe!" He tried to sit up but the young man rose quickly to press him back down.

"Keep still," Tashad said softly. He placed a cool hand over Seth's forehead. "You need to rest. Your parasite is gone."

Seth stared at the Human without comprehension.

"He took it." The youth gestured at the equipment beside the table. "Some resonance he's been working on. Sort of like the reverse of the tune that attracts them."

"No! That can't be. Is she all right? What did he do with her?"

"She?"

Seth nodded and closed his eyes. "Yes, she." Knowing better, he tried to call to her, the way he sometimes did when she had withdrawn. Nothing. Just a cavernous vacancy where she used to fit into his senses. He lifted his arm, not surprised to see his data sleeve gone. He sat up, shaking off Tashad's hand. The room tilted crazily and he closed his eyes again. "Where is my transmitter?"

"They took it. The Shri-Lan. To get into your ship. Please let me help you."

Seth pushed his hair out of his face. "I think you've done enough."

"This was hardly my doing. I didn't come here to force people into having their brains altered. I was promised a research opportunity with the Trida team and instead I end up working for the Shri-Lan. I'm stuck here." He went to a cabinet and stood before it as if undecided about what he wanted there. "But I have records. Notes. Conversations. If I ever get off this rock and somewhere safe I'll have my say about what goes on here."

Khoe? Dammit. Wake up! "Where are they keeping her? She destroyed the storage thing where the others were being held."

"They're gone. They took the *Stoyan* off-planet. The research ship. Not very long ago. Told me to keep you alive until they get back in case he needs to work with your brain some more. He wasn't sure you'd wake up." Tashad sorted through the medicine packets on a shelf. "I'm studying astrophysics. What am I supposed to know about keeping you alive?"

"Where did they go, dammit," Seth snapped. "How long have I been out?"

"About six hours. They are going to jump, that's all I know. He's got at least five cruisers with him." He peered at an ampoule in his hand. "I'm thinking if he doesn't get results he's going to keep right on going. Things are a bit of a mess here right now."

"Your mess," Seth growled. "You should have turned in the lot when you first saw something going on here. Now people are going to die or worse." He pushed off the table and carefully tested his weight before standing. His legs seemed agreeable to holding him up. He shuffled to the boy and nudged him aside to rummage through the cabinet. None of these medicines were in pill or vapor form and he resigned himself to an injection. "Those," he said. "Just painkillers."

The boy turned and Seth saw tears stream over the delicate face. "I couldn't! They would have killed me!" Tashad cried. "First the doctor was trying things out on rebels and I didn't care. Those people are rude and mean. You have no idea about the things they've said to me. I barely dare to step outside anymore. I know what the Shri-Lan do to people they don't like." He raised his hands in a helpless gesture. "But then Jael died. My teacher! She went mad and then just died. I don't even know where they put her after that!"

Seth closed his eyes briefly, thinking of the bodies Khoe had found outside.

"And now he's got those others," Tashad continued. "Volunteers from the other agencies. Some of them are my age, trying to learn something out here. What if this new test doesn't work out?" His red-rimmed eyes pleaded with Seth. "What if it does?"

Seth frowned, sorry for his harsh words. "Is there no one left here of your team?"

"No. Just a half dozen guards outside and the doctor's wife, Isalia. She refused to go with him. She's locked herself up."

"Seems sensible. If your doctor doesn't return they're going to start getting angry. Lock yourself up, too. Contact Air Command and let them know what's going on here."

"Air Command? They'll arrest me. And they'll arrest *you*. Why do you want them here?"

Seth took a deep breath and halved the amount of painkiller he was going to take. His mind was fogged and the lack of Khoe in his head kept threatening to drop him in a bout of vertigo. Of course the boy would think of him as Shri-Lan. He caught a glimpse of himself in the mirrored front of the cabinet. The irises of his bloodshot eyes were pale, a sure sign of illness among his people. The dark shadows under them went well with the cheeks covered in a few days' growth. He certainly looked the part today, too. "Well, wait till I've gone."

Tashad wiped his face with his forearm. "It'll take days for Air Command to get here. Weeks maybe. There's nothing here for them. Tague destroyed everything that you didn't already. He's the only one now with the research data."

Seth gestured for Tashad to administer the medicine. Gritting his teeth, he looked away from the needle slipping into his skin. It hardly helped to remind himself that the pain in his burned fingers felt far worse than the injection; he'd never feel comfortable around needles. "I'm going after them. There's got to be something flyable left down here."

"Your ship is still here. They weren't able to break into your cruiser, even with your transmitter." The youth's hand lingered on Seth's bare arm and his voice took on a pleading tone when he continued. "Stay here until help comes. Or take me with you. You got rid of that alien. You're free. I'm so scared here. And alone."

Seth gently removed Tashad's hand. "I might have… given you the wrong idea earlier. I can take you out of here, if you want. I just can't guarantee that I'm going anywhere you want to be."

The youth's hopeful expression shifted to disappointment. "How are you going to get away? Your ship's under guard. They want it."

"Of course they do. It's a damn fine plane." Seth perched on the edge of the examination table and ran his fingers over the ship tattooed above his elbow. The burn mesh made it difficult but after a little experimenting he tapped the code onto three of the *Dutchman*'s torn sails. A gentle buzzing sensation confirmed access and he lifted his arm to touch the embedded data sheet against the implant at his temple. "I may have to get rough with them. Still want to come with me?"

Tashad looked away. "No. I'll stay. I'll call the Slian team to come get me and Isa after you've gone. I don't dare to walk over there in the dark." He fished Seth's clothes from a shelf under the table and shook them out. "Those rebels scare me more than the lizards."

Seth winced when the pain in his hands made fastening his shirt problematic. "Lock yourself up until someone gets here. Don't give those rebels out there a reason to…" He hesitated, but his glance at Tashad's slender body told the boy what he meant. "To hurt you."

Tashad nodded uncertainly.

Seth tried to recall the layout of the facility, willing his brain to work properly. "I need your help to get out of this place. Go down to the module that sits higher up, at the far end. Know which I mean?"

"Yes, the recycler."

"Find something to make a lot of noise to get their attention. Break a roof panel or something. If I make it to my plane I'll try to get them to follow me away from here. You'll be fine then."

"I can do that. You're being very kind after… after what

we did to you."

"We don't always get to make our own choices," Seth said and then sneered at his own philosophical tone. "I sound like my old man just before I get a trouncing. See where that got me?"

Tashad tilted his head and gave him a weak smile. "You're not really a rebel, are you?"

Seth winked. "Sure I am. Hail the mighty Tharron and his bastard offspring." He pondered this for a moment. "Well, actually, if you can leave my name out of this, I'd appreciate it."

"I will."

"Are there any weapons here?"

"Yes. We have all the stuff that used to belong to the… the first test subjects. In the closet near the stairs. I saw guns." Tashad tugged on Seth's sleeve to stop him from stepping into the hallway. "I'm sorry I didn't warn you when you first got here. I'm to blame for this and I'm worried about your condition. You could be damaged. I don't know if you should be going off-planet at all. Never mind going through subspace any time soon."

Seth had to agree with that opinion. "If you ask me, a good place to be right now is inside a big tub of hot water with bubbles and a trio of dancing girls but there's no point in wishful thinking."

Tashad pointed toward the west side of the building. "The main door is sealed now and guarded. But there is a tunnel down in the labs leading outside to the other side of the building. I… I don't want to go down there. I don't think I can stand to see the bodies. I'm sorry."

Seth touched his slight shoulder. "That's all right, Avi. You didn't come to Csonne for this. Just promise me to check out your next study assignment a bit more carefully. Shri-Lan are bastards to work for, believe me."

Tashad smiled. "Please be careful."

Seth watched the youth disappear down the hall and then turned in the opposite direction to the lab area of the facility.

There he found the stolen items Tashad had mentioned behind a sliding door, pathetic reminders of the lives lost here because of Reylan Tague's misguided research. He dug through a small stockpile of projectile weapons, rail guns, simple lasers and even a flash mod among com badges and other tools taken from the victims. He chose two rails and a bare-bones scanner that made him wish for his own top-quality data sleeve. A finely crafted K'lar knife caught his eye and he tucked it away in a pocket. No need to leave the valuable goods for those who would soon loot this place.

He came to the stairs and moved silently down into the shielded lab, not surprised to find the bodies of the dead Dyads still scattered on the floor. He stepped over them and into the narrow tunnel. It rose toward the open exit doors at the back of the main building.

The area behind the compound was a shamble of dropped bundles and supply cases, some piles of sheeting that looked like more of the shielding he'd seen below, and a large empty space that used to be taken up by the *Stoyan*, the doctor's research ship. A Human, listlessly shoving a few boxes onto a trolley, muttered to himself when his cart tipped off balance. Another paced nearby, rifle poised although the glare of overhead lights kept the wildlife at bay.

Seeing no one else out here, Seth squeezed the trigger of his new gun to drop the first rebel who obliged him by falling onto the cart. His aim brought down the other before he ducked for cover. He heaved him onto the trolley as well and shoved it into the tunnel opening. After scanning the area and finding no more guards here, Seth sidled around the sprawling modules of the compound, glad for the design that placed windows onto the domed roofs rather than the walls. Eventually, he rounded the farthest bend to see the *Dutchman*. It now didn't seem so clever that he had parked at a distance; the space between the main building and the plane looked inconveniently broad and exposed.

He crouched down and waited with an eye on the scanner to alert him to the creatures in the dark. Two rebels stood by the main entrance, chatting and bent over the display on the woman's wrist. He heard her laugh. A Centauri paced aimlessly by the rebels' remaining ship, occasionally crossing paths with a masked Caspian. Seth's scanner detected two more people aboard the cruiser. It would not be long before their own sensors found him hidden here.

The Caspian at the far side of the rebel ship heard the humming first. The others, too, looked up when it grew louder. A sharp whine accompanied it and then even the ground seemed to vibrate along with the air. The two rebels at the door seemed undecided about leaving their post but the others moved curiously toward the maintenance module at the other end of the compound. Seth grinned when whatever mechanism Tashad had managed to overload tore itself apart and exploded the module into a hail of shrapnel and glass.

He raced toward the *Dutchman*. The ship, already in standby mode at his remote command, whined into readiness. The first of the rebels' bullets tore up the ground by his feet by the time he reached it. Some ricocheted off the hull as he ducked around the back and pressed his hand onto the keypad.

"Damn!" he cursed while he fumbled with the bandages on his fingers. They peeled off along with some of his skin but the sensor looked beyond mere fingerprints and he was finally allowed aboard.

Once inside the ship, Seth leaped into the pilot couch and slipped into his headset. Screens overhead came alive to show his surroundings. Some of the rebels were running toward their ship, the only weapon powerful enough to damage the *Dutchman*. Seth went through the launch processes while taking potshots at the people outside, hoping that fewer rebels meant less trouble for the people still inside the research station. Some of his fire took out the rebel cruiser's landing gear but its pilots had prudently lifted off the struts as soon as they guessed Seth's intent.

Something slammed into the *Dutchman* and Seth launched

to engage his shields, aware that the rebel ship was doing the same. He swept around the other ship and into a diagonal escape path out of Csonne's atmosphere. The *Dutchman*'s much-modified crossdrives soon outpaced the rebels but they remained on his tail, even when he slipped outside of weapons range. Seth recalculated his flight path and set the scanners to track down the small fleet carrying the doctor and his experiment toward the nearby keyhole.

He found them nearing the breach, five hours in the distance. With luck, the convoy would stop before entering the keyhole to prepare whatever the doctor needed to prepare before attempting to prove his newest theory. If they entered the uncharted breach before then he had neither the fuel nor the aptitude to follow. And if they didn't, Seth was most certainly flying into battle against five rebel ships.

And for what? Seth left the cockpit and paced around the small, untidy cabin, feeling alternately anxious and exhausted. The painkillers had wrestled his headache into a manageable state but what damage had been done to him? The Shantir on Magra had warned of brain damage. Seth ran his hands through his hair and realized that they were trembling.

"All right, Kada," he mumbled to himself. "You're upright, your brain's working, so be happy with that." He reached into a cabinet to find a medical scanner. "See?" he said after running it along his body. "Nothing leaking in there, nothing missing. Stop your damn worrying."

He looked toward the cockpit. Maybe it was time to cut his losses and let Air Command clean up this mess. The alien was gone from him and wasn't that what he had set out to do? His well-developed sense of self-preservation told him to return to Csonne, scrounge some coolant from one of the outposts there, and then head straight back to Magra, even if that took weeks without a proper spanner. Then he's see his little Bellac friend whose medical skills would ensure he'd not suffered from having been turned, however briefly, into a Dyad. And then put it all behind him as another peculiar adventure in his peculiar life.

And maybe someday the bottomless hole Khoe left in his mind would close over. He stared at the lounge where they had spent hours talking, arguing, studying and dreaming up ways of using their bodies that weren't even physically possible. He could almost see her hovering at the edge of his vision but her gentle touch inside his head was now only a memory. *Khoe!* he shouted silently as if some last remnant in his brain was still somehow tangled up with her, somewhere. There was no answer for him.

If the doctor had removed her without harm, was she still Khoe? Had she turned back into the shapeless net of particles that first arrived on the *Dutchman*? Would she remember him at all? Seth rubbed his eyes, trying not to imagine her caught inside one of those collector disks. Was she in pain?

"I was right," he said and returned to the cockpit to take helm control back from the autopilot. "I've lost my damn mind."

There was nothing more to think about. He brought the ship about and headed back, demanding top velocities from the *Dutchman*'s engines. Within minutes he entered the pursuing rebel ship's weapons range and began a series of evasive maneuvers as he targeted their shield seams. The weapons system aboard the *Dutchman* was designed for Air Command's Eagle class ship and the surprised enemy had little opportunity to return fire. Volley after volley of precisely plotted missiles slammed into their shields. The *Dutchman* shuddered when it passed through the debris field left by the disintegrating rebel plane.

"One down," Seth said, taking no time to relish the victory. He turned and once again raced toward the keyhole and the remaining rebel ships.

They were waiting for him. Instead of rushing toward him, as he expected, the rebel cruisers formed a tight defensive line around the *Stoyan*, hovering close to the invisible breach in space. Puzzled, Seth ran his scanners over the field. Individually, he would have little trouble engaging them with the *Dutchman*'s superior weaponry and a lot of faith in his skills as pilot. Engaging all five of them at once took more recklessness than even he possessed.

He shifted his attention to the research ship. The *Stoyan*'s design dedicated most of the available space to labs and equipment rather than passengers. And yet his scanners reported over fifty individuals aboard, far in excess of what the ship could support for long. Unwitting specimen in the doctor's laboratory.

He took full control of the *Dutchman*'s weapons system while issuing navigational commands via his neural interface. After belting into his pilot couch, he rerouted all of the ship's resources, including those used by the gravity spinners, to the shields. The *Stoyan*, like most ships of that class, had few defensive systems and, if he could get the rebel cruisers out of the way, a standoff might just be possible.

"Stand down, pilot." The order came over his com system as he approached effective weapons range. "You have no business here."

"Just passing through." Seth began his calculations of the enemy's formation to find the best possible spread for his weaponry.

Khoe would have supplied him with the mathematical odds of succeeding in an effort to be sensible about the whole thing. Then again, he thought, she also advised him to shoot himself in the foot to test her theory, so perhaps sensibility had little to do with anything today.

"Crap!" he shouted when the *Dutchman*'s alarms showed that the keyhole was beginning to expand. "Crap, damn, crap!" So much for his plan to trail the *Stoyan* into subspace if she couldn't be stopped out here. Without a spanner on board, he could not follow on his own. And with those damn rebel ships in his way, making a run for that gap was quite simply suicide.

He swung into position for his attack, still mystified by the rebel ships' reluctance to take the offensive. The keyhole was opening at an alarming rate and the *Stoyan* would soon ramp up her engines to reach the required velocity. Surprisingly, the rebel ships turned and also got into position to enter the breach.

"Well, now I'm feeling like you just don't care," Seth grumbled.

The *Dutchman* reported that the keyhole had now turned into a sufficiently broad jumpsite. Seth took a deep breath. This wasn't the first time that he would ride someone's wake through a breach without knowing anything about its terminus, but he'd never get used to it. It wasn't a highly recommended practice among deep-space pilots.

"What the…" he said, gaping at his screens.

The wide-open gate before them suddenly spilled two battlecruisers and their accompanying fighter planes, the small and agile Kites, into real-space. At the rear came the mighty Ghoster, clearly having recovered her engines. All but one vessel bore Air Command's proud emblems.

The five rebel cruisers veered aside, spreading in a wide formation as if they had hit a wall which, it would seem, they had. Seth dove out of the way when Air Command opened fire in pursuit of the ships, harassing them with the Kites to get them away from the jumpsite. His long experience with Air Command battle tactics made clear that those pilots were enjoying the chase.

He left them to it and veered around the *Stoyan*. The Explorer had sprinted away in surprise and now came about again to take another run at the keyhole, now the only route to escape. He took after it, aware that one of the other ships now gained on him.

"Dutchman!"

Seth blinked. "Delphi?"

"This is remarkably exhilarating," Caelyn said over the *Dutchman*'s com system. Seth nearly severed the link before he realized that Caelyn had coded his transmissions with a convoluted Delphian encryption he had given to Seth not long ago.

Seth frowned as he checked his scanners. "You're on that

rebel ship behind me? Tov Pald's boat?"

"Yes, isn't it exciting? Apparently, it's a very good quality ship. We've been here for hours. Major Terwood's been slipping probes through the breach to wait for you to get here. He didn't want to land on—"

"I need your help," Seth interrupted. He rolled out of the way when his sensors warned of an incoming volley from a rebel ship. A second one blasted his shields. He dove toward one of the Air Command Kites and then got out of there when the pilot took after the rebel. Caelyn's cruiser streaked after the *Dutchman* when he turned toward the keyhole and away from the battle.

"That Explorer over there, the *Stoyan*, is going to jump," Seth said. "They're just going to cut a new terminus because they don't need to get anywhere. I could really use a spanner with me in case I lose them." He glanced at his depleted coolant levels. "And to get back home, actually."

There was a short silence before Caelyn replied. "Major Terwood orders you to stand down, Seth. I'm sorry."

"We are going to lose the *Stoyan*!" Seth snapped. A quick check of the displays showed that the Ghoster had made its ponderous turn back toward the breach, leaving the rest of the small fleet to chase down the rebels. "They won't get here before that keyhole opens." He got into position to follow the *Stoyan* into the breach. "Dammit, you'll have to chase me, then."

"That'll work," Caelyn said. "Palas just received that order. Are you sure about this?"

"They're using civilians for their test," Seth said. "And they've got Khoe. Yes, I'm damn sure."

"Khoe's not with you anymore? You're free? That's fantastic news."

"We'll celebrate later. Listen, you need to remove your interface links for the jump. All of you." A ticking sound alerted Seth that someone had already decrypted their exchange.

"That hardly seems advisable," Caelyn said.

"Just trust me. You can't be plugged into your ship unless you're looking for a hitchhiker."

Pause. Then: "Heard, Dutchman."

The confiscated rebel cruiser joined the Dutchman as the three ships reached maximum velocity. By the time the transport entered the breach into nothing, Seth and Caelyn were close enough to slip inside without needing to create their own chart. Wherever the Stoyan went, so would they.

THIRTEEN

Seth was slow to recover from the jump that had taken all three ships through the unimaginable distance between the spanned keyholes. Convinced that he was upside down, or perhaps the contents of his head were, he groped around for something he might recognize. Gradually, he realized that his arms had floated up during the leap and that the *Dutchman* was still tumbling through space with reduced gravity.

Shaking his head clear of the fog that came with a long jump, he ran through a quick diagnostic before spinning the gravity up to something a little more comfortable. His head still pounded steadily and his stomach was also not happy with the general state of things.

"Centauri," he heard Caelyn's voice over the cockpit speakers. "Are you back with us?"

"Barely," Seth said. He reconnected his neural interface to take a look around. An annoying ringing in his ears had joined his headache. "That one hurt. Where are we?"

"Precisely nowhere," he heard another voice, clearly Delphian and clearly irritated. "There is nothing out here within travel distance. We'll need to go back through that breach to return to Trans-Targon. What is that Explorer doing out here?"

"Collecting more aliens," Seth said.

"I've sent a message packet back to Major Terwood to let him know where we emerged," Palas said.

Seth scanned the *Stoyan* now at a near standstill. The life signs aboard had dwindled to just over thirty. It did not take advanced mathematics to see that, indeed, her air reserves would barely support even that many people for the long trip back to Csonne. He opened another channel to hail the ship.

"*Stoyan*," he said after manipulating the output to disguise his voice. "I took damage back there. Going to have to lock on." He held his breath as he waited for some reply that made clear that they knew who he was.

But his gamble paid off. Instead of using what little armament they had to let him know what they thought of his ruse, they seemed far too busy with their own problems to realize that it wasn't one of their own that had escaped the battle with Air Command. Were those even rebels in control of that ship, or merely the *Stoyan*'s own crew?

"Lieutenant Palas," he said, using the Delphian encryption when the *Stoyan*'s shields dropped. "Please lock on to that Explorer when I do. Expect casualties and maybe some armed resistance."

He swung around the side of the vessel to nudge the *Dutchman* into one of the docking ports while Palas executed the maneuver on the other side. He did not expect anyone to welcome him aboard when he stepped through the airlock but the pandemonium he encountered didn't seem routine, either.

Two technicians hurried past him, followed by someone in lab gear. He heard shouting and curses. An alarm that nobody heeded was buzzing to itself somewhere. Environmental controls had been set to conserve resources and he smelled not only overused air but also something burning.

The airlock opposite him opened and the two Delphians entered. As always, that otherworldly Delphian serenity seemed to promise that these tall, blue-braided individuals could never fall prey to misfortune and, despite himself and knowing better, Seth felt safer for having them aboard. The Human in engineer coveralls entering hesitantly behind them gave him the opposite impression.

"Gods, what's happening here?" Caelyn said when someone screamed nearby.

Seth felt a pang of guilt when he saw the device protecting Caelyn's arm. "Get up top and tell the flight crew not to re-enter the breach. Figure out how long we can stay here before we have to return. Use force if you have to." He appraised the hulking build of the crew member they had brought aboard. The man looked up to the task but there was something unsettling about him. He hunched tiredly, looking about himself with bloodshot eyes in a pale face. His lips moved soundlessly. "What's the matter with this one?"

The Human's eyes shifted to Seth. "Just a bit of a bug, sir. Missed my last med check. Don't be reporting me."

Seth frowned. "Get the bridge figured out. I'll meet you up there."

The others headed that way while Seth followed the sound of chaos down the cramped corridor. It was meant to be a wide passage, connecting the air locks to the lab and service area with plenty of room to move equipment. Now it was crammed with bins and racks surely not meant to be stored here permanently. Some of the equipment was strapped to the floors and walls with temporary restraints.

More disorder greeted him in the main lab. Two rows of triple-level bunks took up much of the space. On some of them, people lay motionless with wires leading from their neural interface nodes to a bunched conduit along the wall. Some of the volunteers seemed unconscious, others moved weakly as if trapped in a nightmare. Technicians scurried frantically from one to the next, restraining those who were clearly in the throes of unimaginable terror. Some of the bunks were abandoned and motionless bodies had been pulled from the walkway between the bunks to line up against the wall.

A young Centauri stumbled toward him, clawing at her own face. "Get it off, get it off, get it off!" Seth caught her in a bear hug until a medic came to press an inhaler to the girl's face. She slumped in his arms and he lowered her onto a cot.

"Cazun…" Seth breathed, looking up at the wall of hastily installed equipment. Piping ran along the bulkheads from an intricate device that looked very much like the storage system in the lab on Csonne. It crouched here like the malevolent mechanical monster of a children's tale.

Among the chaos a few of the test subjects rested placidly, even smiling, staring at the ceiling as if something entertained them up there. He bent over a Feydan woman whose lips moved without a sound. He tugged her headset away from her neural interface. Like all of the victims here, she was probably a technician or research assistant who shouldn't have left Suncion this morning. Did they even know what was happening here?

She blinked up at him. "Colors," she said. "They're colors. And so pretty."

He straightened up to grab the arm of a passing crew member. "Where is Doctor Tague?"

"Tague? Crazy bastard is hiding in the control room." She put her hand over Seth's to squeeze it urgently. "Are you one of those Shri-Lan that's been coming around? By all that's still sacred around here, get us back right now. We were told to let them sleep and listen to their program for a few hours and then we'd head back. I don't know what is going on or why we were attacked but these people need help now."

"Disconnect the interface to the program you're running. Do you have something else?" He looked around, having nothing to draw on but his experience with Khoe. "Music or stories or even a damn weather report. Just something of no importance that'll keep them busy."

"I… I don't understand…"

"Just do it!" Seth pulled away and headed to the end of the lab to a door that the technician seemed to have meant. It slid aside to reveal a dark, small space crammed with equipment. Nothing here looked even vaguely familiar.

A lab worker whirled around when Seth entered, looking utterly frightened. Crumpled on the floor before him lay Doctor Tague, motionless.

"Who are you? What do you want?" He peered more closely at Seth. "You're the Centauri that had the alien. The one we took out. How did you get aboard?"

Seth bent over the doctor. "What happened here? He's dead."

"I can see that. Something got to him." The technician gestured at a tilted control board along the wall. "Some feedback maybe. He was connected to the ship during the jump."

"Kind of a novice move, considering what's going on here."

"This area and the ship's mainframe is shielded and closed off from the outside. The Alpha itself is linked to the com system. Only the test subjects were exposed to anything in subspace."

"That didn't work out so well, did it?" Seth pointed up at several monitors recording the testing area outside. "At least not for your volunteers."

"We have six viable fusions so far," he said, not without a hint of pride. "Six! We hoped for perhaps one or two. He was right. The incursion needs to happen in subspace. We've accomplished much here today."

Seth was not a man who easily lost his temper but now he grasped the front of the tech's jacket, ready to snap his neck. "You're sacrificing all those people for that? For six Dyads?"

Tague's assistant tugged ineffectively on Seth's wrists. "The Brothers demand results. We are giving them that. They're already on their way to Csonne to see these for themselves."

"Reverse it!" Seth shouted and shoved him to the console. "All of it. The way you got the alien out of me. Those people are dying."

"I have no idea how to reverse it. And I'm not about to

link to any part of this ship." He pointed to the body on the floor. "Who knows how that happened."

Seth ran his hand over his eyes. The pain in his head sent shards of broken glass from his forehead all the way down the back of his neck. "Then how the hell do you think we're going to get back? That Alpha is just going to keep calling to its kind. None of us are safe."

The technician shook his head. "This room and the cockpit are fully shielded. We'll make it just fine if we don't engage."

"And who knows how many entities will escape into real-space on the other side? There is a lot of Air Command waiting to arrest your scrawny neck. They will be exposed." Seth looked over the control console. Only one way remained to shut this down. "Where is she? The alien you took from me."

"Stored in the containment chamber of course. It's a perfect example of a viable entity. Tague meant to offer it to the Brothers once we render the process safe for other species."

Seth shook his head and drew his pistol. "I'm voting against that," he said, adjusting the gun's setting.

"What are—" The Human dropped the floor, unconscious.

Seth went to the com panel mounted above the main control board to hail the bridge. "Caelyn? Are you up there?" He squinted through his headache at the monitor.

His fears about the flight crew proved correct when he saw the pilots in the grip of the subspace entities. The Centauri captain stared at his hands as if in deep contemplation. Caelyn hunched beside the com officer sprawled by the door. The navigator, like some of the volunteers in the back, mumbled to himself as he rocked back and forth in his bench.

"The crew is disabled," Palas looked up through the camera at Seth. "Acting very strangely. That man over there is dead. The ship is in emergency standby mode. You were correct about the air supply. If we don't leave here soon we won't make it to Csonne."

"So much for shielding the cockpit," Seth grumbled. "Hold this position. We're not ready to jump back."

"What do you mean? Systems are green. We need to rejoin Major Terwood's fleet in case we have to offload these people."

"Just stand by," Seth said, a little irritated. "Get the shields ready for jump, but hold off."

Palas turned from the camera when Caelyn said something too low to understand.

Confident in Caelyn's ability to keep the pilot from rushing back into subspace, Seth stepped over the body on the floor to study the lab's control console. None of it made any sense. He was at home in just about any cockpit but this system resembled nothing he had seen before. It was not made with Union-made components although he recognized a few Caspian symbols. Hesitantly, he hovered his hand over what seemed to be the main input panel to see if it would even allow him access.

Seth smiled when he realized that the system was engaged and unaware that Tague no longer needed it. "You've lost your mind," he said to himself. "But we've established that." He reached for the one control that he recognized, the one that was part of any sophisticated processor. The one that linked to the operator's neural interface.

"Khoe?" he spoke aloud when he made contact, his eyes closed as he leaned heavily on the board. "Khoe, are you in there?"

He waited. Anxious voices filtered through the door, but no one was shouting now. The monitors showed a calmer situation. Most of the victims had either succumbed, had been sedated, or were actually getting to know their visitors. He saw a few of the doctor's staff move through the space, shifting bodies. Someone sat on a cot, crying.

"Khoe? We're kind of in trouble here. Please answer me!" He directed his thoughts around the unfamiliar processor, eyes on the overhead displays, finding nothing he dared to explore. He was so used to his familiar, comfortable interface with the *Dutchman* that looking around this machine seemed like entering an alien world. "I'm here, Khoe. Can you feel me?"

Nothing.

Are you alive? he thought, fighting a terrible surge of grief threatening to overwhelm him. Perhaps she had simply disintegrated in her shielded prison, cut off from him and from the Alpha that had given her life to begin with.

Khoe, please! I can't do this without you. He concentrated, no longer worried about touching the wrong thing inside the processor. He felt a little like a madman ransacking through a cluttered room in search of a dropped jewel.

Nothing.

He disengaged the link and returned to the com panel by the door. "Caelyn, we've got to find a way to shut this experiment down before we jump back. I could use your help up here. Maybe you can figure this out."

Again, nothing.

"Caelyn?" Seth peered up at the screen. The bridge was empty of all but the unresponsive crew. He cursed. "Can that Delphian not stay where you put him for even a minute?"

He opened the door and hurried through the main lab. Some of the people here looked up curiously when he rushed past them and a technician moved to stop him but Seth paid no attention.

When he stepped into the small control room outside the cockpit the sight of a Delphian on the floor forced a strangled cry from his lips. He rushed to turn the man over to see that it was Palas, not Caelyn who had fallen here, dead.

He drew his gun and rose to move silently into the cockpit where he adjusted the surveillance system to check each camera in turn, looking for clues. The control room with the dead doctor and his assistant. An empty storage room. The main lab, crowded with people. A cramped access way.

And then a view of a gangly body on the ground near the air lock, the long blue braid clearly visible on the monitor. Seth froze, then forced himself to breathe evenly. He could hear his teeth grind when he shoved his sudden fury and guilt aside to focus on his next move. Where was the Human crewman they had brought aboard?

He shifted the camera again, zooming into the image until he saw the uniform among the people in the main lab. The Human stood like some unmovable boulder in the room, talking to apparently no one. Seth watched as he grasped a passing technician by the throat, shouted something, and tossed him aside. The others shrank back when he aimed a gun and simply shot one of them. Cowed, they rushed to the far wall of the lab and sat on the floor, apparently by some command.

The engineer moved to the containment system and placed his hands on it as if very familiar with the mechanism. As soon as he did, a row of yellow indicator strips lit the monitor panels above him.

A soft hiss escaped Seth when he realized why something had seemed not quite right when this man came aboard. Something felt oddly familiar, even without Khoe in his head to hone his instincts. This was another Dyad, like him, here aboard the *Stoyan*, murdering people without provocation. And now he had his hands on the machine that entrapped Khoe and the Alpha.

Seth crept through the ship's control space and tried a panel set into a bulkhead. From what he had seen on the surveillance system, this access should lead around the main lab to a side entrance, far less conspicuous than the main corridor.

The space was narrow – little more than a service way to the ship's environmental apparatus. He slipped out of his jacket and dropped it when it snagged on the edges of some conduits, slowing him down. The sound of only one voice reached him when he stepped out of the passage.

"I don't care," the Human said when Seth peered into the

lab. He was shuffling through the narrow space between the bunks toward the control room. His eyes twitched, as did his lips and even his chin. The muscled legs seemed barely able to keep him upright and he shifted continuously to keep his balance. "That's not what you said earlier," he said to no one.

Seth stepped into the room and fired his gun.

Nothing.

Deve looked up when the movement caught his attention. He glared at Seth blearily. "No guns allowed," he said in a strangely high-pitched voice accompanied by a giggle. "He broke them all." He seemed confused by the pistol in his own hand and tossed it aside before taking a few lurching steps toward Seth. "You're the other. One of us."

Seth ducked around the lumbering Human toward the mechanical monster holding Khoe hostage. Although slow, the man had a terrific reach and surely wielded considerable strength. More worrying than that was the certainty that, just like Khoe's, his touch was deadly.

"Back," Seth said, now standing in front of the containment system. He put his hand onto a control panel. "We've re-coded the transmitter. Any closer and we'll kill your Alpha. You know we can."

Strangely, Deve stopped, apparently fooled by Seth's feeble bluff. Perhaps, Seth thought, the presence of so many newly-created Dyads here simply confused his senses.

Seth rubbed his arm, feeling for the thin edge of the com chip hidden beneath his tattoo. He shifted a miniscule tab to open the link from his neural interface to the embedded transmitter. *Dammit, Khoe. Wake the hell up! I need you.*

"They're evil," the Human before him said. "Did you know that? They'll destroy us all."

Seth frowned. "Who?"

"Who the fuck to you think!" Deve roared. "He told me. He's going to bring them all here. And they'll kill anyone who gets in their way." He suddenly doubled over as if someone had kicked him hard in the middle. Foam spewed from his lips when he grunted in pain. "All right! Just stop it.

Just stop!"

The processor behind Seth whirred and coolers kicked in when something went into operation. Information that meant nothing to him scrolled over a slotted display and indicators had something to say to those who understood the message.

"He's found it," Deve cried. "Found the sire. You can't harm us now, Centauri."

Seth took a step forward. Something terrible was going on in the man's mind. Deve wrung his hands as if fighting to keep them to himself. His body shook from taking blows only he felt. A trickle of blood seeped from his nose, unnoticed.

"You don't want this," Seth said. "You can be free of that thing in your head. I can help you."

"Shut up!" Deve barreled at him, fists raised. He slammed into Seth to pitch him back, over the cots and onto the floor. Stars exploded before Seth's eyes when his head met the edge of a bunk but there was none of the deadly surge of power he had expected. The Dyad was used up; unable to generate the energy it took to kill Seth.

He rolled under the next cot and then the one after that while Deve simply crashed through the obstacles in his way. He sprang to his feet and then ducked when one of the bunks flew through the air. Blood trickled down his cheek but when he groped for his interface node he found it still firmly seated in his temple. Some of the techs who hadn't already crept from the lab during this confrontation scrambled for the corridors.

"Stoyan," they suddenly heard a harsh voice emit from the com band on Deve's forearm. It took a moment for both men to realize that Air Command had arrived, ready to deal with the aliens and their dying hostages. "Prepare for boarding."

An alert sounded, accompanied by a discreet change of illumination. Seth cursed when he realized that the *Stoyan* was powering up. The creature inside Deve's head had taken control of the helm, ready for the return to Csonne.

"You can't outrun them," Seth said. "That's a Ghoster out there."

Deve's broad lips stretched into a smile. "They won't kill us. They want to get their hands on us. Let them follow. They'll all wake up with a new friend in their heads. I'll even wait for them to catch up." He stalked toward Seth, lifting his feet only with tremendous effort. "But I don't need you along. You're dangerous. Both of you."

"Stoyan! Respond immediately or we will destroy you."

Deve halted and pressed his hands to his head. "Stop this," he pleaded. "Stop me. Make *it* stop, dammit!"

Seth reached into a pocket on his thigh and withdrew the folding knife he had taken on Csonne. It snicked open, gleaming with double-edged menace. He moved to his left, forcing Deve to turn. Surely, the Dyad, weakened by whatever had taken its toll on the Human's body, would not be able to control the Alpha, pilot the *Stoyan*, and fight a faster adversary all at once. That, then, left only Deve to oppose him.

His knees buckled when he felt a bolt of pain drill into his skull, only to fade as something familiar took hold right there inside his head. He felt it expand and then realized with a breathtaking sense of relief that whatever shaped Khoe in his brain had returned. She touched him, recognized him, and remembered these past days with a growing sense of joy.

"Seth?" He felt the word in his head like a sweet melody. "You're here. I was so lost!"

Find the Alpha, he sent urgently as he lunged at Deve. *Keep this Dyad away from it.*

Khoe squealed in fear and surprise when he dove under the fist that Deve, driven by Lep Ako, swung at him. The other fist glanced along his shoulder, instantly numbing his arm. He spun and stabbed his knife deep into Deve's chest.

The Human bellowed in pain and stumbled backward, staying on his feet to take another shambling run at Seth who barely dodged out of his way.

"He's with the Alpha!" Khoe exclaimed. "He has the Alpha! Don't kill him. Please don't kill him!"

Too late. Deve pounced and Seth thrust the knife forward, feeling it slip between two ribs to find the man's heart. He sidestepped the heavy body as Deve crashed to the ground, his groans bringing bubbles of blood to his lips.

"Don't let him go!" Khoe cried.

Bewildered, still breathing in harsh gasps, Seth crouched and put his hands on the Human's wound. There was nothing here to stop the bleeding. He felt a surge of energy trickle through his fingers, barely there, and then the dying man gave up, taking his invader with him.

Seth came to his feet and looked up to see that the control displays on the containment system had calmed. Only a steady hum remained. He couldn't remember if it had hummed before. "Do you have it?" he said to Khoe. "The Alpha. Is it there?"

"Wait."

She finally shimmered into view, looking like she always did, with long braids tangled around her shoulders and a pretty smile on her lips. But she hovered uncertainly in his mind, weakened by her isolation, deprived of the energy she needed to draw from him.

Seth pulled her into his arms, needing to assure himself that she was really here. "I thought I lost you." He kissed her and then kissed her again.

"I'm back in your head. It feels so good!" She gave him a confused half-smile. "I'm not sure that was the plan. Was it?"

"No. But I need you in there. Don't leave."

"What are you saying?"

He drew back, as surprised by his words as she was. "I guess I meant that. I just about died when I realized you were gone." He stroked her pale cheek with his thumb. "I'm a Dyad now. I want you with me. Here in real-space."

She smiled hesitantly. "You want me to stay? With you? That's big." When he seemed at a loss for words she looked around. "Are those people dead? Where are we? What is this place?"

"We've gone through subspace and brought out more of your kind. It didn't go well. You need to get into the doctor's program. Download what you find to the *Dutchman* and then wipe it out. Everything. Then figure out a way to shut the transmission down."

"That resonance is created by the Alpha. You can't shut that down."

"His assistant said something about changing the frequency they were using to capture your people. It's the way they separated you and me. See if you can find that. If that's not possible, maybe we can get at least the Alpha back home. It's not fused with anyone."

She nodded and shifted her attention to the lab's processors. "I'll write a program that'll drop the shielding on it as soon as we're in subspace. Once it's back home it'll stop others from leaving."

The *Stoyan* shuddered when a warning shot from the Ghoster glanced off her minimal shielding. Seth headed for the main corridor leading to the cockpit. "Air Command is coming for us," he explained. "We need to get out of here now. They won't let us jump."

"Want to see if I can deflect their guns?"

He turned to her to see if she was joking when something in the dim passage caught his eye. "Caelyn!" Seth rushed to the air lock where one of the medics knelt beside the Delphian. He sagged against the wall, holding a bloodied bandage to his head.

"Next time, Centauri…" he began when he saw Seth.

"Yes, I know. Remind you to stay home. We need to jump back right now. Are you up to it? Khoe is feeling a bit wobbly."

Caelyn came to his feet, aided by the medic and Seth. "Khoe? I thought she's gone."

"I got her back! I was scared green for a while."

"Why?" Caelyn peered into Seth's face, acquainted with the species well enough to read his expression. "Gods,

Sethran. Don't tell me you fell for the girl!"

Seth shrugged and grinned with a sidelong glance at Khoe.

"Listen to me. She can't stay with you. Quine said—"

A tremendous blast off the portside of the ship nearly threw them off their feet. Seth hustled the Delphian into the cockpit where he rather impolitely shoved the captain out of his bench. The man barely blinked when he slid to the floor and Caelyn took his seat.

"Come on! Air Command isn't going to play much longer. Can you get us some juice, Khoe?" Seth closed the cockpit door, grateful that the medic had dragged the dead com officer away with him.

She was already pouring every bit of the ship's energy into coaxing top speed out of the vessel. Caelyn brought the *Stoyan* into its trajectory to the keyhole. "I don't know if we can keep this up. That Union ship is going to overtake us."

Seth tipped the catatonic navigator out of his chair and dropped into it. "We have one chance. And only if you get that resonance worked out."

"Sethran," Caelyn said. "Wait."

"We have no time to wait!"

Khoe floated into Seth's lap and tipped her head in Caelyn's direction. "Tell him not to worry."

"Huh?"

"Please."

Seth looked from her to Caelyn. "She said for you not to worry."

Caelyn seemed just as confused for a moment. Then his brow smoothed. "Oh." He leaned back into the ship's headset and busied himself with the cockpit controls. "All right, then." He closed his eyes and took a deep breath. "Not a tough jump if the shields hold. I have my doubts about that, though. Are you ready?"

"He's a good friend," Khoe said. "You shouldn't get him into so much trouble." He eyes grew distant when she returned her attention to the Alpha. "It's so beautiful," she murmured. Her smile became radiant. "And so simple."

"What is?"

"The Alpha. Its harmony. I understand the resonance we need to separate the Dyads again. Oh, Seth, we can do this! We can send them all home."

"Let's do this, Caelyn," Seth said. Slowly, the keyhole before them expanded. Khoe gripped his arm when another volley from the Air Command ship blasted their failing shields.

Seth flipped an overhead control. "Prepare for jump," he warned the others aboard. "Brace for impact," he added belatedly.

"Going negative."

Khoe cut off the strident voice of the officer who continued to nag them to stand down and be boarded. The cockpit fell silent when they reached the threshold into the void.

"Thank you," she said to Seth. He felt her soft lips brush over his. "It's so hard to understand from your books, but I think I got to feel love."

His smile was short-lived when he saw her tears. "Khoe..."

"I can't stay with you," she said. "The Alpha is with me now. I had to take it from that man or we would have lost it. It is the only way. I will make sure my people are safe." She ran her fingers through his hair. "And yours, Sethran. Without the Alpha here we will both die. I know that now."

"Khoe, no." Seth felt the air punched out of his lungs. "There has to be a way."

She kissed him again and the touch lingered when they entered the breach. The Big Empty. Where no sound or light existed. Where reality ended and only a growing terror remained when all senses failed.

And yet he perceived an eerie note thrumming through every atom that made up the ship and their bodies. It was both sound and color and it was beautiful. So immeasurably beautiful without form or dimension or any of the things she had found so fascinating in his world. He sighed, possessed by a sudden, painful longing to stay here, too. He felt her withdraw to expand into some infinite vastness even as he still saw her before him, fading.

Then she slipped away, releasing his mind with a gentle whisper as she drifted out of view. The last thing he felt was her smile.

EPILOGUE

From up here, it was almost possible to believe that no other place existed.

Seth propped his elbows on the sun-warmed stone parapet of the tower and gazed out over the valley to Magra's endless horizon, moving from mountain wilderness to lush farmland and finally to the ocean itself. The spires of Magra Alaric's towns rose glittering in the distance like smooth stalagmites reaching for the sky. One could imagine that the ships buzzing around those spires looking for places to land were birds coming home to roost. He closed his eyes to smell the trees and let the sound of the wind fill his mind.

"Not going to jump, are you?"

Seth smiled when Caelyn came to stand beside him. He looked down to the foot of the research tower, pleased to find that the last of the annoying vertigo had finally released him. The headaches, too, had ended. "One gets tired of all these stairs, Delphi."

"That's why we've installed the elevator, Centauri," Caelyn replied. "Shan Quine sends greetings. He came by Delphi the day I was leaving."

Seth took a closer look at Caelyn's hands resting on the stone wall. "They did a good job with that."

Caelyn lifted his hand and slowly closed and opened it again. It obeyed his mental commands to pick up a tiny sliver of stone from the parapet and move it deftly between his fingers. The engineers had matched his other hand down to the texture of his hairless skin and the blue cast of his fingernails. "It's almost like it belongs there," he said.

Seth watched him for a while, feeling an unpleasant mix of guilt and a bizarre, unreasonable envy at seeing Caelyn's loss replaced while his own would never be.

"I didn't think I'd still find you here," Caelyn said.

"Would have been gone but Shan Saias said you were coming back early so I thought I'd wait to have a look at that paw. It's amazing work."

"It is. And you? How's the head?"

"Back where it belongs." Seth did not look at Caelyn when he said that. Quine had arranged for another Shantir, one schooled in the ancient Delphian methods of dealing with neurological conditions, to attend him here at the tower. Out of reach of Union interference and out of sight of Air Command, Seth allowed him to heal the physical scars left by Khoe on his brain. The ones left by her on his mind would probably never heal and he didn't even mind that very much.

Some strange ghost of Khoe still haunted his thoughts now, weeks after leaving Csonne in Air Command custody. At times he almost saw her face or felt her smile tickle something deep inside his head. She was not the first woman to have touched him this profoundly but none had left him as empty and rudderless as she had.

He berated himself for having fallen like a schoolboy for the strange being who excited his mind and had done incredible things to his body. They had shared a few thrilling days of his life, but she was gone now and it was time to get back aboard the *Dutchman*. But still he loitered here, among these kind but distant people, reluctant to face the empty space waiting for him inside his ship.

But more than that, and not something he tried to express even to the Delphian Shantir, was the certain feeling that Khoe had not left him as he once was. For a short while, he had been someone else, a member of a strange new species who might never be seen out here again. What he had not realized at the time was that he had, for those moments, completely embraced the change, relinquished whatever it was that made him Centauri. He had lost himself and it didn't even hurt. Perhaps a piece of her still lodged in his brain or maybe it was that brief glimpse of subspace that filled him with a peculiar sense of *otherness*.

"Shan Chion detected some strange structures still in my head that they can't figure out, but it doesn't seem to cause any problems."

"Structures?"

"Yeah. Maybe some part of Khoe's neural net." He tossed a stone chip off the parapet and watched it disappear among the trees below. "It's just there. Nothing that'll let me hack into rebel networks, unfortunately."

"I was about to ask."

"I'll stop by the enclave on Delphi if Quine can talk them into taking a look. They seem interested. But it'll mean landing the *Dutchman* on the Air Command base there. So that might be a while."

"Don't leave it too long." He regarded Seth for a while before speaking again. "I worry, my friend. She's still on your mind."

"Nothing to worry about. She's not the first woman to dump me. Won't be the last."

"She was not just any woman."

"No, not *just*."

"She would have killed you if she'd stayed. Or destroyed her own kind if you'd kept the Alpha here. That isn't a choice."

Seth nodded. Shan Saias had spent many hours poring over Reylan Tague's rambling notes and reviewing the Delphian research that had originally discovered Khoe's strange species. Rushed, blemished by speculation and guesswork, Tague's work offered a few more insights into the formation of the Dyad here in real-space. All of it depended on the presence of the Alpha either here or in subspace but not both.

It was only behind closed doors, in collaboration with Targon's own physicists, that the possibility of more than one Alpha was raised. Such an event was likely a necessity if Khoe's species were to survive and thrive, but what did that, eventually, mean for real-space inhabitants?

"At least you can say that, for a few days, you were a member of a whole new species."

"Can't," Seth said. "Classified, remember?"

Caelyn laughed. "So you're heading out now?"

"Tonight. I'm going to meet Colonel Carras on Aikhor."

"Carras! The Vanguard commander? I'd think you'd want to avoid him for a while."

"All is forgiven, apparently. Vanguard agents don't exactly enjoy a long lifespan."

"You trust him?"

Seth turned his back to the valley and leaned against the parapet to look up at the glittering antenna array above them. A row of gray-plumed birds peered back down. "Yeah. I do. He's the one who pointed out to Air Command that I got those people back safely. At least the ones that survived the first trip."

"Nothing said about stopping an alien species from invading Trans-Targon?"

"Nothing they'll admit to. Carras is going to make me an offer, I think."

Caelyn raised an eyebrow. "Will you accept?"

Seth shrugged. "I'll see what he has to say." He grinned. "Probably their way of keeping tabs on me."

"Clever. I'm sure getting back into some sort of mischief is exactly what you need right now, Centauri."

"You're damn right, Delphi."

* * * * *
*

ABOUT THE AUTHOR

Chris Reher is a first generation Canadian currently and out of necessity residing on planet Earth (which, in the general and interplanetary scheme of things, could *really* use a catchier name. Imagine heading past Proxima Centauri and someone asks you whence you came and you tell them "dirt". All theological implications aside, that just won't do.)

When not finding ways to defy the laws of physics or torture her subjects or entice them with inter-species hanky-panky, she designs web sites or writes about designing web sites. She enjoys long walks on the beach or, given the local beach shortage, writes about beaches far beyond Proxima Centauri.

www.chrisreher.com

Also by Chris Reher

Terminus Shift

Entropy's End

Sky Hunter

The Catalyst

Only Human

Rebel Alliances

Delphi Promised